The Fila Epiphany

Space Colony One
Book 2

J.J. GREEN

ii

ISBN: 978-1-913476-01-4

Cover Design: <u>Vivid Covers</u>
Editing: <u>L.M. Lengel</u>

Sign up to my reader group for a free ecopy of *Night of Flames,* the prequel to Space Colony One, and for more free books, discounts on new releases, Review Crew invitations and other interesting stuff:

<u>https://jjgreenauthor.com/free-books/</u>

(I won't send spam or pass on your details to a third party.)

CONTENTS

CHAPTER ONE

From out of a clear blue sky the shuttle descended. A glint of sunlight on its metal skin was the first sign, then the vessel itself appeared. Snub-nosed, wedge-winged, it swooped down from the upper atmosphere gracefully.

Then it blew apart.

A fireball split the hull into flaming pieces and shattered the wings. A heartbeat later the deafening explosion arrived. Shattered wreckage shot out across the sky at crazy angles, spinning, whirling, and finally falling like fiery hailstones. Screams of those watching mixed with the thuds and clanks of smoking fragments hitting the ground.

Cariad would never forget the first time she saw the vid of the shuttle explosion, which had arrived on her interface screen only a minute after it happened. Horror and dismay had gripped her. She'd nearly been sick. Next came the realization that she was supposed to be aboard the craft. A dreadful, guilty relief had flooded her.

Now, as she gazed at the carefully collected and tagged remnants that the Guardians had collected, the vivid memory of the disaster and its accompanying emotions washed over her again.

"Are you feeling all right?" Strongquist asked.

Cariad had almost forgotten the Guardian standing beside her. "Yes. I'm okay. Just remembering."

"It was a terrible shock to the colony," Strongquist remarked. "Weren't you scheduled to be aboard?"

"I was." Cariad glanced at Strongquist. It was a surreptitious peek that had become somewhat of a habit. She still found it hard to believe that her companion wasn't human. Ever since the Guardians had confessed they were androids, she had become almost obsessed with trying to find visual evidence of their artificiality. As always, she could see nothing that gave it away. Yet the creepy feeling the Guardians had given her right from their arrival had increased tenfold.

"You were very lucky," Strongquist remarked.

"What? Oh, yes. Yes, I was."

They were inside the large warehouse the Guardians had built to store the debris from the shuttle explosion. The place was so large they had been forced to build it outside the settlement site, which was already becoming cramped as the planned buildings went up. The warehouse was therefore also outside the electric fence that protected the colonists from the local predatory wildlife. It was daylight, which meant the threat of an attack was minimal, but Cariad was uncomfortable nevertheless. Her and Strongquist's voices echoed in the large space and the artificial lights were painfully bright.

"All the evidence we found during our investigations of the stadium bombing and the shuttle explosion is in the *Mistral's* database," Strongquist replied, "but I thought it might be helpful if I pointed out the most significant pieces of wreckage and explain their importance. You can ask me any questions you may have before I deactivate."

"Right. So what is it you want to show me?"

Strongquist set off across the gruesome sea of shuttle remains and Cariad followed him, carefully tiptoeing between the pieces to avoid disturbing them.

She wanted to get this transfer of responsibility for the investigation into the Natural Movement saboteurs over as quickly as possible. After realizing the detrimental effect of their presence to the colony, the rest of the Guardians had already deactivated. Strongquist would be the last of them to voluntarily put himself in suspension for an undefined duration, possibly forever.

Cariad could hardly wait. The two groups of colonists—the Gens, descended from the first contingent of passengers aboard the *Nova Fortuna*, and the Woken, who had spent the nearly two-hundred-year journey in cryonic suspension—would finally be able to learn how to work together to survive.

With the Guardians out of the way, only the Natural Movement would remain as a fat fly wriggling in the ointment. Determined to prevent the success of humanity's first deep space endeavor because it was not how humans were "supposed" to live, the movement's followers had terrorized the colonists since their first night planetside.

"Here we are," said Strongquist. He'd brought Cariad to a corner of the warehouse where tiny pieces of shuttle strewed the ground like macabre, twisted, metallic confetti.

"What did this use to be?" Cariad asked, wondering if the Guardians had even managed to identify the minute scraps.

"We believe these pieces are all from an area around the fuel supply. Material of this composition isn't found anywhere else on the *Nova Fortuna's* shuttles."

"Did you find the fuel supply section itself?" Cariad asked.

"No. We found no sign of it despite extensive searching. We concluded that it must have been atomized by the explosion."

"So do you think that's where the bomb was?"

"We made that inference, yes. It makes sense that if the bomb immediately exploded the fuel that it would increase the devastation. A bomb in another section of the shuttle might not have had the same effect. If the vessel had only been blown in half, for example, it was so close to the ground there would have been a slim chance of survivors. The shuttles were built for maximum safety."

"If only they'd been built to prevent sabotage," Cariad said.

"Indeed. It's reassuring that you came to the same conclusion as we did so quickly. Perhaps you'll have more success in the investigation than us."

"I'm certainly going to try my best. It's clear that the saboteur knew what they were doing by attaching the bomb to the fuel supply."

"Yes," Strongquist said. "Do you know where that section is on the shuttles?"

"I'm not sure. Isn't it under the tail?"

"It is, but very few Gens would know that."

"Okay. I get it," Cariad said.

"I'm sorry I can't tell you more than that regarding this detail," the Guardian said.

"Well, we have the Natural Movement tattoo that we found on our suicide, Twyla," Cariad said. "Dr. Montfort is carrying out full body examinations of every colonist. By the way, there's something I forgot to ask you—how did you identify the saboteur on the First Night Attack?"

"You'll find extensive records in the *Mistral's* database, but basically, several people volunteered the information that a woman had been loitering around the switch on the electric fence that day as dusk was falling. After we apprehended her, we had barely begun to question her when she confessed, just like that. She said she would rather die than live unnaturally on an alien planet, though when the time came for her execution, her fear showed. I wonder now if she gave up so easily in order to throw us off the scent. At the time, I don't think anyone suspected that there might be other saboteurs."

"I think you're right. Is there anything else you wanted to tell me?" Cariad was itching to leave. The pressure of threats from outside and within the colony bore down on her. There was so much she had to do.

"Yes. You should know that the chemicals used to create both the stadium and the shuttle bomb were the same. The main ingredient of both bombs was derived from fertilizer."

"Fertilizer? So one of the terrorists could be a farmer?"

"Possibly, but I believe the connection is weak. Anyone could have accessed the supplies. However, the fertilizer wasn't used in its original form. It was refined."

Cariad said, "All right. I understand. Refining chemicals isn't typical knowledge for a Gen. Perhaps it was information that was passed down along with their central beliefs."

Strongquist acknowledged her response with a nod. "Would you like to accompany me to the *Mistral*? It will give you the opportunity to ask me anything you feel is important before I deactivate."

They stepped carefully between the shuttle remnants as they went to the warehouse doors. Outside, the soft sunshine was a pleasant contrast to the artificial glare inside the warehouse. They walked the short distance to the settlement fence, treading over the rubbery ground cover that clothed the open space. Tall fern-like plants dotted the landscape.

Inside the protective fence the streets were busy. The Gens were re-settling the tiny town after the most recent Natural Movement sabotage had destroyed their breakaway settlement at an oceanside cave system. Cariad and Strongquist navigated the streets that led to the shuttle field.

Although her new responsibility weighed heavily on her, Cariad was glad of the distraction. She had said good bye to her Gen friend, Ethan, only two days previously and she already missed him badly. Even the task she had of replenishing the colony's gene pool after the great loss of life hadn't been sufficient to stop her constantly worrying about him.

She was also worried by Strongquist's earlier revelation that a nearby star system held sentient life. Though the presence of extraterrestrial intelligent life forms was an amazing discovery, there was no way to tell whether they were friendly. In its current state, Concordia could not withstand an attack.

The truth was, the situation on Concordia was dire. Not for the first time, Cariad wondered whether giving up her life on Earth and leaving behind her family and friends had been worth it. But she had no choice except to go on.

CHAPTER TWO

After two days of searching, Ethan had been forced to conclude there were no survivors of the flooding at the caves. As he flew the flitter away from the last few remnants of the disaster that had been washed ashore, his mind turned to the journey that lay ahead of him.

He'd been forced to pack hastily for his expedition, aware that injured Gens might be clinging to life on the beach, hoping for rescue. He had warm clothes and blankets, plenty of dried food, a full water tank, and a device that purified water. The portable appliance had been quickly put together by a mechanic called Osias. Ethan also had an instrument that tested for substances that were poisonous to humans. Cariad had advised him to only use it if he became desperate for food. The plant and animal life on Concordia could contain unknown toxins, she'd said.

The most essential items Ethan had stowed in

the flitter were two weapons. He had the gun he'd been issued as a farmer and a second weapon that Cariad had given him—one of the Guardians' that she'd persuaded Strongquist to donate.

Whenever Ethan left the flitter he would be vulnerable. As well as the creatures that had preyed upon the colonists during the First Night Attack, capturing and quickly digesting their victims, Concordia was also home to predatory aquatic thread organisms. Ethan's friend, Cherry, had nearly been dragged into a lake by one of them.

What other threats the planet held, Ethan didn't know but he hoped to find out. Concordia wasn't supposed to harbor any animal life any larger than the average insect, but the information the probes had sent back was inaccurate or it had been tampered with by Natural Movement followers. Now, no one knew what might be out there.

Cariad had tried to persuade him to take an interface along. If he got into difficulties, he could comm the settlement and they could send a flitter out to rescue him. She'd said he would be able to access the network via satellite from anywhere on the planet. It might take a while to reach him, depending on how far he roamed, but it would be a safety net.

But Ethan had refused. He knew he was risking his life by going off alone as he was. He couldn't expect others to risk their lives too in order to help him. Also, he didn't want to be in contact with the settlement. He couldn't explain exactly why he felt so opposed to the idea, but it was something to do with the reason for his need to get away. His gut told him the answer to his problems lay in solitude out in the wilderness. The only electronic device he'd brought was a small recorder. It hung around his neck, ready to vid his journey and any organisms he came across, especially anything that seemed dangerous.

Night was beginning to fall. The sun had set and the ocean waves and beach were growing shadowy in the dusk. Although the flitter had lights, Ethan preferred a full view of his surroundings in the uncharted territory. He would have to stop soon, but he decided to while away the short time remaining by recording the events of the previous two days. He turned on the recorder and began to speak.

"This is Ethan, and it's the third day of the fourth month, year one, Concordian Calendar. It looks like no one but Cherry survived the cave disaster. I haven't managed to find anyone else still alive, though I saw one victim five minutes' flight down the coast from the caves." He paused and swallowed as he revisited the memory. "I was stupidly optimistic. When I saw the body, it didn't occur to me that the person was probably dead. I flew straight at the figure, but then as I got closer, I realized that the body's position and stillness could mean only one thing. I lowered the flitter to the sand and climbed out.

"It was a man. He was lying face downward, the waves lapping at his feet, his arms at awkward angles. I lifted his shoulder and turned him over. His face was swollen and disfigured, and small sea creatures had already begun to eat it. I guess I should have made a vid of the creatures but I couldn't bring myself to. The sight was too horrible. I backed up. It wasn't possible for me to tell if I'd known the man.

"I retraced my steps to the flitter. I called out several times, hoping other survivors might be lying nearby. When I didn't hear a response, I took out a weapon and went to investigate the undergrowth, thinking someone could be unconscious in there and hadn't heard me shouting. As I got close to the vegetation, I called out again, asking if there was anyone there and if they were injured. I told them to make a noise if they couldn't reply. I didn't hear anything." All he'd heard was the waves on the shoreline.

Ethan had recorded a vid of the plants that bordered the beach, which were different from the trees in the area surrounding the settlement. They were smooth-skinned and branched out from a central point in the ground. Each limb split into four or five more at intervals roughly as long as Ethan's forearm. Cup-shaped receptacles stuck out from the ends of each branch.

He'd peered between the plant stems to look for survivors but hadn't been able to see anything. The plants were clumped so closely together, it wouldn't have been possible to move through them without leaving a trail of damage, and there'd been none that he could see. Leaving the undergrowth, he'd checked up and down the beach for signs of disturbance, but it was unsullied by any footprints other than his own.

"I searched for hours that day and the next, but I didn't find any more bodies. Even the wreckage of the supplies that had been washed out of the caves petered out quite soon. There are plants here on the shoreline that are different from any I've seen before, and animals have left tiny tracks on the sand, but otherwise I seem to be the only living thing for kilometers. I don't go near the water so I don't know what's in the ocean. That's it for now." He turned off the recorder.

Was that the kind of information he should be recording? He guessed so. He was the first explorer of Concordia and his discoveries could prove invaluable to the rest of the colony. Ethan resolved to record his observations every day.

The sky was darkening quickly. Ethan brought up the flitter's display, which showed a map of the local terrain. He spread the map wider with his fingertips. The settlement was at the corner of it now. In one direction lay his farm and the lake that bordered it. Cherry was taking care of his land while he was gone, though he didn't know if he would ever want it back. He was finally doing what he'd always wanted to do, and not the occupation that the Manual's role allocation system had decided for him.

Cherry had been one of the few people he'd said goodbye to before he stowed the last of his goods on the flitter and drove through the gates of the settlement. Saying goodbye would have involved difficult conversations and questions that Ethan didn't know how to answer.

In another section of the map lay the ocean and the cave system that had recently been destroyed. The rest was unknown territory. The continent that Ethan was about to explore was the largest on the planet, which he assumed was one of the reasons it had been chosen as the site for humanity's first deep space colony. He had plenty of space to roam. For the first time in a long time, a feeling of calm and peace settled over him. He closed the flitter's roof, shutting out the rapidly cooling nighttime breeze.

He was traveling south, keeping the vehicle a short distance above the beach so that he had a close view of it and the bordering land as he went along. In the fading light, the landscape was changing rapidly. The many-branched plants were giving way to low, spindly bushes similar to the ones that had once covered his farm. The terrain inland was turning flat, and the sand extended from the beach between the bushes. He hoped to find some kind of hilly ground soon. Sleeping inside the only raised object for kilometers around would make him feel exposed.

No hills appeared, however, and consulting the map told him there were none for kilometers. When he could no longer see into the distance, Ethan stopped the flitter and increased its elevation until it was about his own height above the ground. He set it to hover. A breeze was blowing in from the ocean that would probably push him inland overnight, but that wouldn't matter much. If the flitter encountered raised ground it would automatically alter its direction to avoid a collision.

Ethan was about to take out a food parcel and eat his evening meal when he thought of something else he wanted to record. After turning on the device hanging around his neck, he said:

"From as far back as I can remember, I was told

that I was coming to a new home. Everyone said we were special because we would be the first Gens not to die aboard the ship. They also told us that we were deep space pioneers. If we succeeded in building a settlement outside the Solar System, it meant that humans weren't confined to a place that would eventually no longer support life. If we could build a deep space colony, it meant that, as a species, we could be immortal. They said our descendants would grow so numerous and so advanced that one day a colony ship would depart our new planet just as the *Nova Fortuna* had departed Earth. And so on and so on, throughout the galaxy, perhaps even billions of years into the future, maybe even spreading to another galaxy and on into eternity."

He paused briefly to collect his thoughts, then went on, "I was a kid at the time I was told that, and not a smart one. I didn't really get what they were saying. But I think I understand now. I'm the first human who ever saw the things I've seen today and the first to pass over the ground I traveled. And for the rest of my journey it'll be the same, whether I make it back or not. In a way, I don't care if anyone in the future remembers what I've done. I don't want this land or that ocean named after me. But I finally get what I was told all those years ago. Though others will come after, I'm the first. When my ancestors decided to come down from the trees they didn't know what they were doing. They had no understanding of where it might lead, and to be honest I'm not sure my own understanding is that much better. But I do get this. I feel it. I'm at the very tip of a finger of human life that's reaching out. I just wanted to say that I'm glad and happy to be doing this, no matter what happens."

He turned off the recorder, deciding not to play it back to check it. He'd probably spoken nonsense and made a fool of himself, but he'd spoken from the heart and he felt better for it.

Outside the flitter, all was dark except for starlight. The moon hadn't risen yet. Ethan turned on the flitter's light and pulled out some parcels of food. A lot of the food supplies he'd brought were dried and required rehydrating and heating up, but some of them were ready to eat. He chewed some protein strips and washed them down with water. He also took out fresh algae cakes. They weren't a favorite but they were nutritious and light to carry.

After his long day's travel, Ethan found he was soon ready to go to sleep. He packed up loose items scattered around the cabin and pushed down the flitter's seats to make a bed. One folded blanket served as a pillow. He covered himself with the other. The soughing of the waves quickly sent him to sleep.

***

It was nighttime and Ethan was barefoot on soft, mossy ground. Darkness surrounded him except for a row of lights that shone from behind, their glow quickly fading into black night. He was heading away from the lights, looking for something though he didn't know what exactly. Something had disturbed his sleep and he wanted to know what it was. The air was strangely thick and he was having to force himself through it.

A shape moved in the darkness ahead. Darker

than the surrounding black, it was long and low down to the ground. The creature seemed to glide rather than walk and it was moving across his view. Was this what had made the sound he'd heard? He wasn't sure if he wanted to get close to the thing. For some reason, it scared him.

Yet Ethan followed the creature, moving deeper into the night until he couldn't see it any longer. It didn't matter. He had something else to head toward. Lauren had appeared ahead. She was wearing a little girl's playsuit, though she was grown up. She saw him too and waved.

Relief overwhelmed him. He felt he'd lost her for a long time but now he'd finally found her again. He began to run toward her. He wanted to reach her before she went away again. He would tell her he wanted her to stay with him forever, and that she mustn't ever leave.

Then he saw the creature had returned. It was ahead of him, moving toward Lauren. He shouted out a warning but she didn't seem to hear. He yelled again and again, and all the while the creature was getting closer to her. Why wouldn't she move? She only smiled and waved and waited for him.

He was running as fast as he could but he was getting nowhere. He couldn't catch up to the creature. It glided along swiftly, bearing down on unsuspecting Lauren. It would reach her before he could. It would—

Ethan started awake, his hands reaching for Lauren. He almost cried out to warn her, to tell her a predator was about to kill her, but then the realization that he'd been dreaming hit him. His arms slumped down and the words died before they left his mouth. Where was he? He saw the starlit sky through the flitter windows and heard the waves. His memory of the last few months returned.

Lauren was dead, and so was Dr. Crowley.

Ethan sighed, turned over, and tried to go back to sleep. The same dream about Lauren had visited him many times. His subconscious mind couldn't seem to accept that she was gone. It wanted to give him the chance to save her over and over again. Recurring nightmares were one reason that he'd wanted to go on his expedition, hoping that the journey might give him time to process his girlfriend's death and that of his close friend, Dr. Crowley.

Dr. Crowley had always been full of good advice. Ethan liked to think back over his conversations with her, but he couldn't remember her saying anything about how to cope with the death of someone you loved. He guessed that if she'd been comfortable with death or wise about how to accept it, she might not have joined the *Nova Fortuna* Project. The doctor had outlived her natural lifespan by at least one hundred and eighty-four years. It was a shame she'd only spent one night on the planet she'd worked so hard to reach.

Sleep was refusing to return to Ethan. He moved onto his back and stared at the roof, wondering if he should give up and read for a while. Cariad had uploaded all the Wokens' data covering what they'd discovered about Concordia. Maybe he might read something useful.

Suddenly, the flitter tipped, rolling him over. He sat up, trying to maintain his balance as the flitter leaned farther to one side. Something was pulling at the vehicle or trying to climb onto it in the darkness. He felt for his weapon. His fingers touched cool, smooth metal.

Where was the thing? It was too dark for a clear view outside. Then he saw it. Tens of scrabbling legs appeared at the window. Ethan knew those legs. It was one of the sluglimpet creatures. He had to get it off the flitter fast. The creatures exuded a powerful acid and if the thing disabled his vehicle he would be at its mercy.

Ethan lowered the window and fired into the organism's underside. The flitter immediately filled with choking, acrid smoke. He couldn't breathe. He opened the other windows. The flitter was tipping precariously on its side, borne over by the creature's weight. Though he'd hit it squarely, the sluglimpet continued to cling on. He fired at it again and another burst of suffocating smoke erupted.

He couldn't touch it to try to push it off or his skin would be eaten by the corrosive, digestive acid. Ethan pulled a boot onto a foot and kicked at the thing. He'd managed to break it free a little, so he kicked harder and fired at it again. At last, the creature released its grip. A thud resounded from below as it hit the ground.

Ethan raised the flitter higher and took off his boot, taking care not to touch the sticky gloop. He quickly wiped the sole clean and dropped the rag from the open window. Peering out he saw the predator hobbling slowly away into the undergrowth by the shore, black against the shadowy gray sand. It wasn't the only one, however. As it retreated, more were emerging. Ethan quickly raised the flitter higher still, doubling its previous elevation. He'd thought that setting the vehicle at roughly his own height above the beach would provide sufficient protection from the local wildlife. He'd clearly been wrong. These sluglimpets were larger than any he'd ever seen before.

Had they followed him all the way from the area around the settlement? It seemed unlikely. The creatures appeared to be widespread on the continent, living in low undergrowth as well as among trees. Ethan watched the animals as they milled around and lifted the front halves of their bodies every so often, reaching up toward the flitter with groping legs. They knew he was there. What were they sensing? His body heat?

He turned on the recorder and pointed it downward to capture a vid of the organisms. Then when he thought he'd recorded enough, he flew the flitter down the beach away from them. Although the predators wouldn't have been able reach him at the flitter's elevation, he didn't think he would be able to sleep knowing they were roaming underneath, hungry and waiting.

Was nowhere on the continent safe from the sluglimpets? Wherever he went, would the horrible creatures always be there waiting to attack as soon as the sun went down? Ethan flew on, wondering what the coming weeks or months might hold.

CHAPTER THREE

It chilled Cariad to the bone to see the forty or so deactivated Guardians. They were standing still and silent, lined up in ranks in an empty room on the lowest deck of the *Mistral*. Part of the creepy effect was because they'd deactivated while upright, not lying down like humans in cryo. Yet they looked as human as ever, aside from the fact that none of them breathed or moved even a micrometer. Some hadn't even bothered to close their eyes before shutting themselves down. They stared blankly ahead, their gazes unfocused. The lighting in the room was dim, yet it was bright enough to glint on the Guardians' eyes as if they were moist.

Cariad mused that the Guardians' eye tissue probably wasn't damp. She imagined that if she reached out to touch an eye it would feel smooth and dry, or perhaps greasy. The impression given of moist eyes was an illusion, like everything else about these strange androids from an Earth she had never known.

"I'm not sure whether you will believe me," Strongquist said, diverting Cariad's attention from the motionless Guardians, "but I would like to assure you that neither we nor our creators meant any harm to the people of Concordia. I hope the fact that we have voluntarily chosen to take this hiatus from the colonization is evidence of that."

"To be frank," Cariad replied, "I still don't know what to make of you all or what you intended to do here. And I think I speak for most Woken and Gens. We feel deeply deceived. I don't know how long it's going to take us to process and understand what you've done." As she spoke, Cariad's obsession with staring at the android's skin and hair reawakened. Strongquist looked perfectly imperfect. Uneven skin coloration, five o'clock shadow, flecks of gray in his eyebrows—everything about him was convincingly human. Cariad marveled at the skill and artistry that had gone into making him.

"We are aware of the problems resulting from our presence, but—"

"Are you?" Cariad asked. "Do you really understand what you did? Are you even capable of understanding? It isn't only that you disrupted the colony, dividing us into factions by lending your support to one group. There are wider effects that I can barely guess at. When it was just Woken and Gens, everyone knew the score. Sure, the two groups didn't mix much, but they would have been brought together by the work of colonizing the planet. We had the Mandate and the Manual and we had to make a go of the colony as best we could because there was no going back. We were on our own, sink or swim.

"Now we don't know anything any more. Our foundation has been ripped from us. You've come here and told us we aren't only the first deep-space colony, but we're also probably human civilization's last gasp. Can you understand how that feels? I don't think you can. You aren't human. You have no empathy, and you don't even grasp basic human rights. If you did, you wouldn't have sedated Aubriot. You've behaved like the machines you are from the moment you arrived. I don't know why it took us so long to see it."

Strongquist looked down, as if in shame or regret. Was he only mimicking the emotions, responding appropriately to the conversation? Cariad didn't know. The Guardian Faina had said their minds were programmed with information from many human personalities, giving them some semblance of humanity, but Cariad didn't know what to think about the Guardians anymore. "Is there anything else you want to say to me before you deactivate?"

"Aubriot has been taken out of sedation," he replied. "And there are some things I haven't told you—things that we deemed inexpedient to divulge at the time."

"Like what?" Cariad replied. "What have you got to say now? Are you going to tell me everything you said about what's happened on Earth isn't true?"

"No, not that."

"Why should I believe you?" Cariad gave a huff of frustration. "You could have been lying when you told us about what's happened on Earth since we left, or you could be lying now. Why did your creators make it possible for you to lie?"

"We were never given any information on the rationale behind our programming," said Strongquist. "If I were to guess, I would say that it wasn't possible due to the organic origins of our mind, or to prevent us from divulging information that could be harmful to the success of the colony, or in order to make us seem more convincingly human."

His final comment took the wind from Cariad's sails. The android had a point. Humans could be just as deceitful as the Guardians had been. Strongquist's guess also reminded her of something she'd wanted to ask him about before he deactivated.

Although he had explained the reactivation process, Cariad had no intention of waking up any of the Guardians ever again if she could help it. She wanted to get all the important discussions over while Strongquist was conscious or "switched on."

"Do you have anything else to tell me about the Natural Movement terrorists?" Cariad asked. "You didn't lie about that, did you?"

"I believe we've been entirely transparent about our investigation into the Natural Movement infiltration of the colony. If there's anything we didn't tell you, it was an inadvertent omission. In any case, all of the files relating to the investigation are on the *Mistral's* databases along with the historical data from Earth that we brought with us. You may be able to discover information there that eluded us."

Cariad said, "There was something else I wanted to ask you about that: Why did you invite me aboard the *Mistral* when you wanted to show me the vids of Aparicio? It occurred to me later that you could have just sent them to the *Nova Fortuna*."

"The reason for that ties in with something we didn't tell you because we feared it might destabilize the colony. Cariad, from the moment of the stadium bombing, we undertook extensive covert assessments of the psychological profiles of each of the Gens and Woken. Our initial motivation was to attempt to discover the bomber. However, as events unfolded, we began to use the assessments to look for individuals who were best suited to steer the colony in a more favorable direction."

"What the hell are you talking about, Strongquist?" Cariad snapped. "You were spying on everything we did and said?"

"Not exactly, but we did look deeply into each individual's history of behavior as far as it was possible," Strongquist explained. "I'm aware we may have appeared ignorant to exactly what was happening politically among the colonists, but we understood more than you probably supposed. We were seeking ways to attempt to heal the schism that was developing between the Woken and the Gens. To do that, we tried to support those we identified as most likely to be able to move the divided relationships in a better direction. One of those we identified was you."

"Me? So you invited me to the *Mistral* to...?"

"As an act of conspicuous support. We were aware of the aura of mystique we had. By inviting you to our own vessel—you were the first person we invited, remember?—we were attempting to raise your profile and status among the Woken. Your personality type isn't the kind to seek out power over others, yet we felt you possessed the qualities needed to bring the two sides together."

Cariad wasn't sure how to take the android's statements, but his words spurred another question. "So was it for the same reason that you helped me defuse the situation when the Gen farmers refused to hand over their weapons?" At the time, Strongquist had dropped a broad hint that gave Cariad the means to assume temporary control and prevent any of the farmers from being hurt.

"That's correct. We could not openly defy Anahi after she declared herself Leader, so we did what we could to support you, knowing your actions would calm things down."

His words kind of made sense but Cariad wasn't convinced. If the Guardians had truly wanted to play politics to promote the success of the colony, they would have thrown their support behind someone else. If anyone was born to lead the colonization of Concordia, it was Ethan.

Cariad said, "Is there anything else?" It felt like long past the time to say goodbye to the android, hopefully forever. She couldn't wait to leave and close the door on the room of eerie mannequins.

"Only one more thing," said Strongquist. "I see that you're irritated and impatient. You don't feel any confidence in anything I have to say."

"You got that right."

"It's regrettable, but perhaps inevitable in the circumstances. Well, in that case I'll deactivate myself in a moment. The reactivation process is simple if you ever need our services in the future."

"Yes, it's easy enough to start you all up again," Cariad said, almost flippantly. Yet now that it came to saying goodbye to Strongquist, her emotions did a somersault. Her irritation gave way to something else. She could hardly believe it, but she felt a little sorry for the machine. After all, it was self-aware, or it seemed to be, yet it was turning off its consciousness without knowing if it would ever reawaken.

Cariad was reminded of the moment she'd been sedated prior to her cryonic suspension for the long trip to Concordia. She'd fallen asleep not knowing if she would ever wake. If she was honest with herself, she'd been terrified. Right up to the moment the anesthetist put her under, she'd been reconsidering her decision to join the colony. In the end, it was partly the notion of how foolish she would look backing out at the last minute that had prevented her from calling the whole thing off.

As he watched her, Strongquist suddenly looked more human than ever.

"Doesn't it bother you?" Cariad asked. "Turning yourself off, I mean? We might never reactivate you, you know. Especially not after everything that's happened. I don't think anyone will want to take the risk."

The Guardian gazed directly into her eyes before answering. "I have no choice in the matter. As I've always said, the success of the colony is prioritized in our programming. We understand that our presence at this time is detrimental, so we must deactivate. However, I would be lying if I were to say that the action carries no personal cost. I try to think of it like this: While I am shut down, I shall be in the same state as I was before I was created. It didn't bother me then. Why should it bother me now?"

To Cariad, Strongquist's words sounded like mind games. "Maybe we will need you again at some point. I guess we should stop drawing this out. What was the final thing you wanted to tell me?"

"It's only a suggestion. There is a holo on the *Mistral's* database that might help you and the other colonists, but I would advise you to watch it alone before showing the others. You may judge it to be too alarming. I wasn't able to show it to you previously because it gives away the secret of our origins, but I'm aware you doubt the veracity of our statements regarding the conditions on Earth prior to our departure. This holo was prepared for the time when we revealed our true identity. One of our creators explains the history and reasons behind our manufacture. I'll send it to your personal files. If you view this holo, I'm confident you'll be assured that we were not lying when we told you that Earth is all but uninhabitable now. It's imperative that the colonists remain on Concordia and do their best to build a thriving settlement. There's no future for them on Earth."

"Okay," said Cariad. "I'll watch it."

Strongquist said, "Very well. It's goodbye, then." He smiled. It was a sad smile, and a rare event for the android.

"Goodbye," Cariad replied, then she realized he couldn't hear her. He had already deactivated. The smile on the android's face was frozen and would remain so until someone decided to wake him up.

Cariad wished Strongquist had given her time to leave before he'd turned himself off. Now she was the only living thing in a room of figures like life-sized mechanical dolls whose gears had wound down.

She quickly went out and closed the door, then pressed the key that locked it. Despite all of Strongquists' words, she didn't fully trust the Guardians not to reactivate themselves. As well, Natural Movement members roamed free among the colonists, and there was no telling what any of them might do. She wouldn't have been surprised if one of them tried to reprogram the androids and turn them into killing machines. Not very "natural" killing machines, it had to be said, but the terrorists had already shown themselves capable of truly impressive feats of cognitive dissonance. Bombs were also "unnatural" but that hadn't bothered them.

Cariad paused outside the locked door. There was so much she had to do, yet for a moment, she couldn't move. Although the Guardians' interference had nearly brought the colony to its knees, their presence and the high tech they'd brought had felt like a safety net. Now, the colonists of Concordia were on their own.

***

Cariad walked through the corridors of the *Mistral* to the bridge, where the second-in-command of the

Nova Fortuna had taken control. Addleson was reclining in the captain's chair where the Guardian Faina had once sat. Addleson was a very different character from the cold, aloof android. He was suave and convivial and had a penchant for luxury. Cariad wasn't sure where the man's traits had come from. They weren't ones she had deliberately selected for among those that were genetically heritable. Perhaps they were an unforeseen expression of certain genes or were conjoined with other attributes. Though Cariad had been at the top of her field when she'd departed Earth, the discipline of genetics still held mysteries neither she nor other experts had managed to solve.

"Cariad," Addleson said when he noticed her enter the bridge. "Been tucking our friends in? It was way past their bed time."

"You can say that again," she replied as she went over to him. "What have you found out about the *Mistral*?"

"Well, first off, she seems to be pretty much an open book. We haven't hit any security lockouts. Everything we encounter in the ship's system opens easily, but frankly, a lot of what we're finding is beyond our understanding. We're reading the instructions the Guardians left behind."

"They left instructions?"

"Yes. It's all set out in English."

Cariad recalled how Strongquist had told her that English had evolved and the Guardian spoke a version the colonists wouldn't understand. It looked like the Guardians had prepared well for their deactivation.

"When do you think you'll be able to take full control of the ship?" she asked.

"Probably another couple of days. One thing that concerns me a little is the weapons. We don't have anything like them aboard the *Nova Fortuna*. All we have on there are a handful of pulse lasers to blow apart asteroids we encountered on the voyage. If we have to use the *Mistral's* weapons, I don't think I'll have much of a clue what I'm doing. Are we likely to need to use them? When I realized the *Mistral* is equipped with rail guns etcetera, I thought it seemed overkill. Did the Guardians think we might attack them when they arrived?"

"No, they weren't intended for us." Cariad recalled Strongquist's earlier divulgence that there was sentient life on nearby star systems.

"No?" Addleson said. "Then who...? Whoa. I hope you don't mean what I think you mean." His customarily upbeat expression took a hit from the new information.

"I do," said Cariad. "So maybe you should prioritize familiarizing your crew with the scanners. We have to keep a close watch for unexpected visitors."

"All right. I'll get on that."

"Do you have all the people you need?" Cariad asked.

"I have enough for the moment, but don't tell me I said that if we find ourselves under attack. Do you think it's likely?"

"We've been here for months. As we haven't been attacked yet, I'm guessing there's nothing nearby that wants us dead right away. And Strongquist didn't mention anything about spotting alien starships, only that they'd seen signs of sentience. Our luck should hold out for a while, I hope."

"Right. Still, I'll have someone analyze all the recent scanner readings."

"That would be smart."

Addleson rubbed his hands together. "This isn't too bad. I have a ship of my own to run, which makes a change. What's more, the *Mistral's* so up-to-date, it's like it's from the future. Scratch that. To us, it *is* from the future, right?"

"Yeah."

"Best of all," Addleson continued, "Geisen's green with envy."

Cariad laughed. Geisen was the pilot of the *Nova Fortuna,* and Addleson had been bridesmaid to that bride for his entire career.

"What are you going to do now?" Addleson asked. "Are you going to interrogate Garwin? He's been pretty quiet in his cabin the last couple of days."

"I guess I should. To be honest, I don't know what to do with him. He's devastated by Twyla's suicide. I feel like I should leave him alone, though I won't of course. I have to do something about the Natural Movement and Garwin's my only source of information at the moment."

"I don't understand how he can grieve over that bitch."

"Me neither. But love's strange. He did seem to really love her."

Addleson wrinkled his nose. "I'm happy to let you deal with him. I'll stick to flying starships."

Cariad left the bridge. At first, she walked

toward the cabin where Garwin was confined, but then she changed direction. She'd given in to her urge to postpone that difficult conversation. She needed more time to get her thoughts in order about the man. As far as she understood it, according to what Gens had told her, he'd been playing a double game for a long time. While pretending to be a placatory, appeasing spokesperson for the Gens, he had actually been organizing their dissent. The alternative Gen settlement had been his idea and he'd been instrumental in its construction and the transfer of the supplies.

Yet Cariad also thought that despite appearances, Garwin could easily have been fully aware of Twyla's involvement in the Natural Movement. If he was capable of such deep deception, he could even be the Natural Movement ring leader for all she knew. Perhaps he'd wanted to move all the Gens to the caves to concentrate the population and make them easier to kill. She would have to approach interviewing him very cautiously.

Meanwhile, Strongquist's mention of a holo made by the Guardians' creators that explained the reasons behind their manufacture had piqued her curiosity. To the Gens, Earth was ancient history—an exotic country they would never visit, or so Ethan had explained. Perhaps it was almost a myth to them. But Cariad was deeply curious about her former home. From her perspective, she'd departed it less than three years previously. She felt a strong desire to see it in its most recent form.

She walked to the room where Strongquist had shown her ancient holos of the original Natural Movement infiltrator, Frederick Aparicio. The room was empty, so she went inside. It took her a while to figure out how to access her personal files from the interface but eventually she managed it. A motionless holo of a young man appeared in the room's center. It was the beginning of the recording, but Cariad hesitated before she let it play.

It was the man's clothes that made her pause. They were extremely worn and patched—little more than rags. Yet according to Strongquist this person had helped to build the *Mistral* and create the Guardians. Also, though the man was young, his face was haggard with tiredness. He didn't look ill, however. Strongquist had said a disease had wiped out most of humanity, breaking down the last remains of civilization. The look of desperation, sorrow, and perhaps anger on the man's face was also striking. What had happened to her home planet?

Cariad started the holo. The man spoke, but the movement of his lips didn't match the words she heard. His speech was being translated into English she could understand. The distraction of the effect was short-lived as she heard what he said.

"Hello, person of the future." The man's tone was sarcastic. "Or are you from the past? One of the cryonically suspended ones? Congratulations on surviving your long freezing. What was it like, I wonder, going to sleep then waking up a couple of hundred years later aboard a starship? I guess I'll never know. None of us will. To be frank, we're screwed. We'll never leave Earth because we gave our lives for yours."

CHAPTER FOUR

On his third morning out in the wild, Ethan decided to do something he didn't think anyone had attempted yet. He would see how high he could take the flitter. As he ate his breakfast, he looked down at the beach below. After the sluglimpet attack, he'd flown as far as he could until tiredness overcame him.

Yet now, as he looked down, he could see what seemed to be traces of more sluglimpets in the sand. Their many legs had left long scratches all over the ground as they'd tried to reach him. Ethan doubted the creatures could have followed him after his long flight the previous night so these were new ones. He gave a shiver. If he'd tried to go on his journey without a flitter, he probably wouldn't have survived the first night.

As he watched, waves were washing away the sluglimpet tracks. The tide was coming in. Soon, the shore would bear no trace of the predators.

Concordia was a dangerous place to live.

Ethan finished his breakfast and brushed the crumbs out of the flitter. It was time for his experiment. He closed all the windows and set the controls to rise. Maintaining the same position, the flitter began to lift. Ethan turned on his recorder and settled back into his seat, looking all around at the view.

The beach was soon a strip of gray between two blankets, one blue, one green. All around, the sky was clear and the sun hung suspended just above the horizon. According to the flitter's control panel the outside temperature was dropping quickly, and Ethan began to feel it as cold air filtered inside the vehicle. He wrapped a blanket around his shoulders and wondered how high the flitter would go. Would it rise into space if he let it?

Clouds became visible at the ocean's edge, then Ethan realized the clouds were hanging over land. He could see the continent that lay to the east. He remembered from lessons at school that Concordia had one large continent, two smaller ones, and an archipelago of large and small islands in a string across the largest ocean, which Ethan was looking out over. He wondered if what he was seeing wasn't a continent after all but one of the larger islands.

The flitter rose higher still. Ethan turned his attention inland. The first feature he noticed was a mountain range that ran down the continent. Then as he went higher, he saw a river beyond it. The river seemed to begin in the range's foothills then grew wider and wider until it flowed out of sight.

Ethan was getting very cold. His breath was

fogging and fine water droplets were appearing on the inside of the flitter's windows. He also felt light-headed. Of course, he realized, the flitter wasn't airtight like a starship. He was running out of oxygen. It was time to return to the beach. He set the controls to take the flitter down. He'd only been up at a high elevation for a few minutes but it wasn't safe to remain there for long. Going into space wasn't an option after all, which was no bad thing. He'd spent most of his life out in the black but now he preferred the wide spaces and sweet-smelling air of Concordia.

When he'd returned to the surface, Ethan decided it was time to leave the beach and head into the interior. If he stuck to the coast, he might only see the same landscape and wildlife all the way around the continent, but venturing into the heart of the land would lead him to something different. He also wanted to try to escape the horrible sluglimpets. Perhaps there was a region they didn't inhabit.

He set a course for the mountains. As he flew, he turned on his recorder and began a report on the sluglimpet attack the previous evening. He described how the pulse fire from his weapon had barely deterred the creature and that it was only physically pushing it off the vehicle that had saved him. He paused as he remembered how the sluglimpets were not so easy to remove when they were stuck to a living being. Ethan opened a window and examined the side of the flitter the sluglimpet had clung on to. The paint was entirely eaten away and the metal underneath it was seared, as if the vehicle had been on fire.

Ethan continued speaking into the recorder: "The sluglimpets are a menace. As long as they exist, life is going to be hard for us on this continent. A fast adult can outrun them, but they move quietly and can easily sneak up on people. Once a sluglimpet catches you, the fittest person doesn't stand a chance. If you're attacked in an enclosed space, it might not be possible to escape.

"Outside the electric fences, no one will be able to go out after dark or leave doors or windows open if there are sluglimpets in the area. Even inside the fences we aren't completely safe. During the First Night Attack the creatures climbed the fence over the dead bodies of others. It's lucky for us the sluglimpets aren't intelligent or it might be nearly impossible for us to settle the planet. We would have to go to war with them."

Ethan hesitated before he went on, "I hate the sluglimpets. They killed two people who were very close to me. Yet on the other hand, the animals were only acting on instinct. They live by eating other animals, and we're just food to them. While a part of me wants to see them all exterminated, another side of me thinks that would be wrong. Concordia was their planet before it was ours. We're the interlopers. And though I was horrified by what they did, what Cariad and I did to them was horrible too. We burned them alive. It was what we had to do, but that doesn't seem to make it right. I guess we have to accept that colonizing this planet is an aggressive act. We're taking what isn't ours so we can live. We shouldn't kid ourselves about that."

Turning off the recorder, Ethan focused on the

landscape ahead. He'd set the flitter's elevation to one hundred and fifty meters and the mountains were slowly drawing nearer. Maybe the different landscape would be free of the sluglimpets. He still had a long way to go to find out. According to the flitter's interface he wouldn't arrive until nightfall, even though the vehicle was flying at its top speed. To help pass the time, Ethan watched and recorded the view of the ground below.

Trees similar to the ones that surrounded the settlement covered the surface in a wide forest. Ethan wondered what might live among them. As his eyes became accustomed to the steadily flowing sea of green, he noticed tiny flashes of brilliant red moving among the trees. Could they be some kind of birds? Ethan grew excited. He angled the flitter downward for a closer look.

They were birds! Or if not birds, some kind of flying creature. The wings of the animals moved so fast they were a blur. Ethan angled the flitter lower, wondering if he might be able to catch one. When the underside of the flitter was brushing the tops of the trees, he opened a window. However, before reaching out to attempt to catch one of the airborne creatures, he had second thoughts. What if they were poisonous or wanted to bite him? He retrieved a pair of long, thick gloves from his pack.

His hand encased in a glove, Ethan reached out of the window. The flitter's presence seemed to have sparked an explosion of the scarlet creatures. They were flying up in huge numbers from the trees. Yet though his hand swept through the fluttering clouds many times he couldn't seem to catch any. He didn't want to grab too roughly and hurt one of them.

The red fliers had begun to land on the flitter, though none approached the window. Ethan turned on his recorder to capture a vid and also described what he saw. He was delighted with his find. Concordia wasn't only home to creatures that wanted to kill.

The scarlet aerial animals were settling on the flitter's hood and the closed windows, and they clung to the doors. As soon as they landed, their wings stopped beating and Ethan could see them better. As well as their four roughly triangular wings, which were thin as plaspaper and translucent, the animals had eight legs in four pairs along bodies a little thinner than Ethan's pinky finger. Their wings were four or five times the size of their little bodies. The creatures didn't seem to have eyes or mouth parts, and he couldn't tell which was the front or back as the creatures didn't seem to have heads. He wondered how they ate.

More and more of the flying animals landed. Ethan could no longer see out of the windshield so he peered out the window. The flitter was entirely obscured by a great mass of scarlet beating wings. They were piled so thickly the shape of the flitter was entirely lost. It was a giant homogeneous lump of red wings.

A rustling came from beneath the flitter, and as green vegetation rose in the window, Ethan realized the flitter was sinking down into the trees. The weight of the creatures clinging to it was so great, it was overwhelming the a-grav. Not knowing what lay beneath him and alarmed at the idea of being buried alive in a heaving red mass of life, Ethan set the flitter to maximum lift. It didn't rise, but it did stop sinking. Ethan had to find a way to lighten the load. He reached out and brushed the hood of the flitter as widely as he could reach, wiping off a swathe of flying creatures. But as soon as they'd lifted up, the fliers settled down once more.

Ethan wasn't sure what to do. If he turned off the flitter's drive it would drop into the vegetation, and who knew what unknown creatures might lie below? Yet he couldn't force more lift out of the a-grav. And if he waited much longer, more scarlet fliers would land and make the flitter so heavy even the maximum lift couldn't keep it up.

The only thing he knew about the flying animals was that they wouldn't enter the window. What if he lowered the cover? Maybe enough of them might fly off to give him a chance to get out of there. Alternatively, they might get over their reluctance and land inside the vehicle. Ethan had no other option than to try.

He lowered the hood. Immediately, the sky was obscured by a rising red cloud. Relieved of the weight of the aerial animals, the flitter zoomed upward, and it traveled so fast the acceleration forced off the other red creatures too. Within less than a minute, the jungle was far below. All that remained of the flying animals was a couple that were stuck to the flitter's hood. They'd been crushed by the weight of the others. Ethan slowed down the vehicle and reached out to peel off the dead creatures. He brought them inside and put them on the seat next to him.

Maintaining the safe elevation, Ethan resumed the course to the mountains and resolved not to take any more detours. Though the creatures had been pretty, his investigation of them could have been his downfall. He'd had enough of new Concordian life forms for that day. As the flitter carried him onto the next place he planned to explore, Ethan recorded a vid of the two dead fliers along with an account of his encounter.

By the time Ethan reached the foothills of the mountain range it was dark. He didn't want to explore the new terrain at night, not knowing if the sluglimpets lived there too. Instead, he set the flitter at a safe elevation above a mountain slope and ate his dinner.

It was his third night away from the settlement. Though he wasn't ready to return there and didn't think he would be for a long while yet, Ethan was beginning to feel the absence of company. He thought about Cariad. If she'd been able to come on the trip with him he wouldn't have minded, but she was busy replenishing the colony population. In two or three years, the place would be overrun with children she would create to replace the many lives that had been lost.

For the time being, Ethan would be forced to undertake his journey alone. He wrapped his blanket around himself tightly and fell asleep.

CHAPTER FIVE

The young man's face was intense, angry even. He glared into the camera, and Cariad saw despair mixed with fury in his eyes.

His jaw rigid, he said, "If I'd had my way—"

"Steen... " A woman walked into the camera's view and went to the young man's side. She didn't look much older than him and was similarly dressed in worn-out clothes. She grasped Steen's arm softly, trying to calm him.

"No," he said, wrenching his arm from her grip. "Leave me alone. *I'm* doing the message. That was the agreement. This was the only reason I helped you. If you weren't going to let me go on the ship, I get to tell the bastards what I gave up for them. What we all gave up."

"I'm not saying you can't do it... " She looked toward the camera. "Is that still recording? Turn it off."

"No, don't," Steen said. "I want them to see

everything. I want them to see every detail."

"All right, all right," said the woman. "Just remember, this was our decision—"

"It wasn't *my* decision."

"It was the majority decision. But that isn't important. It wasn't *their* decision. The *Nova Fortuna* colonists didn't choose this. They aren't responsible for what's happened here or what we've decided to do. You don't need to be so harsh. It isn't fair."

"What *is* fair, huh?"

For a moment, the woman's chin trembled. "Nothing's fair. Nothing." She clenched her hands into fists. "But you don't have to take it out on them. What's the point?"

"It might make me hate them and all of you just a smidgen less."

The woman tilted her head and gazed into Steen's eyes, not speaking.

After a pause, Steen's body relaxed. "Okay. I hear you. I'll be *nicer*."

The woman gave him a look of warning and stepped out of sight.

"So," Steen said, returning his attention to the camera, "dear future person, if you're seeing this it's probably because our little secret has been revealed. You know that the friends we sent to visit aren't all they seem. But they're pretty convincing, right?" He smiled smugly. "Did you like their skin? Mina did that—the lovely Mina who was here a minute ago to tell me to tone it down because none of this is your fault." He scowled. "Well, it might not be your fault, but it isn't my fault either. And you're the ones who get to live while we die in this poisoned, diseased dump once known as the beautiful planet Earth. Allow me a little anger on that account, okay? I think I deserve it."

"*Anyway,*" he went on, as if he was telling a friend an anecdote, "I don't know how much our friends told you, so you'll forgive me if I repeat things you already know, won't you? A good story's worth telling twice. I promise I won't leave out the best parts."

Steen put his hands in his pockets and began to stroll to and fro. "To summarize, nearly everyone is dead. The flu that killed them was nasty, but at least it was quick." He stopped and waved a finger at the camera. "Pretty painful though from what I heard. I don't really know. I never caught it. A little quirk of nature, a strand of protein on a chromosome, made me immune."

He leaned toward the camera and cupped his mouth with his hand as if telling a secret. "If you *really* want to know what the symptoms were like, ask Mina. She's even rarer than me. She got sick but recovered. It was a crying shame the same couldn't be said for the rest of her family. Now *there's* a sight you don't want to wake up to."

Cariad flicked the switch to stop the holo, freezing Steen in his close-up. He was so angry and bitter and the story he was telling was so awful, she felt sick. The holo wasn't at all what she'd been expecting. Though Strongquist had warned her she might find it alarming, she'd thought it would a simple message or report, or even some kind of documentary like the ones that had been made about the *Nova Fortuna* Project. The holo was so raw and full of hatred, Cariad didn't want to hear any more right then. She turned it off, banishing Steen to her personal files. Maybe she would watch more later. Whatever it was that Steen wanted to say, it wasn't urgent. It was all history from before the Guardians had departed Earth.

She had more important things to do. She had to speak to Garwin.

Cariad left the *Mistral's* viewing room and walked to the cabin where Garwin had been confined ever since his wife's suicide. Cariad hoped he would have recovered a little from the shock of his wife's death, and that he might be able to tell her something that would help her root out any remaining saboteurs.

When she arrived she unlocked the door and went inside. Garwin hardly seemed to have changed from his almost catatonic state of two days previously. He was slumped on a chair in the corner of the cabin, his chin on his chest and his hands hanging loosely on his lap, looking like a sail that had no wind to fill it out. He didn't look up or make any other movement that acknowledged her arrival.

Compared to the Garwin who had confidently addressed the crowd of Gens and Woken at the stadium, and the man who had successfully played a double game that had won him favor on both sides of the Woken/Gen conflict, he was barely recognizable. It was like Twyla's death had sucked away his life too.

Cariad sat on the bed. Montfort had checked Garwin for a Natural Movement tattoo and found nothing, and Cariad had decided the best course of action was to act as though she believed Garwin wasn't a follower. If he was, despite having no tattoo, he might think he had everyone fooled and grow over-confident, accidentally letting something slip. If he really wasn't, her belief in his innocence might encourage him to help her with the investigation. "Garwin, I'm sorry about what's happened. You must feel terrible."

Garwin shook his head and put his face in his hands. He took a breath and looked up. "She wasn't involved with them. I know how it looks. She was there when we found the aquifer, but it wasn't her who blew it open. She would never have done anything like that. She taught kindy. Do you think she would have killed kids? She loved kids."

Cariad saw she had no easy task ahead. She hadn't imagined that Garwin would be so deep in denial about his wife.

"Why do you think Twyla killed herself?" she asked.

"Isn't it obvious?"

"Well, yes," Cariad replied, thinking *She feared exposure and execution*. "But I'm not sure we're thinking along the same lines.

"She was the prime suspect, wasn't she?" Garwin asked. "Just because she knew about the aquifer and Ethan saw her leaving the caves. What could she say to prove her innocence? No one would have believed her. The truth was, anyone could have done it. Anyone could have explored that area and found that aquifer. The bomb could have been planted at any time. But they all would have wanted someone to blame for all those deaths. They would want revenge for what happened. She didn't stand a chance, and she knew it."

"If that's so, how come you're still here?" Cariad asked.

"What do you mean?"

"You knew about the aquifer too. You were also under house arrest after the disaster. What makes you think you wouldn't have been scapegoated as well as—or even instead of—Twyla?"

"Because I was *liked*," Garwin exclaimed. "I should know. I worked hard enough for it. You Woken all liked me, right? The Gens loved me. Twyla wasn't like that. She didn't work at being popular. She didn't enjoy being around people. That was why she worked with kids."

Cariad folded her arms. To make him tell her anything about Twyla that might be useful to her investigation, Cariad would have to convince Garwin that his wife was a Natural Movement saboteur. She hated to do it, but she needed to get tough with the man if he was going to give her anything useful. "Are you sure about that? You're sure the reason she worked with kids was because she was uncomfortable around adults?"

"Yes," Garwin said. "I am."

Cariad took out an interface screen and brought up the image of the tattoo on Twyla's thigh. To Cariad, it was unmistakably the logo of the Natural Movement. The stylized N and M was branded on her mind. It had caused her many moments of frustration and irritation on Earth when the group had protested the *Nova Fortuna* Project or fought hard against rationality and reason in many fields of civilized society. However, as a Gen, it was possible that Garwin might not be so familiar with the logo. She turned the interface screen toward him. "Do you know what this is?"

He studied the image for a moment. "Someone drew something on their skin? I don't know what it's supposed to be." Cariad thought she believed him. In his current state of mind, the man's carefully constructed outward persona was by the wayside. The Garwin she was seeing seemed to be the real one. She told him the meaning of the sign.

"So?" he asked. "Why are you showing it to me? I've never seen it before."

"Maybe you haven't." Cariad inwardly squirmed over what she was about to say. "Garwin, this tattoo was high up on Twyla's thigh. It was located in a place where only someone who was intimate with her would have seen it."

The effect of her words on Garwin was instantaneous. His mouth fell open and a flicker of revelation crossed his features, but it was quickly supplanted with rejection. Garwin's jawline firmed and he looked away. "I don't believe it."

"I can take you to see it if you want."

"I don't want to see it," he shouted, rising to his feet. "How dare you come to me with lies about my poor dead wife? Who do you think you are? Get out of here. Get out!"

Garwin's sudden rage frightened Cariad. She ran out of the cabin and locked the door. From inside the room came the sounds of objects being thrown about. This was a side of Garwin no one had ever seen. Cariad had clearly pressed a sensitive button, and part of her hated to be so blunt with the man, but it had been necessary. Cariad was sure the reason Twyla had been a kindergarten teacher was so that she could indoctrinate a handful of young children and pass on cultish Natural Movement teachings to them.

If Natural Movement followers remained among the settlers, they wouldn't rest until the entire colony was wiped out. Garwin might know something that would help her prevent that from happening. But right then she would have to give him time to process what he'd seen. While she waited for Garwin to calm down and hopefully accept the truth about his wife, she go planetside to check on the examination of all the colonists for evidence of a tattoo. But first she needed to sleep.

***

Cariad remained aboard the *Mistral* during the quiet shift. Addleson allocated her one of the spare cabins. The ship contained enough to accommodate all the Guardians. Cariad wasn't sure why, as the androids probably didn't have any requirement for sleep or privacy. Perhaps the berths had been added in order to maintain the deception of the Guardians' humanity, or because their creators had thought there might be a need to transport *Nova Fortuna* colonists somewhere. The cabin Cariad slept in seemed unused. The fact added weight to her suspicion that no Guardian had ever slept in it, though it was also possible that the ship's invisible nanobot sanitation kept it pristine.

The next day, Cariad went to the *Mistral's* shuttle bay. The starship carried two shuttles and each held forty passengers, which had been double the entire ship's crew. Cariad wondered what had been the rationale behind the Guardians' creators in providing them with one more shuttle than they needed. Perhaps Steen might explain when she found the time and fortitude to endure another bout of his anger and desperation.

The Gen pilot who had been assigned the role of flying one of the Guardians' shuttles was happy to take Cariad down to the surface. As she was the only passenger, the pilot invited her to sit in the flight cabin.

All the pilots were Gens, and the one flying the shuttle was called Zhang. Cariad knew her vaguely. There weren't many pilots among the colonists so they stuck out. There was something Cariad had wanted to ask Zhang. Though some time had passed since the shuttle explosion, the woman might know something useful.

When the shuttle was out of the *Mistral's* bay and the dome that was Concordia was spread out beneath them Cariad asked, "Does flying the shuttles worry you now, since the explosion?"

Zhang replied, "I have to admit, it does a little. But they're thoroughly inspected before each flight now so that helps put my mind at ease. How about you? Does it worry you, traveling as a passenger?"

"I do feel a little nervous sometimes. I was supposed to be aboard the one that went down. It was only a fluke that I wasn't."

"Really? I didn't know that. What a stroke of luck."

"Yes, I was very fortunate. Do you mind if I ask you something personal?"

"That depends what it is."

"Well, I wanted to ask if you were friends with the pilot who died."

"Walston? Yeah, of course. We all know each other. I wasn't really close to him, you know, but he seemed like a good guy. His wife is pregnant. She found out a week or so before he died. Did you know?"

"No, I didn't." Cariad's hatred for the Natural Movement saboteurs moved a notch higher. Still, the fact made her conjecture less likely.

"Was that all you wanted to ask me?" Zhang said.

"No, it isn't. I was wondering... Do you think it's possible that it was Walston who brought the bomb onto the shuttle?"

"Huh? And kill himself along with everyone else aboard? Do you honestly think that's a possibility?"

"I agree it's a stretch," Cariad said. "I didn't think of it at all until after Twyla killed herself. Then it occurred to me that fanatics often have a death wish, only they want to take as many people out with them as they can. I wondered if the stadium bomber had died in that explosion, and if someone aboard the shuttle had detonated the bomb."

"If the saboteur was aboard," Zhang replied, "that's good news for us. It means there are fewer of them to worry about. But from what I know of Walston, I doubt he wanted to die. He had too much to live for. Who gets his wife pregnant then kills himself? Doesn't make a lot of sense to me."

She was probably right, Cariad reasoned. Still, Zhang hadn't experienced the growing excesses of the Natural Movement on Earth. The pilot hadn't lived at a time of festivals for deliberately exposing children to infectious diseases and "back to nature" communes on remote islands that resulted in people starving to death. To Zhang, if she knew anything about such events, they were dry facts of a disconnected past. Cariad had been around while such events were taking place. When she thought about it, there was nothing she couldn't imagine a Natural Movement follower doing to further their cause.

After disembarking the shuttle, Cariad walked directly to the settlement hospital, where Dr. Montfort was carrying out the examination of every colonist for signs of the Natural Movement tattoo. There were too many colonists to make everyone line up for their examination. Instead, they had been given an appointment to attend. Cariad waited outside the examination room until the doctor was free to speak to her.

"I won't take up too much of your time," Cariad said as she went into the examination room. "I only wanted to find out how everything was going."

Montfort said to his medic, "Alasdair, would you mind waiting outside?"

After Alasdair left, Cariad asked, "Did you find anything yet?"

"As is to be expected, not anything definite," Montfort replied. "If it had been possible to immediately examine everyone the moment the suicide's tattoo was discovered, we might have stood a chance. Now, unless any remaining saboteurs are very stupid, the best we can hope for is the remains of a botched attempt to remove the ink."

"What's the story you gave to explain the reason for the examination?"

"I said we suspect that Concordian bacteria might be causing an infectious skin disease, but of course Natural Movement members will know what I'm looking for. I haven't found anything except some grazes and scrapes in areas similar to where Twyla's tattoo was positioned."

"And the injured claim the lesions are due to accidents that occurred when the caves were flooded," Cariad said.

"Obviously. And undoubtedly some of them are. We've also been dealing with broken bones, concussions, internal bleeding, sprains, and plenty of other traumas."

"Of course you have," Cariad said, suddenly guilty. "I'm sorry, I should have done more to help. It's been a long time since my training but I could have done something."

"That's okay. We all have a lot on our plate. The Gen doctors are doing an excellent job. Erm, as you're here now...?"

"Sure. Where do I wash up and find clean scrubs?"

"Sorry, I meant we need to get your own examination out of the way," Montfort said.

"My examination? But I... " Cariad had spent the last several months trying to help catch the Natural Movement saboteurs. She'd nearly died at their hands twice. Yet the doctor had a point. No one could exempt themselves from examination. She sighed. "Okay. Where do I get ready?"

The doctor indicated a curtained cubicle. Cariad walked over to it and parted the curtains. The sight of the narrow examination bed covered in sanipaper caused knots in her stomach. She had a particular dislike of being prodded and poked. After quickly stripping off her clothes and piling them on a chair, she put on the medical gown and lay down on the bed.

Dr. Montfort asked if she was ready before he entered the cubicle. The first thing he did was wipe inside her mouth with a probe. He removed the detachable end and popped it into a DNA reader.

"Not sure it's me?" Cariad asked, joking to ease her tension.

"That's right," Montfort replied. "You sure look like Cariad, but, who knows, maybe you're an insane cultist in disguise." His light-hearted tone relaxed her a little, but when it came time for the examination, she tensed up again. The doctor thoroughly examined her skin, recording a vid as he went along. He even examined the skin of her scalp under her hair. "Okay," he said finally. "You're done. It looks like you aren't planning to kill everyone after all."

Cariad adjusted her gown to cover herself. "Not today anyway."

Montfort smiled. "I'll leave you to get dressed. Take your time. You're my last victim this morning."

As soon as he left, Cariad put on her clothes just as quickly as she'd removed them, anxious to leave the cubicle. Montfort was at his desk recording his notes. Alasdair hadn't returned.

"You have notes on everyone who shows signs they might have had a tattoo before they got rid of it?" she asked.

"I have a list of them here for you," he replied. "I don't like recording their names because I'm probably casting suspicion on innocent people. But I don't see a way around it."

"So this list includes everyone who has a lesion in an unusual place?"

"Exactly. All the ones I've seen so far. I still have around half of the colonists to examine. Normally injuries from physical accidents are located on knees, elbows, hands, heads, and backs. And often the feet too if the accident is a fall of some kind. All the areas of the body where you might expect impact injuries if the person is conscious and trying to save themselves from harm. If someone has a mysterious lesion in an odd place like the inside of the thigh, for example, they make it onto the list."

"Are there many of them?"

"More than makes me comfortable. Do you want to see it now?"

"Yes, I do."

Montfort turned around his interface screen to show Cariad six names. She didn't recognize five of them, but one was a big surprise. "One of these is a Woken," she exclaimed.

"Rene?" said Montfort. "Yes, she's on it. I was very surprised to see a lesion on her."

"She wasn't at the caves," Cariad said.

"I know." Montfort's usually amenable expression turned grave. "Of course, it doesn't have to mean anything."

Cariad paused as her surprise settled down. Rene was one of the few people who had shown her support when Cariad had been the only Woken who was prepared to stand up to the leadership-usurper, Anahi. Also, Cariad hadn't considered that any of the Woken might be a Natural Movement saboteur. After the discovery that the cult had probably passed down its teaching from one generation to the next over the course of the voyage, Cariad had assumed that if any saboteurs remained, they were Gens. The revelation that a Woken could be one of the traitors threw a whole new light onto her investigation.

"Did you ask her what happened?" Cariad asked. "How she hurt herself?"

"Yes, of course. I asked all of the people on the list where they sustained their injury, and they all had some kind of an explanation. Except for Rene. She said she didn't know."

"She didn't know?" Cariad echoed. "How could she not know? I take it this wasn't a bruise or something slight like that?"

"No. She'd lost quite a bit of skin. She said she didn't even know the abrasion was there until I showed her. The lesion is at the top of her thigh, just under her buttock. Not many nerve endings there, but still, the injury wasn't slight. She should definitely have been able to feel it."

"Can you think of any reason she might not have known about it?"

Montfort looked down. "Nothing's jumping out at me at the moment."

Cariad said, heavily, "Well, could you send me the list?"

"I will." Montfort asked, "So you're taking charge of the investigation now the Guardians are out of the picture?"

"Yes. I wanted to be involved right from the start after the stadium bombing but the Guardians seemed to hold all the information. Someone has to do it so it might as well be me."

"I can't think of a better person." Montfort smiled warmly, but his effort to cheer her up had little effect. The revelation that her friend could be a Natural Movement terrorist had left her feeling hollow inside.

"If I can be of any more help to you, just let me know," Montfort said.

"Just let me know if you see any more suspicious injuries. Do you need me to help with the examinations?"

"Thanks for the offer, but I think I can manage. You have your plate full as it is, and Alasdair is a wonderful help."

"Yes," Cariad said. "He's a good medic." She stood to leave.

"How's the repopulation program coming along?" Montfort asked.

"Okay so far, but it's early days. Like you, I have great help, so that's something to be thankful for."

"Uhuh," said Montfort. His gaze strayed down to his interface. "Oh, the Leader election result's just come in."

"Really? Who won?"

"Someone called Osias."

"Osias?" Cariad repeated. "Should I know him?"

"I think he was one of Garwin's mechanics."

"They elected a friend of Garwin's? I wouldn't have predicted that."

"Maybe they aren't friends," Montfort replied.

"They might only have worked together. I don't know... Gen society is something of a closed book to me. We Woken grew distant from them during the disturbances."

"Yes, we did, and the two sides were never close from the beginning. I hope we can put that all behind us now."

"Me too," Montfort said.

As Cariad left, she mentally added paying a visit to the new Leader to her list of things to do. His cooperation while she carried out her investigation could be vital.

CHAPTER SIX

Ethan was awake before the sun came up. A chill air had invaded the flitter overnight and he was shivering. Somehow, his blanket had fallen off. As he sat up stiffly, drawing his blanket over his shoulders, he saw that the flitter's windows were covered in condensation. He wiped one clean with a corner of a blanket. Aside from pale stars in a lightening sky, all was dark outside. Lowering the window, he listened. The sounds of something shuffling around on the ground came from below.

He stuck his head out the window and peered down, but he couldn't make out anything in the blackness. Only the shadowy shapes of the surrounding foothills were visible in the starlight. Keeping his gaze on the spot where the noise seemed to be coming from, he turned on the flitters' lights. A flurry of movement resulted. Whatever they were, the things moved too fast for Ethan to see them clearly. All he could make out were the hairy backs of animals about half the size of the sluglimpets.

In a moment, the creatures were gone from the circle of light that beamed out from the flitter. Had the nocturnal life forms been only wandering around, or had they been attracted by his presence like the sluglimpets had? One thing was sure, they were another large life form that hadn't been recorded by the probes sent from Earth to assess Concordia. Were the organisms dangerous? Another type of predator, perhaps? If they were, what was their prey? Whatever the sluglimpets ate had never been established. There was clearly a lot more information on the animals of the continent for Ethan to discover.

He watched the lit-up area of ground for a while, but the creatures didn't return. Lowering the flitter to a couple of meters above the patch, he saw the dry ground had been disturbed by small, many-toed feet. After recording a vid of the tracks, he raised the flitter to a safe height. The sun was coming up over the thin line of ocean just visible in the distance.

Ethan made his breakfast, adding water to a cereal mix and then pushing the button that activated the heating function. He stirred the mixture as the chemical heat permeated it until steam rose. Ethan spooned down the porridge quickly, grateful for the warmth that helped banish the chill that had invaded him while he slept. When he'd finished eating, he recorded his thoughts.

"The creatures that were moving beneath the flitter when I awoke were the fourth life form I've encountered so far on Concordia," he said, "and the second nocturnal animal. I don't know if these creatures are dangerous. It could be a coincidence they had congregated right below where the flitter was hovering and they weren't trying to reach me. But after my experience with the flying creatures yesterday, it still clear that settling Concordia will probably be harder than we thought."

As the sun rose, Ethan guided the flitter higher up the mountainside. He wanted to see what was up near the summits and also find a pass that led through the range. He wanted to go down to the river that lay on the other side.

The sun was high in the sky and the mountains were flooded with light when he reached a spot near the top. The temperature had dropped considerably, so Ethan put on another layer of clothes, topping them off with a thick jacket. He hadn't thought to bring a hat and so he had to protect his head as best he could by turning up the jacket collar to cover his ears.

No animal life seemed to be around on the rocky slopes, which were littered with loose stones and pebbles. Ethan lowered the flitter to ground level when he reached a flattish spot, and, taking his weapon with him, he climbed out of his to investigate the surrounding area. The slope wasn't very steep and he could walk it comfortably providing he took care not to slip on the scattered stones. It felt good to stretch his legs after days cooped up in the flitter.

Ethan recorded everything he saw. Between the larger rocks, sinuous strands like extremely elongated leaves wound, creeping out over the loose flakes of stone. When he stepped closer he discovered that the surface of the ribbon plants was pitted and fissured and oozed a gelatinous material, though the plants didn't seem to be injured. He forbore from touching the stuff but he recorded it close up.

As he drew nearer to the edges of the slope, where the land rose too steeply to walk and the slope met a wall of rock, he saw holes gaping at intervals. The holes were wide and flat, and their impenetrable blackness indicated they were deep. Were they where yet another nocturnal creature lived? After recording a vid of one, Ethan backed up and stayed well away from them.

He wandered for a while in a wide circle but remained within fifty meters or so of the flitter. He didn't want to risk being cut off from the vehicle, which was his life line. He'd already traveled so far he would starve before he could walk back, assuming he would be able to find his way and avoid being eaten.

After he'd seen and recorded as much as he could, Ethan decided that his next step would be to spend the afternoon taking the flitter down to the river. As far as he could, he'd established that the mountain regions might not be particularly safe. It was time to explore further afield.

He flew the flitter into the air, searching for a gap between the mountain peaks that would avoid the necessity of traversing the high-altitude, snowy regions. Spotting a low pass, he flew toward it and through. In the country beyond the range a wide, brown ribbon divided the mountains from the land. Ethan oriented the flitter in the direction of the river, and began another long journey.

The other side of the range was much more perpendicular, and Ethan found himself passing great walls of gray rock, similar to the cliffs of the cave settlement, though these walls were cracked in long, broken strips. He passed them in their shadow as they blocked the light from the sun. As he went, the rocks' resemblance to the ocean cliffs reminded him of Cherry's near-death, which also reminded him of all the people who had died at the caves, and in the shuttle explosion, and at the stadium bombing. Then, inevitably, his thoughts turned once again to the horrible deaths of Lauren and Dr. Crowley. A somber mood settled over him. His recorder hung unused around his neck.

It was late afternoon by the time he arrived at the river. He hovered above the southern shore of the gigantic body of water, in the shadow of the mountain range. From his low elevation the northern shore wasn't visible. Ethan had seen plenty of vids of large rivers on Earth but this seemed even larger than those. It was more like a sea.

The sun was still some distance above the horizon. Ethan estimated that he had enough time to land and look around before any nocturnal animals like the sluglimpets would venture out for the night. He lowered the flitter to the sandy shore, though as he landed he saw that the sand was different from that by the ocean. It was dark gray and so fine it was almost like dust except that it was moist and gritty.

Ethan was careful to take his weapon with him again when he left the flitter. He was also careful to close the doors firmly. He didn't want to find something inside waiting for him when he returned.

The plants that grew alongside the river had high roots that arched out from the central stem down to the ground, and they had long, thin branches that dangled among the roots. Ethan had to step high to walk between them. It was hard to tell where one plant ended and another began. As he walked away from the shore, the fine sand gave way to sandy earth and then a rich, black soil that he reached only five minutes' walk from the river. In this rich earth, the plants grew tall. The ones Ethan soon found himself among were three times his own height.

He glanced back toward the flitter to check that he hadn't gone too far. As in the mountains, he was determined not to let the vehicle out of his sight. When he couldn't see it immediately, he began to retrace his steps. His footprints were plain to see in the soft soil so it wasn't difficult to return along exactly the same route.

Each step that he took, Ethan expected to catch sight of the flitter, but it didn't appear. His heart began to pound. Where had it gone? He should have been able to see it minutes previously.

The black soil reverted to powdery beach sand and the plants shrank to head height and still there was no sign of the flitter. Ethan ran the last few meters. He reached the same river bank he'd left only minutes ago, but it was bare. He sped over to the spot where he'd left the flitter and saw that the sand was disturbed. Long grooves led down to the water. Ethan walked to the water's edge but he couldn't see anything breaking the pale brown surface or beneath it.

Had the flitter moved by itself? It didn't seem possible. Ethan was sure that he'd turned it off before he left it. And the area was too flat for the vehicle to simply slide into the water. He looked up and around, just in case the flitter had somehow risen upward by itself. The skies were clear.

The only explanation was that his vehicle was in the river. That was what the grooves in the sand indicated anyway. Had something in the water dragged off his vehicle, his only way of returning to the settlement? All Ethan knew was that he was alone on the beach and the flitter was gone.

CHAPTER SEVEN

Cariad did a little research before she went to meet the Gen called Osias who had won the election. The new Leader was young—only in his late twenties—and he was a mechanic who had worked under Garwin, as Montfort had said.

Whether he'd been Garwin's friend or not, perhaps some of the older man's previous charm had rubbed off on him. From what Cariad could tell from his campaign speeches, he seemed to be a good choice. Like his previous supervisor, he was sociable and always ready with a smile, yet he seemed level-headed too. And he was focused on integrating the Woken and the Gens.

Already, only a short time after banding together to reject the Guardians' interference, divisions were opening up again. The Woken spent most of their time aboard the *Nova Fortuna* while the Gens rarely ventured up to the ship, despite the fact that the previous restrictions on travel had been lifted. They were busy with the restocking and continued building of the settlement. Due to the division of labor between the Woken's scientific endeavors and the mainly physical work of the Gens, Cariad could easily envisage a return to the times when the Woken thought the Gens were inferior to themselves and in need of guidance. In turn, the Gens would begin to become annoyed at the Wokens' aloofness and bossiness. Someone needed to do something to encourage the groups to mix.

Only a day into his tenancy, one of the first actions Osias had taken was to claim the Leader's traditional office aboard the *Nova Fortuna* and to open another for his use within the settlement. As was the custom, whether aboard the ship or planetside, if he was in his office, anyone would be able to visit him during the working day to discuss their problems relating to colony life.

Cariad was one of the first at the new Leader's door. She'd chosen to visit him at his settlement office. She was spending as much time as she could planetside to buck the trend the reclusive Woken were setting, though she hated to leave her techs to work alone in the reproductive lab. They had a lot to do.

When it was finally her turn to see the Leader, Cariad walked through to his private office. Osias was on a vid call as she entered, so she waited for him to finish.

"Sorry. Sit down," he said, closing his interface. "It's Cariad, right? I thought I might see you quite soon." He stood up and leaned over the desk, holding out his hand. He was wiry, not the kind of build Cariad would have expected to see in a mechanic. When she shook his hand, however, his grip was powerful. He went on, "I know I'm not supposed to have favorites, but you're my favorite Woken."

Cariad laughed. "You make us sound like pets."

"Well I didn't mean it like that," said Osias, smiling, "but you are a group apart from us, aren't you? We Gens like to watch you from afar."

"I know," Cariad replied. Osias was putting it politely, but she knew what he meant about the aura of mystique that the Woken seemed to hold for the Gens. "We're a slice of history to you, just like the Guardians seemed to come from the future."

"Exactly," Osias said. "So how can I help you? I'm guessing you aren't here to complain about the sanitation in the new residences or to ask to change your profession."

"No, actually. I'm entirely satisfied with both my sanitation and my job." She smiled. "Seriously, I wanted to propose something. It's an idea I had about safety in the settlement. Feel free to shoot it down. You are the Leader after all."

"Please, go ahead. I'm very interested to hear what you have to say."

"I was wondering if you'd given any thought to the policing of the settlement."

Osias' expression darkened. "No, I hadn't, actually. I thought we'd had enough policing from the Guardians."

"I thought so too. Only I'm not sure we've seen the last of the Natural Movement."

"Wasn't Twyla the saboteur?" Osias asked.

"Otherwise why did she commit suicide?"

"You might be interested to hear Garwin's take on that," replied Cariad. "But anyway, it isn't certain that Twyla was acting alone. Garwin might have been in on it too, and though he's under arrest it's possible there are others. I already have a list of potential suspects. I think it would be prudent to act as though we still have saboteurs among us."

"Where did you get your suspects from?"

"Er, I can't tell you that. I'm sorry."

Osias gave her a long look that belied his young years. Cariad felt as though he was searching her for evidence of deceit. While she gazed steadily back at him, she wondered what he'd made of his former supervisor.

Osias leaned back in his seat. "You've taken over the investigation from the Guardians?"

Cariad nodded, tense with the knowledge of how a Gen might view her actions as further interference by the Woken. "I thought I would take on the responsibility. I was involved quite closely when the Guardians were working on it."

"I see," Osias said, his tone implying he was reserving judgment for the moment. "Well, if we are going to police the settlement, the law enforcers will be Gens."

"Of course."

He nodded. "Okay. I'll think about it. Let me know if there's anything I can do to help with the investigation. There are spare rooms in this building, for instance, if you need somewhere planetside to work."

"Thanks," Cariad said. "I won't take up any

more of your time."

She left the Leader's office more light-hearted than she'd felt in a long time. The man's intelligence and open-mindedness were a refreshing change from Anahi's anxiety-ridden attempt at leadership. Also she felt instinctively that Osias was someone the Woken would warm to.

It was time for Cariad to return to the *Nova Fortuna*. She had to check in with her techs. As a team they'd removed the fertilization and gestation equipment out of storage and restarted the reproductive processes. She'd wasted no time in analyzing the gene pool of living, fertile Gens and Woken. Some gametes also remained in storage from the ones collected from donors on Earth. She found their viability was still good despite one hundred and eighty-four years spent frozen. And other sex cells had been collected from Gen volunteers during the course of the voyage. Based on the data, she'd selected the best matches to ensure the maximum heterogeneity and healthiness of new colonists. Her techs were working on creating the embryos.

Cariad had always felt uncomfortable about the section of the Manual that stated that Gens had to be chemically prevented from reproducing naturally until a couple of years prior to Arrival. Donating eggs or sperm had been the only way open to them to pass something of themselves on to posterity, though the identity of their offspring was concealed.

She understood the necessity of the anonymity rule. People who were parents had a disincentive to stick to the colonization plan. Faced with the prospect of their own children being forced to live out their lives aboard a starship would have made them more likely to rebel. During the first one or two generations, the Gens might have tried to turn the *Nova Fortuna* around and return to Earth so that even if they never saw blue skies or smelled grass again, their children might. Later generations might have tried to take the ship off course to investigate the possibility of finding a closer habitable planet. Although this possibility wasn't fantastical, the data on the planet they'd been on course for was the most rigorously assessed and the safest bet in the gamble of deep space colonization.

Though Cariad appreciated the rationale behind the decision to not allow any Gens except the Final Generation to bear their own children, that didn't prevent her guilty feelings. Each natural pregnancy and birth that had occurred since she'd been revived from cryo was a source of pleasure to her.

Still, Cariad had a special enjoyment of her job too. She especially liked decanting the new infants. So although the reason for re-opening the reproduction facilities was regrettable, she had no problems with returning to the task of stocking the colony with new humans.

***

Cariad hadn't ever really noticed the smell of the *Nova Fortuna* until she'd spent time aboard the Guardians' *Mistral,* which was almost clinically clean. Now, each time she stepped off a shuttle onto the old colony ship, it smelled stale and moldy to her. This wasn't surprising given the ship's age and the fact that many thousands of humans had lived and died on it, but that didn't stop Cariad from noticing it.

Cariad walked the familiar route to the Fertilization Lab and went inside.

"Hey, Cariad," said one of her two techs, a Gen called Cassie.

"Cariad?" another said. He was a Woken called Florian. "Who's that? Never heard of her."

"Oh, you know who she is," said Cassie. "She used to work here, like, years ago."

"Come on guys," Cariad said. "Cut me some slack. I haven't been gone that long. I've had a lot to do. I had to say goodnight to that final creepy Guardian for one thing."

"You did?" Cassie asked. "What was it like? And where did they all go? I mean, I keep thinking they're going to spring out of hiding all of a sudden and kill us all in our sleep."

"That isn't likely," Cariad said. "I locked the room they went into. But to answer your first question, it was pretty eerie. They all just turned themselves off. Standing up, too, and wearing their uniforms. Some of them didn't even bother to close their eyes."

Cassie looked horrified. "Well thanks for that, Cariad. Now I feel a whole lot better."

"Sorry, but you did ask. So, what are you both up to? Have you implanted the first batch of embryos?"

"Yes," Florian replied, "and they all took. Isn't that great?"

"That is great," said Cariad. "Well done. You can't get much better than a zero percent failure rate. So the Gestation Room is full. Where are you going to put the ones you're making now?"

"We cleared out a couple of extra rooms like you said," Cassie replied. "The soil biologists weren't too pleased. They were using them to grow microorganisms they'd found in Concordian soil. But I explained that the future of the colony depended on, you know, actual colonists, and they couldn't argue with that."

"Microorganisms?" Cariad said. "I'm not sure those are the best rooms to be growing babies in."

"Don't worry," Florian said. "We sterilized both rooms top to bottom. The only thing that'll be growing in there from now on is fetuses."

"Hmmm... okay," said Cariad, though she remained uncomfortable. She wished her assistants had chosen disused storage rooms or something similar. Concordia remained mostly a closed book to all the scientists. They couldn't assume they could predict the properties or behavior of anything they found there. But the embryos her team were creating had to go somewhere, so she didn't have any choice but to allow them to go into gestation bags in the rooms that had been selected. "How many bags did you find room for?"

Florian replied, "Seventy-three in the extra rooms."

"Right," said Cariad. "So with the fetuses you started yesterday, that brings us up to one hundred and twenty-three new colonists in nine months' time. That isn't enough to entirely replenish the pool."

"Don't forget the pregnancies planetside," said

Cassie. "The last I heard, we were up to twenty-one, and one of them is twins."

"Twins?" said Cariad. "Cool! They'll be the first twins ever born on Concordia."

"Providing they make it that far," said Florian. "Hate to put a downer on the news, but twins do have a higher rate of complications. Better not to count our chickens yet."

"Count our what?" Cassie asked.

"Chickens," Florian repeated. "You know." He made his arms into wings and clucked around the lab, pecking at imaginary corn.

Cassie laughed so hard, she couldn't catch her breath. She wiped her eyes. "No, I don't know, and I don't think I want to. You Woken have some strange sayings. Earth must have been a crazy place. I'm glad I'm going to live on a normal planet."

"I'm glad you're going to live on a normal planet too," said Cariad, also chuckling at Florian's antics. "But if we're going to make a success of that we need to grow some more people. And you're both doing fantastically to help with that. I forgot to remind you, though, to be gentle with the equipment. It's nearly a couple of centuries old. I'd been hoping to never have to use it again."

"Yeah," said Florian. "We know. It's almost as old as you and I, Cariad. We're taking the most care we can."

"Great," Cariad said. "So, twenty-one pregnancies planetside, hopefully resulting in twenty-two babies, brings us up to one hundred and forty-five new people. It still isn't enough. All in all, we've lost three hundred and fifty-two colonists. And it will take at least eighteen years for the babies we have now to grow old enough to reproduce."

"And it wouldn't be a good idea to encourage them to have babies so young," said Florian.

"Very true," Cariad agreed. "We need to up the numbers now, rather than later. On the other hand, a hundred and twenty-three new babies aboard the ship is a lot to handle. The facilities are only set up to handle fifty at a time."

"I'm pretty sure the Gens will make up the shortfall over the next few years," said Cassie. "The people I speak to are getting over the "icky" aspect of natural reproduction and they're thinking about having their own babies."

"That's good to hear," said Cariad. "I wouldn't want to try to force them, but the colony needs all the people it can get right now. Ideally, I'd like to be matching couples for maximum genetic diversity, but I don't think that would go down too well."

"Er, no," said Cassie. "I think the Gens have had enough interference from the Woken to last a lifetime." As she realized what she'd said, the tech turned bright red. "Sorry. I didn't mean... "

"It's okay," Cariad said. "For what it's worth, I entirely agree."

"Yeah, don't worry about it," said Florian cheerfully. "The Gens will soon be breeding like rabbits."

"Rabbits?" Cassie queried. "Are they the animals that purr and sit in your lap?"

"No," Florian replied. "That's cats."

"Please," said Cassie, sensing what was coming

next. "No more animal impersonations."

Undeterred, Florian went on, "You know, miaooowww!"

Laughing, Cariad said, "I'm going to go check on the new embryos."

"You are?" said Cassie. "I don't think they're even visible to the naked eye yet."

"Yeah, well, I'm going to have a look anyway." Cariad caught a glimpse of Florian rolling his eyes at Cassie, but she chose to ignore it. She knew she had a rep for being overly attached to the babies she was responsible for growing. She didn't care.

After putting on sterile over garments, she went into the dimly lit Gestation Room. The seemingly empty transparent sacs hung from the ceiling in rows, each containing a bundle of cells at its apex that would hopefully grow into a healthy baby.

The Gestation Room was one of Cariad's favorite places aboard ship. One of the techs had already started up the recording of a mother's heartbeat and the swish of blood through veins and arteries. Cariad found the sound soothing and she guessed that the babies did too. Cassie had been correct to say the embryos were still too small to see, especially in the dim red light that mimicked the interior of a uterus, but Cariad still took pleasure in walking up and down the rows, checking the bags and imagining the infants that would gradually fill them as they grew, until they would finally be decanted, slimy and squirming and perhaps uttering their first cries.

She recalled Cassie's mention of the "ickiness" many Gens felt about pregnancy and birth. She understood the feeling. It was exactly how she'd always felt too, and the paradox between her sentiment and her role on the *Nova Fortuna* wasn't lost on her. She wondered if she might ever feel differently. She wasn't too old to have her own children if she chose to, and with the current state of the colony, she felt some of the pressure that all women of child-bearing age were probably feeling.

Her thoughts drifted sadly to memories of her parents and sisters, who she'd been forced to leave behind to take part in the *Nova Fortuna* Project. Her mother would have been delighted to have a grandchild. She hoped at least one of her sisters had been able to fulfill that desire.

Cariad heaved a sigh. Her time in the Gestation Room wasn't having its usual soothing effect. She felt more melancholy and anxious about the future than she had before she'd come in. It was strange. Whenever she remembered the family she'd left behind, it always made her more fearful about the failure of the colony. It was as if it would only be if the colony succeeded that she would finally be able to banish the guilt that plagued her. Although her family were long dead, she somehow needed the colony to thrive for their sake. She wanted to be able to assure herself that the sacrifice she'd forced her family to make had been worth it.

Cariad left the Gestation Room and took off the sterile garments before returning to the Fertilization Lab. Florian had ceased horsing around and both he and Cassie were working on creating embryos. She joined them and began to carry out checks on the fertilized eggs from her techs' earlier work.

She worked with her team for a few more hours

until they were all tired and decided to call it a day. Before going to eat in the refectory, Cariad went to her cabin. She wanted some time alone. When she arrived, she sat on her bunk and turned on her interface to see if Montfort had sent any updates to his list of people with lesions that might be a removed tattoo. When she saw four extra names, she groaned. Was the doctor being overly cautious? It didn't seem credible that so many people would have abrasions in seldom-seen areas of the body.

Just as she was wondering what she was going to do about the potential Natural Movement members, another comm arrived. It was from Osias. A man and a young child had gone missing down by the lake.

CHAPTER EIGHT

All Ethan had was his weapon, his recorder, and the clothes he was wearing. As he stood on the sandy riverbank, staring at the place where the flitter had disappeared into the water, he got angry at himself. He'd been stupid to walk away from his only means of transport, and all his food, water, and other vital equipment. Yet who could have guessed that such a thing would happen? And what could have taken his vehicle? It wasn't like the flitter was edible. Why would anything want to drag it into the river, assuming that was what had happened?

Maybe an aquatic creature had been able to smell his food, but it seemed hardly possible. Could an animal in the water smell food on land that was inside tightly sealed packages? He didn't know. He hadn't learned about Earth animals with that kind of ability when he was at school. Then Ethan remembered the thread creatures in the lake near his farm that had grabbed Cherry. He was far from the lake, but the organisms could live in waterways all over the continent or even the entire planet.

He took a few steps backward. If a thread animal had taken the flitter, it could rise out of the river and try to add him to its haul for the day.

The light brown water flowed swiftly past, not giving any sign of what might lie within it. The edge of the sun was brushing the horizon. If sluglimpets inhabited the area, they would be out in an hour or so. Ethan contemplated going into the water and trying to retrieve his vehicle. The flitter's roof might lie only just beneath the surface. If that was the case, he might be able to drag it out again. The vehicle wasn't heavy. But the river was so muddy he couldn't see below the surface. Also, whatever had taken the flitter was probably hanging around. If he went near the water, it could very well try to grab him too.

Should he risk capture to retrieve his vehicle? As it was, he had no shelter and no protection from predators, and he would find it just about impossible to return to the settlement without a flitter. The colony stronghold was many kilometers away and he had no navigation device. Even if, by a miracle, he made the journey without any food or protection from hostile life forms, he could travel within a short distance of the place and still miss it.

The conclusion was obvious. He had to try to retrieve his vehicle, even if it meant risking death. Without the flitter, he was as good as dead anyway.

Ethan gazed at the murky water washing up on the river bank. He couldn't swim. Like all Gens, he'd never learned how. Water had been far too precious a commodity on the *Nova Fortuna* to waste on a swimming pool. Ethan had seen the artificial pools in vids from Earth, but he hadn't been able to imagine what it might feel like to go into one. The idea of submerging his entire body in water and moving through it had seemed weird.

The sun was already halfway below the horizon, and still Ethan hesitated. He was remembering Cherry's screams of terror as she'd fought being dragged into the lake by the long threads wrapped around her legs. If he hadn't been able to cut through them with the plow, she wouldn't have stood a chance.

The memory of the threads reminded him of the thin branches of the plants that bordered the river and an idea occurred to him. Perhaps he could use them to reduce his risk of capture. He strode over the sand to the arch-rooted plants and walked through them until he found one that had extra-long branches sweeping down. He stepped up onto a root, gripping the central stem to keep his balance. The root was slippery with slime. Where one of the branches joined the stem, he grabbed it and twisted. The tissue was fibrous and pliable. He twisted the branch all the way around several times until it finally broke off.

Ethan jumped down from the root and returned to the river. Standing as far away as he could while still being able to reach the water, he poked the end of the branch under the surface next to the spot where the flitter had been. He held the branch loosely, ready to release it if something tugged at the other end. He felt no resistance. Edging a little closer, he tried again. Again, the branch sank effortlessly into the water.

Either there was a steep drop off just beyond the river's edge, or the flitter had been dragged out farther than Ethan had hoped. He moved nearer to the river until he was closer than Cherry had been to the lake when she'd been grabbed.

His throat tight, his gaze scoured the moving water for a sign of anything beneath it. Each slightly anomalous ripple made his heart leap, but he had to get the flitter back. He just had to. If he didn't, he might as well walk right into the water. It would be a quicker and probably less painful end than losing his life to a sluglimpet or dying of starvation.

Once more, he shuffled closer. The river wet the toes of his boots. Yet still the branch met no resistance. In an agony of despair, Ethan took a large step forward, heedless of the cold water that soaked his feet and calves.

He felt the branch touch something solid! He pushed it deeper. Had he found the flitter's roof? If he had, the vehicle was very deep in the water. Another problem occurred to him. Would the vehicle be irreversibly damaged from being submerged? If he did manage to retrieve it, would it still fly?

Ethan probed with the branch. The resistance he felt didn't seem to be what he would expect from the flitter roof. He pushed the branch down hard. It sank in softly and at the same time Ethan's heart sank too. He'd guessed what was happening.

He pulled the branch out the water and lifted it up to inspect the end in the quickly waning light. The tip was coated in thick, black, smelly mud. He hadn't found the flitter, only the riverbed. If his vehicle was anywhere nearby in the water, it was out so far he would have to swim to it to retrieve it.

He flung the branch toward the river and watched it spin in the air until it landed and the current swiftly carried it out of sight. Ethan sat on the soft sand, not caring as its moisture soaked his pants. If he did venture into the water, he would be pulled off his feet by the current too. He'd seen how powerful moving water could be during the cave disaster, when water pouring from a burst aquifer had washed people into the ocean. The river's current would be far too strong for him to resist. The thought he'd had earlier popped into his mind again: *At least it would be quick.*

The sun had set and the wind blowing from over the water was turning chilly. Ethan gazed out over the gigantic river. When he'd left the settlement and set out on his ambitious journey, he'd known how dangerous it would be. He'd known he might never return. Now that he seemed on the verge of his probable demise, he wondered if the short journey he'd made had been worth it.

It had, he concluded. He didn't regret his decision. It had been the right thing for him to do. But it wasn't enough. He wasn't ready to give up. If his experiences of recent days had taught him anything, it was to appreciate what he had. He was going to cling onto his life to the last second and do his best to return to the settlement. And he wouldn't give up hope. During the First Night

Attack, he'd come within a hair's breadth of dying but he'd been spared at the final moment. Something equally unpredictable might come his way and save him.

Ethan stood up and shouldered his weapon. If sluglimpets inhabited that region, the approaching night would be the most dangerous time for him. But if he was careful and kept moving, they might not be able to catch him. He would walk during the night and sleep by day. He didn't know yet what he would do for food. The device that tested for chemicals that were toxic to humans was with the rest of the equipment in the flitter. But perhaps he could try to eat small amounts of plants that he came across. He could wait a day to find out if they made him ill. Maybe he would find something edible.

Ethan brought to mind his memories of the continent's topography. To return to the settlement, he would have to cross the mountain range. The river sprung from its foothills, so he only had to head upstream to find a way into them. With trepidation he recalled the creatures that had gathered beneath the flitter and the deep, dark holes he'd found in the upper slopes. He would face the mountain animals and the cold of the high altitude when the time came.

His first goal was to survive the night, and to do that, he had to walk. He would have to remain within sight or sound of the river to avoid becoming lost, but he would also avoid straying too close to it if he could.

Ethan turned to face the opposite direction of the river's current and began to walk. He had one thing in his favor, he realized. He was on the correct side of the river for returning to the settlement. If he'd chosen to fly the flitter over to the opposite bank, he would have had to travel much farther. He would have had to go around it because he couldn't ever have crossed it.

Smoky wreaths began to rise from the river, almost glowing in the dusk. Ethan had never seen such a sight before. He guessed that the white, drifting clouds were water vapor rising from the surface. The effect mesmerized him as he walked, stepping though the vegetation while keeping an eye on the now nearly black water. The mists looked almost alive as they curved and glided out onto the bank.

As darkness quickly fell, Ethan found the white vapors eerie and unsettling. For some reason, they reminded him of the flitter in its watery grave. He imagined the food packages becoming sodden and contaminated with mud, bursting apart as the water soaked the dried food and it swelled up.

Realizing that his thoughts were turning gloomy and that dwelling on negative subjects wouldn't help him in his quest to survive, he tried to think of something more cheerful. However, everything that sprang to mind sent him down a black whirlpool. If he thought of his time on the *Nova Fortuna*, he was reminded of Lauren and Dr. Crowley. If he recalled the period he was at the settlement, he remembered bombings, attacks, and the Gens being oppressed by the Woken and Guardians. In the overall darkness of his recollections, his memories of the few times he'd spent with Cariad were the only bright sparks. Yet when he dwelt on them, he missed her and his mood lowered again.

Frustrated, Ethan shook his head, trying to clear it. The stars were coming out and he had a long night of walking ahead of him. He needed to improve his state of mind to stand a chance of surviving the difficult journey that lay ahead.

He decided to try a different tactic. Rather than occupying himself with random memories, he would focus on happy recollections. Aboard the *Nova Fortuna* one of the forms of entertainment had been music concerts in Main Park. A group of musicians had been very popular when Ethan was a teenager. He couldn't remember the band's name—it had been something like the Astro Novas or the Going Novas—but he could remember one of their songs.

As he hummed the tune, the lyrics came back to him. He began to sing.

Come into my arms, baby

And I'll never let you go

I'll take you all the way

All the way to Arrival Day

If you let me kiss you

You'll never regret it

I'll take you all the way

All the way to Arrival Day

Ethan smiled to himself. As a young adolescent, the subtext of *I'll take you all the way* had been obscure to him. He continued to hum and tried to remember the rest of the song.

After two or three hours of striding along beside the river—thankfully with no sign of sluglimpets—thirst began to trouble Ethan. The answer to his problem was obvious and lay only a handful of meters from him. Faint glints reflected from the recently risen moon gleamed from the water through the dark shapes of intervening vegetation.

He dreaded going near the river again. It had swallowed his flitter, or rather, whatever was in it had taken the vehicle. Even if he had left that creature behind, the expanse of water could harbor other animals, possibly of huge dimensions.

The moon was only a sliver in the starry sky. The night was so black he couldn't see the water very well. If he ventured to the edge to drink, he would have to be very careful and very quick. But to the water's edge he had to go. He wouldn't survive for long without water.

Pointing his weapon forward, Ethan stepped slowly over the arching roots in the sandy earth. The rushing, swishing sound of the river grew louder as he drew closer. The surface was oily and black.

Tucking his weapon under his right arm, leaving his finger on the trigger, Ethan formed his left hand into a scoop, ready to quickly lift water to his lips. What he could see of the water seemed normal. Nothing was disturbing it beneath as far as he could tell.

Ethan's tongue was sticking to the roof of his

mouth. He bent down, reaching forward with his left hand while keeping his gaze fixed on the dark water. He lifted a handful of water to his lips. It tasted sweet and refreshing though gritty, but the amount he'd managed to scoop up barely wet the back of his throat. He reached forward again and scooped up another small amount of the delicious liquid.

He could feel the cold, sweet fluid going down his throat into his stomach. He would risk one more mouthful then he would retreat to safety.

But as he leaned forward for a third time, something tightened around his ankle. He leapt away, dropping his weapon in shock. The grip on his ankle tightened. It was a thread! A thread organism had a hold of him. Ethan lifted his weapon. The thread was tugging on his ankle, nearly unbalancing him. He couldn't get away. He fired at the barely visible, thin, black line, narrowly avoiding shooting his own foot.

He'd hit it. The pulse round severed the thread. Ethan tried to run, but his other leg was caught. While he'd been shooting at the first thread, another had snaked around his other ankle. This one was thicker and stronger. When it yanked, it almost pulled Ethan off his feet. He shot at it, half-severing the thick strand. The wound didn't make the creature let go of him, though its strength was reduced.

More threads were slithering from the water. Ethan fired at them at the same time as pulling with all his might against the thick thread holding onto him. He shot at it again. This time he hit it and cut right through it.

He was finally free!

Except he wasn't. Three slim ribbons had fastened themselves around his calf. They were dragging him toward the swirling black waters of the river.

CHAPTER NINE

Cariad was just in time to catch the final shuttle flight to the planet surface before the beginning of the quiet shift. All the way down, she wondered what had happened to the child and man who had gone missing. Osias hadn't replied to any comms since he'd sent her the message, but Cariad guessed he thought the disappearances had something to do with the Natural Movement and that was why he'd contacted her.

It was the first time she'd arrived at the settlement by shuttle after dark. Lights shone in a line around the shuttle field and at the landing stages, and the small town's streets were also marked out by dim yellow solar lanterns, glowing softly with the energy they'd absorbed during the day. The only other sign of the impact of human civilization in its new home was a single string of illuminated spots that marked the road out to the farming district. Used to seeing the spread of buildings within the protective electric fence, Cariad was struck by how fragile and ephemeral the settlement appeared when only its lights were visible within a surrounding ocean of darkness.

As soon as the shuttle landed, Cariad rushed past the line of Woken who were waiting to return to the ship after spending the day working planetside. Her comm chirruped, and she was relieved to see Osias wanted to speak to her.

"Sorry, Cariad," he said. "I made a mistake. I shouldn't have contacted you. This isn't anything to do with the Natural Movement."

"Are you sure? What's happened?"

"Yes, I'm sure. I didn't get the full story until I arrived at the site, but there's no doubt about it. The victims were attacked by native wildlife. Sorry to waste your time. There's no need for you to attend. We can handle it."

"Attacked by native wildlife? Was it sluglimpets?" Cariad was outside the shuttle field, wondering if she should turn around quickly to board the final flight to the ship that day. But even if the attack didn't involve the Natural Movement, she still felt she might be able to help. She'd had close encounters with sluglimpets herself.

"No, not sluglimpets. Aquatic creatures in the lake out at the farms."

"Huh? How did it happen?" There had already been one attack by organisms in the lake. As far as Cariad knew, the place was now entirely out of bounds.

"I'm sorry," Osias said. "I can't explain right now. I have to deal with this."

"You're at the lake now?"

"Yes."

"Okay," Cariad replied. "I'm coming out there."

"No, there's no need for that."

"Well, I'm planetside now and I'd like to help. Woken should be involved in fixing colony problems."

"Hmm... Okay. But I don't know how you're going to get out here."

Cariad was already striding in the direction of the flitter shed. "Don't worry. I'll figure it out."

However, when she arrived at the shed, it was closed and locked. She knocked on the door but no one answered. Walking to the lake was out of the question. It would take her too long and, more importantly, the sluglimpets came out after dark. Cariad was wondering if maybe she shouldn't have been so set on helping out when someone walked past on the street. She caught up to the Gen, a young woman who seemed to be on her way home.

"Excuse me," Cariad said. "Do you know where I can find the person who's responsible for the flitters?"

"Verney?" the woman replied. "That's easy. He lives right there." She pointed at the small, single-story next door to the flitter shed.

"Of course," Cariad said. "Thanks."

Verney came to his door wiping his mouth. His hair was thin and close-shaven. He didn't appear to mind being interrupted while at his dinner until Cariad saw the signs of recognition in his eyes. Immediately, his expression grew narrow and suspicious. She was familiar with this attitude toward her as a Woken. It wasn't without just cause, so she never took offense. But she needed this man's help.

"My name's Cariad," she said. "Sorry for disturbing you."

Verney didn't reply. He only waited to hear what else she had to say.

She took a breath. "There's been an attack out by the lake—"

"I heard about it," Verney said, shoving his hands in his pockets and tilting his head.

"I want to go out there, only... "

"Only you need a flitter."

Cariad gave a small nod.

Verney looked her up and down. "Think you can help?"

"I want to, if I can."

"From what I heard, they were dragged into the lake a while ago. I don't see what's to be done about it now."

"Still... "

Verney paused another moment before saying, "Ah well. It won't hurt. Have you flown a flitter before?"

"Er, no." It was a problem she hadn't considered.

"In that case, you're not taking one out by yourself at night."

Cariad thought Verney meant to take back his agreement, but he came outside and closed his door. "Come on." He walked the short distance to the flitter shed and opened the security lock. "I'll take you."

Cariad rushed over and into the shed, where Verney was turning on the lights. He opened a flitter door and told her to get in before walking around the other side and climbing into the driver's seat. After starting the drive and maneuvering the vehicle out into the street, he hopped out for a moment in order to return to the shed and lock it.

Soon, they were at the gate in the electrified fence that surrounded the settlement. Cariad saw men and women with long poles walking along the interior of the fence.

"What are those people doing?" she asked as they passed through the gate.

"Looking for dead sluglimpets," Verney replied.

"Really? Why? Oh wait, I know. They push off the corpses, don't they?"

"That's right."

During the First Night Attack, after their first attack had been repulsed, the sluglimpets had climbed on the dead bodies of others to scale the electric fence and the settlers had suffered a second attack.

That terrible night had only occurred a few months previously, but to Cariad it felt like the distant past. She'd forgotten that the people living planetside constantly endured the risk of a repeat invasion of predators.

Verney was flying the flitter down the road that led to the farms. He kept his gaze on the dark surface, broken at widely spaced but regular intervals by round glowing patches from the sparse street lights. He didn't seem inclined to talk.

The road surface was smooth and plain, lacking lines to segment traffic as had been usual on Earth. Cariad could hardly believe that one day the road might require such lines, and have signs and junctions leading to other roads. She hoped that day would come.

"Have you been out this way before?" Cariad asked, finding the silence awkward.

"Nope."

Cariad glanced at the man's profile, almost a silhouette in the scant light. *Ah well*, she thought, *if he doesn't want to talk, I won't make him.* She had the impression that Verney considered he was already granting her enough of a concession by agreeing to chauffeur her out to the lake, and that engaging in small talk with a Woken would be a step too far.

They passed through the fence that protected the farming district from sluglimpets. The area it encompassed was much larger than the settlement. Cariad imagined it would be a time-consuming job to patrol it.

A knot of seven or eight figures stood by the lake, outside a similar enclosing fence, though Cariad didn't think this one was electrified. It was there to prevent unwary colonists from straying too close to the dangerous waters, not to deter the aquatic predators. As far as she was aware, none had ever been observed to leave the lake. Cariad wondered if that was what had happened. Had an animal from the lake come out after nightfall and climbed the fence?

Verney parked the flitter next to the group of women and men. Cariad recognized Osias' wiry figure but she didn't know the other Gens.

"Cariad. Verney," Osias said gravely when they drew near the group. "Thanks for coming."

"What's been happening?" Cariad asked. "Have the people been found?" However, the answer to her question was already clear from the somber mood.

Osias sighed. "No. There's been no sign of them."

"What happened?"

"A toddler got away from her parents' farmhouse and wandered down to the lake. When the girl's father and mother realized she was missing, the dad went after her while her mother comm'd for help before following him. The kid's dad had tracked the path she'd made across the fields." He paused and pointed to the fence. "He caught up to her just as she made it under. She ran right over to the water and the thread creatures dragged her in. He climbed over the fence to go after her and the creatures took him too. The mother saw sense and waited for help, thank the stars."

Cariad walked across the field toward the fence. "It's safe on this side of it, right?" she asked over her shoulder.

"Yes," Osias replied. "Do you want to see the place where the victims were dragged in?"

"Yes, I do."

Osias followed her and they strode the short remaining distance through the crop field. At the edge of the field, the gap beneath the fence was plain to see even in the scant moonlight. It was a shallow depression that the bottom of the fence didn't reach into. Nothing had worn away the ground. It had been awfully bad luck that the child had happened to go to that exact place while running from her father and that she'd fitted through it. She'd probably been attracted to the expanse of water beyond. The top of the fence was bent where the father had climbed over it.

The lake looked calm and peaceful with barely a ripple in the stillness of the night.

"Where's the mother?" Cariad asked.

"She was so distraught, I asked one of her neighbors to take her to the hospital."

Cariad's heart ached for the poor woman. The child must have been one of the very first conceived when the natural reproduction prohibition was lifted on board the *Nova Fortuna*. Cariad couldn't imagine how it might feel to lose both your child and your husband at the same time.

She recalled with bitterness her first impression of the lake. She'd thought it was pretty and a nice spot for Ethan to have his farm. He'd been lucky that a thread predator hadn't attacked him.

"There's no hope they're still alive," Osias said, also looking out over the water. "Otherwise we might have tried to get them back. As it is, I don't think there's anything we can do except check the fence for gaps and fix them."

"Can't you electrify it?" Cariad asked.

Osias replied, "We're already using every spare generator we have keeping the fence around the farming district supplied to ward off sluglimpets. We're under relentless pressure of attempted attacks."

Cariad peered at the sand where the child and her father had been dragged into the water. As well as signs of scuffling, there were long, whiplike trails cut into the surface. She gave a shiver. Whatever had taken the little girl and her father, it had been large and its reach had stretched nearly to the line of the fence.

"You know," she said, "whatever's in the lake, it might help to get more information about them. Do you know if any xenobiologists have been down from the ship to investigate it? I don't mean today. I mean generally."

"I don't," Osias replied. He turned toward the group of farmers, who were discussing the attack with Verney. "Hey," he called, "Have any Woken been down to check out the lake?"

"Not that I know of," a farmer replied. Her companions agreed. "I don't think any Woken have been here to look for wildlife since they cleared the area for farming."

"The best protection would be to eradicate the creatures entirely," Cariad said. It wasn't the ideal solution in terms of the Mandate, however. A central idea of the *Nova Fortuna* Project was to avoid ruining the planet's environment in the way that Earth's had been ruined. Yet when it came to the colony's survival, they had to do whatever it took. "I think we should scan the lake," she said. "See what's down there. If there are only a few of these creatures, maybe we could catch them and move them to another area. What do you think?"

"Maybe," Osias said, "though I'm not sure that would help over the long term. Maybe they lay eggs and they'll hatch out some time in the future. But it would certainly make the place safer for now."

"Okay," Cariad said. "I'll comm the ship and ask

if anyone has a portable scanner they can send down."

When they discussed the idea with the farmers, they agreed with the proposal. Soon afterward, Verney took Cariad and Osias back to the settlement in the flitter.

"The last shuttle must have left long ago," Osias said. "Where are you staying tonight?"

"Actually, I don't know," Cariad said. It had slipped her mind that the temporary shelters for colonists had been dismantled now that most of the permanent homes had been built.

"I have spare rooms at the Leader's Residence. You're very welcome to stay there."

"I will, thanks. That's kind of you."

"Feel free to stay as often as you like and use whatever rooms are available. I think it would do the colony good to have the Woken spending more time down here."

"I agree," Cariad replied. "I'll do that." Osias was right that a Woken living in the settlement would help reduce divisions in the society. Also, while she conducted her investigation into the Natural Movement saboteurs, she would be spending plenty of time planetside. It would be more convenient if she didn't have to return to the ship every evening.

"How are you finding life as Leader?" Cariad asked.

Osias rolled his eyes. "I think maybe I bit off more than I can chew."

"Really? I think you're doing a great job."

"Thanks. That's kind of you to say. It's going to take time to fix all the damage that's been done, physical and otherwise, but we'll get there. It helps that right now everyone's so busy trying to get everything working, we don't have time to complain and fret."

"It must be hard to stay on track when you're so down on numbers," Cariad said.

"That's right, and that's apart from the psychological shock so many Gens are struggling to overcome."

They didn't speak much more as Cariad was preoccupied with thoughts of the day's tragedy and the fact that two more precious lives were lost from the colony.

CHAPTER TEN

Ethan scrambled backward on all fours. Severed ends of threads lay on the beach, feebly writhing and squirming in their death throes. The living parts had retreated into the water and no more were slithering out to clutch at him. He was clutching his weapon so tightly the stock dug into his ribs, but he barely registered the pain.

As he regained some control, Ethan eased farther from the water, pushing between the roots of plants. Then a thought hit. *Sluglimpets.* He sprang to his feet, his pulse racing once more. The vegetation was full of shadows but he couldn't detect any movement. He hoped the digesting predators didn't inhabit that region.

He couldn't risk returning to the water's edge, but he had to drink. The few mouthfuls of water he'd managed to scoop out hadn't done much to slake his thirst. There was no point in continuing his journey, trying to get as far as he could without water. He would never make it back to the settlement, and probably not even as far as the foothills of the mountains.

Ethan turned the problem over in his mind. Somehow, he had to get the water from the river without approaching it ,but the task seemed impossible. All he had were his weapon, clothes, and boots. He had no utensils of any kind though his boots would hold water. Parched as he was, the idea of drinking from them didn't seem unappealing. If he could get one into the water and retrieve it, it might hold water long enough to reach him. But what could he tie to a boot so he could pull it back? And what if one of the threads took it?

The prospect of walking a great distance with only one boot daunted him. Sweeping his gaze over the vegetation, wary of sluglimpets, Ethan tried to decide whether to take the risk. While he might manage to walk barefoot on the river sand, footwear would be essential to cross the mountains.

No. It would be better to wait until he was nearly dying of thirst before risking the loss of a boot. What about other items of his clothing? Ethan looked down at his shirt sleeves and had an idea. He took off his shirt.

He edged a little closer to the water. Holding the end of one sleeve, he cast his shirt forward. It hit dry sand. He pulled the shirt back, shook the sand out of it, and tried again. The second time he timed it so that the shirt sleeve caught an approaching wash of water. For a few moments the sleeve soaked up precious fluid. Ethan pulled it back, flicking it upward to try to avoid picking up sand.

He wasn't very successful. The cuff of the shirt was coated in fine grains when he lifted it to his mouth, but it was also wet and heavy with water. He sucked at the liquid, ignoring the grainy powder he also took into his mouth. As he drew in the water, his gaze was focused on the river. There was no sign of the threads.

His idea seemed to work. Ethan performed his trick several times. While he slaked his thirst, Ethan also kept a lookout on the ground around him, wary of the approach of sluglimpets. His luck seemed to have changed for the better in that regard too. There was no sign of their low, flat carapaces pushing through the plant growth.

Whatever happened, he guessed he wouldn't die of thirst, or at least not while he walked alongside the river.

When his disgust at the sandiness of the water overcame his thirst, Ethan put on his shirt and continued tramping along the riverbank, out of reach of any threads that might venture from it. He settled into a steady pace he hoped to be able to maintain all night, which would bring the now-dark mountains significantly closer by the time morning came. To give himself something to occupy his mind, Ethan tried to remember more popular songs from his days aboard the ship. The catchy Arrival Day song was hard to shake from his mind at first, but then he remembered a female solo singer who went by the stage name Quasar.

Ethan had been about eleven or twelve when he'd first watched Quasar sing, and she was the first woman he'd ever crushed on. At that time Lauren had been his age and he didn't think of her as anything more than a very good friend. Quasar, on the other hand, had awakened deeper, confusing feelings in him.

He recalled the song she'd been singing the first time he saw her. It was called *Time*.

I see the seconds tick away
In your eyes
In your eyes
Minutes pass
And I come no closer
To understanding you

Should I wait for you?
For how long?
For how long?
A lifetime?
The Countdown draws closer
But you draw no closer to me

Come with me to the Observatory
For a while
For a while
Star watching
Doesn't take long
It takes forever

Time leaves us behind
It won't wait
It won't wait
An eternity
But I'll wait for you

I'll wait forever

Ethan smiled sadly. Quasar had been about eighteen when she'd been popular as a singer. When she grew older she gave up stage performances and concentrated on her job as a ship's engineer. He recalled that she died during the First Night Attack.

So many lives had been lost since Arrival. Ethan had left the settlement before the final tally of deaths in the caves disaster had been released, but he guessed the colony had lost more than three hundred men, women, and children. He hoped Cariad could bring the population up to a sustainable level. He also hoped that his own demise wouldn't add another to the count.

Ethan's thoughts ranged wider, drifting again to the shipboard days.

***

During one of his many chats with Dr. Crowley, she had explained to Ethan the importance of the diversity of the colony's gene pool and why the Gens couldn't replenish their numbers naturally over the course of the long voyage.

"I imagine it must be hard for you to accept," the doctor had said.

"What?" Ethan had asked. "The fact that we couldn't have our own children?"

"Yes," replied Dr Crowley. "It's one of the many sacrifices the project founders forced upon you. Perhaps the largest one. The impetus to reproduce is instinctive after all. We denied Gens the right to fulfill their natural desires."

"I never thought about it like that," Ethan said.

"After the prohibition on natural reproduction was lifted and contraceptive-free water became available for people who wanted to conceive, Lauren and I talked about having a baby. She wants to wait, at least until after Arrival, and maybe longer, even forever. She says the idea of something growing inside her, even a little baby, is really weird, and that the pregnant women she's seen on Earth vids look so uncomfortable and kind of grotesque. I got the impression she really doesn't like the idea of conceiving but she's trying to get used to it for the sake of the colony. I don't mind either way. I like kids but if I never have any of my own I'm okay with that. And even if I wasn't, it isn't something I would ever try to persuade Lauren to do against her own will. It isn't me who would have to carry and give birth to the child.

"So," he went on, "I don't think it's as much of a sacrifice as you think. I never heard anyone complain about it, not even women who are too old to become pregnant now."

"I see," said the doctor. "Do you mind if I ask you something personal? Did you or Lauren ever donate?"

"To the gamete bank? Yes. We both have. Why do you want to know? Do you think it makes us more content not to have our own children if we know there are little Laurens and Ethans running around somewhere?"

Dr. Crowley laughed. "No. I was wondering if your lack of desire for children is an effect of the contraceptive. So, when you both spent some time free from artificial manipulation of your hormones you didn't feel any different about conceiving? I mean, I know it's only for a month or so, but you might have noticed a change."

"I didn't," said Ethan, "and if Lauren did, she didn't tell me about it. She only said it made her feel more emotional than usual."

"In that case, maybe the desire for children is a social thing." Dr. Crowley sighed. "I guess we'll never know. I certainly hope the distaste for the experience you talk about doesn't continue long after Arrival or we could have a problem on our hands. We'll need the Gens to begin to reproduce naturally as soon as possible then. I've been very glad to see there are a few pregnancies aboard already."

"I think things will be okay in that area," Ethan said. "Just because Lauren might take some time to get used to the idea, doesn't mean all the women are the same."

"No, but it's a problem we didn't account for," said Dr. Crowley. "We thought the opposite would be true—that frustrating the impetus to reproduce naturally would cause discontent and unrest. Some of us speculated that we might awake from cryo to find the ship jam-packed with many thousands of people and they would be starving due to using up all the supplies. I don't think anyone imagined we might have the opposite problem." She smiled wryly. "I hope you're right. I and many other Woken are far too old to personally make up the shortfall in new blood."

Ethan wondered if it was an appropriate moment to ask his friend a question he'd long wanted to put to her. He decided to go for it. "Do you mind if I ask you a personal question too?"

"Not at all. I'm an open book."

"Okay. I wanted to ask, did you leave children behind on Earth?"

"Ah. Good question. No, I didn't. I was unmarried, had no siblings, and both my parents were dead. I don't—didn't—have any children. So joining the project was a no-brainer for me. For one thing, I was getting on in years. Who would pass up a chance to live another couple of centuries, even as an ice cube? It was different for others, of course. Some of the Woken made very hard decisions in order to be one of the first humans to set foot on an extra-Solar planet. Very hard decisions indeed."

"You mean some of them did leave their kids behind?"

"Yes, they did. It was deemed ethically unsound to place children into cryonic suspension. The process had never been tested for the length of time we would be frozen. Only those who had a full understanding of the risks could take part, and children were too young to give their consent. What's more, even childless Woken often left behind a spouse. Each application was assessed individually, you see. The standards the applicants were judged against were so rigorous, it was often the case that only one half of a married couple met the criteria. There was a lot of bitterness, anger, and acrimony surrounding the entire selection process. It was a difficult time."

"But not so difficult for you," said Ethan, "because you were only leaving behind your friends."

"In that way, yes," replied the doctor. "To tell

you the truth, after my work occupied nearly all my time while we prepared for departure, I had precious few friends either. Since my revival, I've worked hard to correct that error." She smiled at him. "However, in other ways it was quite hard. You see, once you received your acceptance into the cryonic suspension program, you couldn't tell anyone about it. It was too risky, so I had to constantly guard my words. There was a sad case of a scientist who was murdered by someone whose application had been rejected."

"Murdered?" Ethan exclaimed. "That was a bit of an overreaction, wasn't it?"

"Of course, but those were desperate times. The murderer probably felt a strong desire for revenge and that he had nothing to lose. The Natural Movement were quickly gaining followers and power, and anyone with any sense could see the way the world was going. With the anti-technology, anti-"interference with nature" sentiment that was building, it was apparent that we were gearing up for another descent into the Dark Ages. I wouldn't want to live in such a world either. Such a shame. We seemed on the verge of so many amazing breakthroughs."

Ethan didn't know what the Dark Ages was, but he got the idea. As with many of his conversations with Dr. Crowley, he was left wondering what living on Earth had been like, or living on any planet for that matter.

Ethan's thoughts returned to his present predicament. Now that he'd experienced life on Concordia he preferred it to the life aboard the ship, despite all the terrible things that had happened since Arrival. He didn't know if it was the wide open environment or the fact that his safety was no longer guaranteed, but he felt more alive than he ever had on the *Nova Fortuna*.

***

He walked for hours, memories of life aboard ship and of Dr. Crowley and Lauren crowding his mind. So much had happened after their deaths—the Natural Movement bombings, the division between the Gens and the Woken—he hadn't had much time to think about either of them or to go over the happy times they'd had and what both of them had meant to him.

As he went along, he became aware of a rushing sound. It was like the sound of waves on a shore, but it didn't rise and diminish, it grew louder. The sound seemed to be coming from behind him, but the night was so dark, he couldn't see much more than the faintly glimmering band of the river, surrounded by shadowy vegetation.

The noise increased as Ethan watched, and then he saw it: a line of gleaming foam. A high wave was running up the river, against the current. It was heading toward him.

Ethan sped away, colliding with and tripping over roots and dangling branches. After a few minutes' running he halted. If he went too far, he might lose sight of the river and become lost. He could still see the glint of reflected starlight on the water's surface.

The rushing sound was louder than ever. He wondered if he should try to climb into one of the arching trees but they had no horizontal branches, only limbs that hung down to the ground. He heard hissing and gurgling as the water swept toward him, a black liquid flowing along the ground. He backed up farther. Would the threads come with it?

But before the wave reached him, it shrank and receded. Within moments it was gone. The rushing sound grew fainter as the wave swept on upriver. Cautiously, Ethan returned to the river's edge. He couldn't risk wandering aimlessly through the vegetation in the dark.

The ground was much wetter after the wave. The soft, fine sand was rich with organic matter, and Ethan's boots were soon sodden and squelching with every step. He continued trudging along, ignoring the empty ache in his stomach. Hours passed. He grew more and more tired but he didn't dare to stop. A pause of more than a few minutes might be enough time for sluglimpets to home in on him, if any lived in those parts.

Eventually, Ethan lost track of time. The night seemed to stretch on without end, and his thoughts were reduced to the impetus to put one foot in front of the other.

When dawn finally came, he almost didn't notice. His world had shrunk to the narrow focus of the ground in front of him and the river to his side. He'd even forgotten about the dark mountains that loomed ahead. Then he noticed that the dirt and roots he was staring at were no longer black and shadowy. They were glistening wetly, reflecting growing light.

He halted. The sensation of ceasing his endless motion felt odd. He turned, trying to find the source of the light. In the distance, clouds were glowing with the light of the rising sun they veiled.

Ethan could hardly believe it. He'd done it. He'd survived a night alone in the wilderness.

If he could survive one night, maybe he could survive many more. Maybe he might make it back.

CHAPTER ELEVEN

Cariad was lying on the bed in a spare bedroom Osias had loaned her at the Leader's Residence when Dr. Montfort comm'd to say he'd finished his examination of all the colonists. He sent Cariad two more suspects to add to the list. One of them was a surprise.

"Are you going to arrest them all?" Montfort asked.

"I haven't decided. I don't think I can, realistically."

"Well, my job's done for now. Good luck. Let me know if I can be of further help."

"Okay, thanks."

Cariad put down her interface. She had avoided the step of arresting suspects while waiting for Montfort to complete his task. She hadn't wanted to trigger anger by taking Gens into custody without explanation. Now that she had all the names, she continued to hesitate. It wouldn't be right to arrest anyone without evidence, and the harmony between Gens and Woken was fragile. Any action she took that appeared unjust or overstepping her bounds could result in an out-and-out revolt.

Ruefully, Cariad realized she couldn't arrest anyone, even to protect the colony. She would have to root out any remaining Natural Movement terrorists and prove their guilt before taking such a potentially divisive action.

She hardly knew where to start. Garwin was in custody but the last time she'd seen him he'd clung to the belief that Twyla had been innocent. She would have to speak to him again. She also had to speak to her friend, Rene, and find out if she had an explanation for the lesion Montfort had reported seeing. Also, interviewing the suspects about how they had come by their injury might turn up some answers.

But first she would pay Garwin another visit. He'd lived with a Natural Movement saboteur for a couple of decades. He had to know something, and perhaps what he could tell her might inform her interviews with the other suspects. She had to return to the *Mistral*.

***

Garwin was lying on his bunk, facing the wall, when Cariad went into his room. Addleson had installed a camera in case he turned violent, but from his slumped, unmoving position, the possibility seemed unlikely.

More than ever, Garwin looked like a broken man. It wasn't surprising. He'd gone from a position of high regard and respect among the

Gens and the Woken to a suspected member of a group of known saboteurs and terrorists who were responsible for hundreds of deaths. Not only that, he'd also lost the woman he'd loved.

"I need to talk to you," Cariad said as she sat on the room's only chair, preparing herself for a long wait. Garwin had no incentive to speak to her. He couldn't win back anything he'd lost. She would have to rely on patience and persistence to get anything from him.

But, to her surprise, Garwin turned over and sat up. He'd shed kilos of weight and his once-handsome, bearded face was thin and sallow. The gray in his hair seemed to have doubled overnight. He smiled sadly. "I'm sorry for my outburst last time. I must have frightened you."

"You did. Are you feeling better now?"

"Not really. Calmer, maybe."

"I didn't want to upset you but you didn't give me much choice. I had to convince you that what I was saying was true."

"I know. I realized that. Only some revelations are difficult to bear, especially when they confirm something that, deep down, you always knew was true."

Cariad straightened up. "So you accept that Twyla was a Natural Movement follower?"

"That's what the marking would seem to show, wouldn't it? I can't think of any other explanation, and I don't think you would lie to me."

"I wouldn't lie to you," said Cariad. "I'm interested in the truth." Mentally, Cariad reined in her excitement over Garwin's apparent change of heart. It might be a ploy. The man had played the

Woken while leading the Gen rebellion, by all accounts. If he was such a successful deceiver and manipulator, she would have to proceed cautiously.

"So," she continued, "have you thought of anything Twyla did or said that might help us to catch the other Natural Movement members?"

Garwin rested his elbows on his knees. "Since I accepted what she was, I haven't been thinking of much else. Or perhaps not that exactly, but things I ignored or excused over the years. Unexplained absences, comms that she would take in another room—though to be fair I had plenty of those myself—conversations about the *Nova Fortuna* Project where she would abruptly change the subject. I thought she didn't care about the colonization or the Gens' role in it. I thought she didn't want to discuss the subject because it bored her, not because she profoundly disagreed with me. Although... " He had been looking down as he spoke, but he lifted his head to look Cariad in the eye. "When I finally accepted the truth about Twyla, I thought back over the years of our marriage, trying to pinpoint the moment when she gave up hope of converting me to her way of thinking. I guess I found it. When I saw the incident in its true light, it finally all made sense.

"It was in the first year of our marriage. She'd returned from work, excited and happy. I always wondered how she had the energy to work with those little kids all day and not be exhausted when she got home, but she never was. I think I see why now. She was filled with zeal for her cause."

Garwin's words chilled Cariad. How many

children had Twyla taught over her career? It had to be hundreds. How many had she indoctrinated with the Natural Movement philosophy?

"That night," Garwin went on, "after she came back to our room, we... well, the details don't matter, but suffice it to say, she never wanted the light on when we were intimate. I always thought she was shy. Afterward, I wanted to talk about what we would do after Arrival. It was a common subject among we Gens as you might imagine. This was years before we began to revive the "Passengers," as we used to call you. But Twyla didn't want to talk about it, as usual. She said the time was so far off, it wasn't worth thinking about, and that we should enjoy our days together then and not think about the future.

"She began on a track that, now I think about it, she'd begun many times before. But that night she went further than she ever had, saying how it was unfair that we'd been forced to take part in this experiment on behalf of humankind. She said we hadn't chosen it, and that it was wrong—morally and ethically, and that it was against human nature to leave Earth. I disagreed. I was looking forward to the end of the journey and thought I was lucky I would be around when it happened. We argued. I said... " He sighed. "It doesn't matter what I said. If I'd known about the Natural Movement then, I would have suspected her immediately, based on what she said. But none of us knew about the threat to the colony at that time. No one knew until the Guardians revealed it."

"Of course," Cariad said. She didn't think the

Gens' educational materials covered the subject or that much information on the movement had been included in the ship's data about Earth. The people who had decided what the Gens would be told about humanity's origin planet had been just about as anti-Natural Movement as you could get.

"The reason I remember that night so well," Garwin said, "was because it was after that particular spat that Twyla became cold toward me. At first, it seemed to be the usual. We would fight, then we wouldn't speak for a day or two. But the days turned into weeks, and then we slipped into civility once again. But the warmth was gone. Not on my part, but on hers. I couldn't seem to reach her anymore, though I loved her just as much." He was looking down again.

"I'm sorry," Cariad said.

"Not as much as me," said Garwin. "I wish I could have realized what she was. I never forgot that argument. If I'd put two and two together, if I'd been willing to admit the truth, if I hadn't trusted her, some people who died might be alive today. But it's hard to accept that the person you've been married to for years is a monster."

After a pause, Cariad said, "Have you thought of anything that might help us find out who the others are?"

The older man slowly shook his head. "You have the names of all the children she taught, right?"

"I can look them up. There must be a lot, though."

"I keep going over our time together, right back to when we met, but nothing has jumped out at me yet apart from that argument. I'll carry on thinking, though."

"Thank you." Though it wasn't much, Cariad felt she'd inched closer to finding out the key that would unlock the Natural Movement's secrets. "Comm me if anything occurs to you, no matter how small. More deaths would be a tragedy, but from a purely pragmatic viewpoint, we can't afford to lose any more people."

"I'll do my best. I want to try to put things right."

As she left Garwin's cabin, Cariad reflected that there might be some redemption for the man yet, though he would never be the same again.

Now she had to speak to Rene, who was the only Woken on Montfort's list of people with suspicious lesions. Cariad dreaded the prospect. Though they hadn't worked closely while preparing for the *Nova Fortuna* Project, Rene was a friend. Cariad could hardly imagine the possibility, but she would be devastated if it turned out that her friend was a Natural Movement saboteur.

Not far along the corridor she met Aubriot, who had apparently come to find her. He'd taken some time to recover once the Guardians had brought him out of sedation. The drug the Guardians had given him had returned him to the state of weakness he'd experienced after his revival.

Cariad inwardly groaned. Aubriot was the last person she wanted to see right then.

As he marched toward her he seemed to have regained all his former strength and drive. He strode forward, head slightly bent downward, his gaze fixed menacingly on her. Yet this time Cariad was not to be intimidated. Despite his overwhelming personality, Aubriot held no true power in the colony. She doubted that Osias would be awed by him and the rest of the Gens wouldn't care who he was. He might try to exert control over the Woken again but they were no longer running the show.

She didn't even give him a chance to speak.

"What do you want?" she asked.

Aubriot halted in surprise.

"Don't forget that I'm not your employee any longer," Cariad continued, walking forward, "and I'm *not* at your beck and call." She pushed a fingertip into his broad, well-muscled chest. "What's more, I think you would be wise to remember that while you might have been someone once, we're a long way from Earth now. Here, you're just another Woken, only you don't have any skills that are useful to the colony. The ability to shout and boss people around don't count. Do I make myself clear?"

Aubriot didn't answer. His mouth was hanging open.

"Good," Cariad said. She stalked past him, leaving him speechless.

CHAPTER TWELVE

Hunger had become a problem much sooner than Ethan had guessed it would. By the time his fourth day without food arrived, weakness and fatigue were plaguing him.

As usual, he'd walked all through the night. Since losing the flitter, he hadn't seen any sign of sluglimpets or other nocturnal predators, but he'd nevertheless stuck to his plan of keeping moving during darkness. But by the time the sun had begun to rise that morning, he'd been barely able to stay upright. As soon as he could see its glow on the horizon, he allowed his trembling leg muscles to give way and he collapsed where he stood, lacking the energy to move any farther.

He lay on his stomach, his head turned to the side. The ever-present river surged past a few meters away. On the second day, the spindly, arch-rooted plants had become interspersed with shorter vegetation that had jagged, spreading leaves and a few other diverse plants. A jagged-leaved plant was growing near Ethan's head, and now that he was close to it he saw it was infested with tiny creatures about the size of his pinky fingernail. They were nearly the same dun green-brown as the leaves, which was why he hadn't noticed them before.

Too exhausted to move, Ethan watched the little animals clambering up and down the plant, cutting off parts of its leaves and carrying them away. He tracked the path of the creatures to a hole in the black, sandy soil. Were they feeding their young or doing something else with the leaf fragments? The organisms seemed familiar.

Ethan closed his eyes. Even thinking tired him. He needed to sleep. After that, he would have to find food. He had no idea how, but if he didn't, he guessed he wouldn't be able to walk through the night again. And not moving at night could mean his death. If it didn't, he would eventually die of hunger anyway if he couldn't make it back to the settlement.

Summoning his fragile strength to lift his head and take in his surroundings, he saw a patch of open ground that was covered in a blanket of the short rubbery vegetation that grew at the settlement. He crawled across to it and, pulling off his weapon, he lay down on his side.

***

Hunger woke him. After losing the flitter, his stomach had griped with pangs for about a day but then the pain had gone away. His digestive system had seemed to accept it wasn't going to receive any food for a while. But this time after a sleep that, judging from the sun's position, had lasted into the afternoon, horrible cramps were wracking him.

Ethan sat up. The weather had luckily remained dry all the time he'd been traveling on foot. However, though the temperature didn't seem to have dropped, he was trembling with cold. He thought of the warm jacket he'd brought along on his expedition, now lying sodden underwater somewhere, courtesy of whatever had taken his flitter—perhaps the thread creatures. He also thought of the packets of dried food that were now ruined by the river water.

His recorder hung loosely on his chest. He hadn't made a recording or a vid since he'd begun his arduous attempt to return to the settlement. Perhaps now would be a good time to make a log of his thoughts. The way things were looking, it was doubtful he would even make it as far as the mountains. He would keep trying to return to the settlement until the end of his strength, but the reality of his situation was clear.

Ethan lifted the device to his lips and turned it on but when he began to speak, his voice cracked. The problem wasn't only that he hadn't said anything for three days, he was also parched. He stood and walked unsteadily toward the river. The mountains blocked the sky to his left, but they didn't seem much closer than they had been the previous day. Ethan guessed he probably hadn't walked far overnight due to his weakened state.

After removing his shirt, he flung it toward the river while holding onto one sleeve, using the method he'd developed to collect water while remaining safely out of reach of the thread organisms. His technique had improved over the days so that he didn't end up taking in sand too, which always made him nauseated. But this time weakness made him clumsy. It took him over half an hour to slake his thirst and his mouth was painfully gritty afterward. His lips were also chapped and sore from sucking on the material with its sandy coating.

Ethan lumbered back to the patch of ground where he'd slept and slumped down. He decided that in a while, he would try to find something to eat. Maybe he could nibble a leaf and wait a while to see if it had any ill effects. Or perhaps he could try to eat the creatures he'd noticed earlier. On board the *Nova Fortuna*, insects had been on the ship's menu. Ethan hadn't liked them much and he hadn't missed them since living planetside, but if he had to eat the Concordian equivalent to survive, that's what he would do.

He turned on the recorder. He explained what had happened to the flitter and what he'd been doing ever since. "I haven't kept up to date with making vids of everything here. Sorry about that. This is what's around me now." He lifted the recorder and turned it three hundred and sixty degrees before bringing it down again. "I haven't seen any sluglimpets or other large animals, though it could be that the wildlife is avoiding me. Nothing's followed me as far as I know, and I haven't been attacked while I slept during the daytime, which was a big concern.

"It's possible that sluglimpets don't inhabit this region. Maybe it would be a better place for a settlement if that's the case. I don't know. That's for the xenobiologists who come after me to decide. But if it is, I hope I can make it back so I can tell you all about it. That isn't looking likely at the moment but I'm going to try."

Ethan paused. If he was going to die in his attempt to get back, there were final messages that he wanted to leave for certain people, things he'd left unsaid because the timing hadn't been right. His body might be found someday and though he would be only bones the recorder could remain intact for decades. He wasn't at his last extremity yet, however. The messages could wait until his final hours.

"I have found some other life forms. I'll show you them." He walked to the clump of vegetation where he'd spotted the small creatures and recorded a vid of them cutting off pieces of leaf and carrying them away. "They don't look very tasty, do they? But I might try some soon. I'm pretty hungry now. It's slowing me down, and I'm probably not being as observant of what's here as I could be. I might have passed other forms of wildlife and not noticed them, especially as I'm doing all my traveling by night."

He returned to his resting spot and sat down, wondering what to record next. He said, "I'm not sure what's going to happen now. I have weeks of traveling ahead of me. I have to get over the mountains for one thing. It's very cold up there, and the local animals could be dangerous. If I manage that, I'll still be hundreds of kilometers from the settlement and to be honest I don't know how to find it." He paused again as an idea occurred to him. "Scratch that. I do know. If I head east until I reach the coast, I can follow it north to the remains of the cave settlement, and then I know the way to the settlement from there. Maybe someone will even come out that way and I'll see them. Yes. That's what I'll do."

Despite his famished, exhausted state, optimism surged in Ethan. He wouldn't have to wander in the wilderness, hoping to one day stumble upon the single tiny spot of human civilization on the entire continent. His new route would be much longer than traveling across country, but he wouldn't become lost. It was a sure way back. If he could only survive long enough, he would definitely arrive home one day.

"Signing off now," he said. "It's the tenth day of the fourth month, year one, Concordian Calendar."

No matter how certain his route, he would never reach the settlement unless he found some kind of food to sustain him along the way. Of course, he could eat something so poisonous it killed him immediately, but that was simply a risk he had to take.

He decided to try the little creatures first. They would be more of a complete food than the plants, as he understood it. He got up and returned to the infested clump. The tiny organisms were just as busy as ever. Ethan picked one up between his finger and thumb and, not allowing himself the opportunity to be squeamish, popped it into his mouth.

The animal squidged between his teeth, releasing a powerfully bitter liquid. Ethan heaved and dropped to his knees. He spat out the remains in his mouth. His mouth flooded with saliva and his stomach forced its way up his throat, expelling the sandy water he'd drunk earlier.

After his stomach had emptied itself, Ethan continued to retch. Finally, his energy utterly spent, he collapsed on his back. Gazing up at the late-afternoon sky, he said, "I guess not those then." He chuckled weakly at his own joke.

He turned onto his hands and knees and spat to one side, trying to rid his mouth of the overpowering bitterness, which was now mixed with the taste of his own bile. It seemed so unfair that now he'd figured out a way to go home, this obstacle of lack of food should stand in his way. There had to be something he could eat. All he needed was something that provided sufficient calories and wasn't poisonous enough to kill him before he reached the end of his journey.

Surely there had to be something.

He watched the little disgusting-tasting creatures carry on their leaf-harvesting task. He didn't want to try the leaves. They probably supplied their pests' flavoring.

Then Ethan remembered something. He knew why the animals had seemed familiar. He'd seen a vid of similar Earth insects that also cut out pieces of leaves. He recalled they did something odd with them. He tried to recall what it was. In a moment, he had it. The Earth insects had grown a fungus on the chewed-up remains of the leaves.

Ethan had eaten plenty of types of fungus aboard ship. If the animals weren't edible, maybe they grew a fungus that was.

He followed the trail to the hole he'd seen

earlier. The creatures were leaving and entering it at a rate of several per second. Ethan also remembered that Earth insects often bit or stung in defense. Yet the creature he'd tried to eat hadn't hurt him. He hoped the rest of them were the same.

He pushed his hand into the soil around the hole and scooped it out. The texture was loose and easy to penetrate. Immediately, the creatures went crazy. They began running around as if trying to find the cause of the disaster. Several ran up Ethan's arm. He brushed them away and continued to dig. Another two handfuls of soil later, he hit what he'd been hoping to find. A mass of soft, pale material that seemed to be the Concordian equivalent of a type of fungus. It was thick with wriggling larvae.

Ethan's stomach turned and threatened to resume retching but he swallowed his saliva and clenched his teeth. He had to eat. If the fungus was edible, he would eat it. It didn't matter if it was disgusting. After brushing away as many of the larvae as he could, and ignoring the creatures that were now running all over him—thankfully not actually hurting him—Ethan took a small bite of the spongy material.

It had little taste, and though it broke into weirdly textured fragments in his mouth, it didn't immediately make Ethan vomit. None of this meant that the fungus wouldn't kill him, either right away or eventually, of course.

He ate a little more. He would wait a while to test its effects. In truth, he didn't think his stomach could have tolerated any more of even the most wholesome food right then. But if the fungus turned out to be sustaining, he would have to eat more before nightfall. He had another long walk ahead and plenty more after that.

CHAPTER THIRTEEN

Cariad had to wait half an hour for Osias to answer her comm. She'd hooked her personal interface to the *Mistral's* system with Captain Addleson's permission and ensconced herself in an empty cabin for privacy.

The new Leader was so popular, he was in need of a secretary. When he could finally speak to her, she told him of the breakthrough with Garwin. "He was with Twyla day by day for a couple of decades. And this was during the time that no one knew about the Natural Movement infiltration except its members, so Twyla might not have been very guarded about what she said or did. Garwin already told me something she said that would have clearly implicated her if she'd said the same today. I'm hoping that with time he'll be able to recall more, perhaps some things that will give us clues on how to track these people down."

"That is good news," Osias replied. "Thanks for

letting me know. What's your next step?"

"Next, I have to interview the other suspects. I'm heading to the *Nova Fortuna*, then I'll be coming planetside. I'll need a room to work in at your residence, if your offer still stands."

"Yes, of course. You're very welcome. Like I said, I want to encourage more Woken to spend time here."

"Well, I don't think I'm going to be very popular when I begin bringing Gens in for questioning, but I appreciate your help."

Cariad said goodbye to the Leader and made a mental note to pack a bag to take with her when she went to the surface. The interview process would probably take several days. After closing her comm to Osias, she contacted Addleson to ask if she could take a shuttle to the *Nova Fortuna*.

"What?" the captain replied. "You're leaving us so soon? You only just arrived. I was hoping to catch up on gossip."

"I am. Sorry. Lots to do. While I'm gone, Garwin might ask to speak to me. If he does, could you pass on the message right away?"

"Sure. If you go to the shuttle bay, I'll make sure a shuttle's ready for you when you arrive."

"Thanks."

Cariad sped through the ship's corridors. She was pleased she was finally gaining some traction in the Natural Movement investigation. If there were any more saboteurs she desperately wanted to catch them before they struck again. She was also pleased to have a distraction that would help prevent her from worrying about Ethan.

Ever since he'd left, she'd been checking his

flitter's tracking signal, which global satellites launched from the *Nova Fortuna* not long after Arrival were picking up. Recently, whenever she checked the signal, the flitter remained in the same spot. She couldn't understand why Ethan would choose to spend time in one area when his intention had been to explore the continent.

She couldn't help wondering if he was in some kind of trouble. The flitter might have broken down, though it was unlikely. In that case, he wouldn't be able to return to the settlement. Trying to travel alone across the country would be a death sentence. Carrying enough food to sustain himself would be impossible so he would be forced to rely on finding edible plants or animals in the wild, but that would be the least of his problems. If the existence of the sluglimpets was anything to go by, Concordia was probably host to all kinds of nasty predators.

Cariad didn't know how to react to the unmoving flitter signal. If Ethan wasn't having problems, it would be ridiculous to try to save him. On the other hand, if he did need help, would Osias agree to risking another life and another flitter on a rescue mission? She wasn't sure he would. And Ethan himself had said he didn't want anyone to come after him if he got into difficulties.

It was too soon to make a decision about what to do, Cariad concluded as she reached the *Mistral's* shuttle bay. She would just have to continue to check the signal and hope that it moved.

***

"Hi Cariad," Rene said. "I haven't seen you in ages. What have you been up to?"

Cariad had gone directly to the soil lab when she arrived aboard the colony ship, but now that she'd arrived, she wasn't sure how to ask her friend about the lesion that Dr. Montfort had discovered on her. "Hi, Rene. Umm... Could I speak to you in private?"

"Ooooh, sounds serious," Rene replied. "How about we go outside?"

The ship's corridor wasn't the ideal place to accuse a friend of being a murderer and a terrorist, thought Cariad, but it would do for a preliminary conversation. "Yeah, that would be good." Rene followed her out of the lab. The corridor was mercifully empty, yet the fact didn't seem to improve Cariad's feelings of awkwardness. "So, how are you doing?"

When Cariad had come out of cryonic suspension she'd shared a room with Rene. Cariad thought they'd gotten to know each other well. Looking at her friend at that moment, she seemed the same amiable, intelligent, sweet-tempered person Cariad had thought she'd always been.

"I'm good," Rene replied. "Hey, are you hungry? It's nearly dinner time. What do you say to us going to grab something to eat while we talk about this private business you want to discuss?"

"No," Cariad replied, "it's better if we talk out here." She had to be professional about her investigation, even if Rene was a friend—*because* Rene was a friend. Cariad couldn't allow her personal feelings to blind her to the truth if Rene was affiliated with the Natural Movement.

"Oh, okay." Rene's friendly expression turned to concern. "What's wrong, Cariad? You look like someone died."

"No one's died, or at least not in the last day or so."

"Is this about that attack at the lake? I heard about it. Just awful. It was a father and his little daughter, wasn't it?"

"Yes, it was. But this isn't about that."

"What is it, then?" asked Rene. "Come on, spit it out. What's wrong?"

Cariad took a breath. "When Dr. Montfort was checking everyone in case they'd contracted the skin disease he's worried about, he found a lesion on you. I have to ask you how you got it." As far as she knew, no one yet suspected the cover story Montfort had made up.

"What the hell?" Rene spluttered. "Whatever happened to patient confidentiality?"

"We aren't on Earth," Cariad said. "There aren't any rules or laws here except the ones we make. Can you tell me how you hurt yourself?"

"Well, that abrasion is pretty hard to explain. I can't explain it myself. But is that any reason for Montfort to tell you about it? And why are you asking me about it now? Why is it your business that I hurt myself?"

"I can't tell you that. So you're saying you don't know what you did that resulted in the injury?"

"I don't know why it should matter to you, but that's right. I got the surprise of my life when Alasdair held up a mirror so I could see it. When I knew it was there, I began to feel sore. Montfort applied a healing gel and sent me on my way. It was weird, but after a while I gave up trying to figure out how I'd done it. It's all healed up now.

But why did Montfort tell you about it, and why are you interested?"

Cariad said, "So as far as you know, you received the injury just hours before you were examined? Do you think you would have noticed it if you'd received it earlier than that?"

"The wound looked quite fresh. I'd say as recently as the evening before, but as to how—"

"Maybe it was an accident that you somehow forgot about, like slipping in the shower," Cariad said.

"I guess that's the only explanation. It's strange that I didn't remember, though. And I didn't have any other bruises or scrapes."

"It seems very strange. You're sure you can't remember hurting yourself?"

"I'm certain."

Cariad didn't count herself as very good at being able to tell when people were lying, but Rene seemed completely honest in her story. "Okay. Thanks."

"Are you going to tell me why you're asking me now?"

"No. I can't."

"Hmm... Right. Okay. So, do you want to come and eat dinner with me?"

"I can't do that either, sorry." Cariad realized she would have to keep a distance between them until her investigation was concluded and Rene was no longer a suspect. "Thanks for answering my questions. I have to go now. I'm going to catch the last shuttle planetside."

"You're going to sleep at the settlement tonight?"

"Yes. I want to be up bright and early."

***

Cariad missed the shuttle by about a minute. As she stood at the closed portal to the shuttle bay, tiredness plucking at her eyes, she realized it was probably a good thing that she would have to spend the night aboard the ship.

After picking up a meal at the refectory, Cariad went to her room. She ate slowly, mulling over her conversation with Rene. Her friend's explanation seemed implausible. How could she have hurt herself badly enough to require a healing gel but not even remember it? Yet it was the doubtfulness of her story that made Cariad inclined to believe her, even setting aside their friendship. An actual Natural Movement follower would have thought up a much more credible lie. They would know about Twyla's tattoo and guess the real reason for Montfort's examination of everyone, and they would have had time to fake an accident or think up something more plausible than *I don't know*.

But if Rene wasn't lying, what did it mean?

Cariad finished her meal, showered, and went to bed. However, as she lay in darkness, sleep didn't come to her. As well as trying to figure out the implications of Rene's story, she couldn't stop worrying about Ethan. According to the signal the satellite was receiving, the flitter had stopped at the edge of the massive river that lay beyond the central mountain range. Horrible images formed in her mind. She saw Ethan's body floating face-down in the water. She saw him trapped in the sunken flitter, struggling to get free, and finally drowning.

She sat up and turned on the light. She needed

a distraction of some kind—something she could do until she was so exhausted that sleep would finally overcome her worries. Cariad recalled the holo message from the Guardians' creators that she'd begun to watch. It wouldn't be pleasant to view more of the bitter Steen's rants, but it would help take her mind off problems in the present.

As she turned on the holo, Steen appeared above the display unit in her desk. He was frozen exactly as he'd been when she'd turned off the holo before, his face set in a sneer. Cariad sighed. He'd directed so much anger and hate toward the colony. If only Steen had known what the colonists lives were really like. If he'd known about the predatory life forms and sabotage attempts, he might have thought himself lucky that he gave up the chance to travel there. She started the holo.

"I was going to tell you all about what you escaped when you flew away in your mega starship," said Steen. "but words can't accurately convey what humanity has been through since you left, so I'll let these images speak for themselves." He paused. "You know, I've seen the reports from the time the *Nova Fortuna* departed. People used to say that the First Generation were heroes. They said they were giving their lives so the rest of humanity could spread to the stars. How terrible it would be to live out the rest of your life aboard a starship, even prohibited from having your own children, people said. But you know what? The First Generation were lucky they didn't have children. Their descendants didn't have to live through *this*."

Steen was replaced by a scene of rioting

protesters. Cariad recognized the context immediately. They were Natural Movement followers. The signs they carried were calling for an end to the interference of Big Pharma in government, including vaccination, contraception, and abortion services. After a few minutes of shouting, screaming, and surging crowds barely held back by riot police, the scene changed. In the next vid, the rioting was more violent. Police were using water cannons on the crowds. The camera pulled backward, opening the shot and displaying the extent of the protest, which spanned tens of blocks.

More scenes followed, showing arguments on TV shows, attacks on medical clinics and research centers, and news sites reporting the banning of stem cell therapies, genetic modification, artificial fertilizer and pesticides, and science education in schools. Politicians followed the trend, giving speeches on the wisdom of people living as they were "meant to" and of humanity returning to more natural ways of life.

The scenes sickened Cariad. The Natural Movement's way of thinking had always occupied a place in most human societies, but she didn't understand how it had taken hold in large sections of the population. She began to skip the holo ahead through the montage. She didn't feel the need to witness any more of it and was only interested in returning to Steen's message. Then a glimpse of a scene piqued her interest. She paused the holo and reversed to the beginning of the scene.

A woman lay in a hospital bed, surrounded by

her family. She was skeletal, as if suffering from a wasting disease or cancer that had gone untreated. Her head was little more than a skull topped by wispy hair, and her arms as they lay on the blanket were almost nothing but bones.

The camera zoomed in on the woman's face. Her lips were moving. A voice said, "What, Mom? What did you say?" The woman tried to speak again but the recorder still failed to pick up the sound. The unseen speaker said, "We're happy you're dying naturally too, Mom. We're proud of you."

Cariad was disgusted. She zoomed the holo forward, unable to stomach any more scenes from the willful return of humankind into ignorance. When Steen reappeared, she halted the holo and let it play on at normal speed.

Steen seemed calmer. "Dear viewer, I want to ask you, are you a scientist? Me too. We're all scientists and engineers, we who are saving your butts. Did you have a job before you left? Maybe in a university or a research lab? Or were you one of the scientists working on the project? It doesn't matter.

"Imagine being forced to do your experiments in secret. Can you even think how hard it would be to practice your passion in hiding, fearful of discovery? Can you imagine the need for a covert underground network of scientists, complete with passwords and secret signs? Does that sound insane to you? It *is* insane, isn't it? But that's what things came to in the end.

"For centuries after the Enlightenment, scientists labored to find out the truth, and in doing that they made things better for people.

Science freed people from disease, suffering, and never-ending toil and drudgery. We improved the lot of humanity, and gave our fellow human beings the opportunity to avoid their natural destinies, but... " Steen chuckled ironically and his expression turned grim. "They. Didn't. Want. It. Not any of it. It turns out that people would rather labor, suffer, and die like animals. They don't want to rise up and live better, saner lives. They don't want intellect to triumph over biological destiny. They don't want civilization." His face turned red with rage, and he shouted, gesticulating violently, "They want to snuffle for their food and eat and shit and fuck like pigs in mud. Because that's what's *natural*."

Steen hung his head and rubbed his eyes before returning his gaze to the camera. "What's the point? This is ancient history to you, right? Hell, it's history to us. I guess I should tell you what happened after and how we came to build the *Mistral*."

He'd arrived at the part that promised to be the most interesting from Cariad's perspective, but fatigue was overwhelming her. She turned off the holo and fell asleep thinking about what had happened on Earth since she'd left, and also thinking of Ethan.

CHAPTER FOURTEEN

The previous night, Ethan had reached hilly ground—the beginnings of the foothills that led to the mountains he would have to cross. When he woke up from his daytime sleep, he saw the river was narrower. He could now see the green line of the farther bank. The vegetation in that part of the country had also changed, perhaps due to the thinner, rockier soil. This worried him. His only source of food was the fungus grown by the creatures that infested a certain type of plant. He'd been forced to search long and hard for the plant the last time he'd eaten. If it didn't grow in the mountains, he would have to find another source of sustenance.

Yet the fact that the topography of the land was changing was a good sign. The river was fed by tributaries from the mountains. The first one he came across, he planned to follow upstream and finally leave the river behind. If the stream was shallow and clear, it might be safe to drink directly from it, free from the worry of thread creatures pulling him in.

Ethan stood up and stretched. His clothes were loose and baggy. He'd lost weight, but otherwise he didn't feel too bad. The fungus kept hunger pangs away and he didn't want for water, providing he had the patience to collect it from the river using the safe method he'd invented.

When he'd first set out on his expedition, he hadn't imagined he would ever be able to survive without the flitter and his supplies, but he'd managed it so far. Dr. Crowley would have been proud of him. She'd seemed to see something in him that he couldn't see himself. Perhaps she'd been right after all. Ethan smiled to himself. Lauren would have been proud too.

Ethan became aware of a rushing sound, like heavy rain falling, but the sky was clear. Then he remembered when he'd heard the same sound the first night after he'd lost the flitter. A wave was traveling up the river.

He was already some distance away from it, but for safety's sake Ethan walked farther into the low forest that bordered the river. Being swept into the tentacles of a thread creature would be a sad end after he'd worked so hard at staying alive.

This time, he had a good view of the wave as it came. The crest was pale foam, the same brown hue as the river but much lighter in tone. Ethan guessed it was perhaps half his own height. The previous wave he'd seen had been taller, he thought, although it had been hard to tell in the dark. He waited until it passed and then returned to the river to see the after effects.

The ground was muddy and the plants were covered in sediment the wave had deposited. He wouldn't find any fungus-growing creatures there, he guessed. He would have to roam farther afield.

Ethan shouldered his weapon and resumed his long trudge toward the mountains. If he had to walk, he might as well walk in the direction he had to travel anyway. He walked on the edge of the zone affected by the wave, searching for the jagged-leaved plant. The weakness he'd felt after not eating for a few days hadn't returned since he'd been consuming the fungus. If he could find plenty of it, he would try to walk for the rest of the day and all through the night.

He was growing thirsty, however. It was time to take off his shirt and approach the river again. Ethan left the drier zone and entered the muddy ground where the wave had passed. His boots squelched and clung to the wet soil and he was forced to pull up each leg every time he took a step.

He drew closer to the river. Ethan had grown to dislike it. Whenever he was forced to go near it, he was always reminded of his lost flitter and thread creatures that might lie only meters away from him.

He had a problem. At the river's edge the ground was too muddy to draw water from, either by hand or by dipping his shirt sleeve into it. The wave had degraded the river's edge to a swamp-like consistency. Yet he had to drink. He was very thirsty, he realized. He hadn't drunk since going to sleep that morning.

How should he attempt to collect water? He moved one step closer. He would have to stretch to cast his shirt far to water, to hit the water but he believed he was at a safe distance.

He flung out his shirt and hit it just right the first time. Thirstily, he sucked the cuff dry. Another cast resulted in another mouthful of water painstakingly extracted from the material. The process was laborious but it was the only one he had.

Ethan threw out his shirt again. This time as the sleeve hit the water, a thread curled around it tightly. Before he had time to react, the thread gave a sharp tug. He was already unbalanced, leaning forward to reach the water and holding the shirt tightly. The tug on it tipped him forward. Ethan couldn't save himself. He fell. His weapon slipped off his shoulder.

As he hit the mud, more threads were already snaking out from the river, lightning fast. The thread that had tugged the shirt abandoned it and slithered over the mud. More threads wrapped themselves around Ethan's forearms. He reared up, struggling against their insistent pull. Managing to rise to his knees, he dragged with all his strength against the insistent filaments. They were wet, rubbery, and powerful, biting into his muscles, which bulged with his efforts to free himself.

Yet more threads were gliding from the water, their ends probing the mud like tongues, trying to find him. Ethan gasped with effort and pain. The threads were too strong for him. His knees were sliding along the mud as he was dragged toward the river.

Ethan fought with every muscle he possessed. He was rigid with resistance as he fought the inexorable drag. A thread wound up his thigh, encircling it. He looked at his weapon lying just out of reach. Could he hook it with a toe? But a thread was already winding around his other leg.

Panic overcame him. His death lay only seconds away, either by drowning or something else the threads would do to him once they had him in the water. Ethan jerked, twisted, and battled with all his might. The threads were cutting deep depressions into his flesh. The water of the river drew closer. It washed over his knees, then his thighs.

No! Please! "Arghhhhhh!"

This was it. Ethan's time on Concordia was over. There was no one and nothing that could save him now. The water was up to his waist. Threads were encircling his torso and winding up to his neck. Ethan hoped it would be over quickly.

The threads pulled him forward and then downward. Just before his head sank beneath the surface, though he knew his situation was hopeless, Ethan took a deep breath.

CHAPTER FIFTEEN

Cariad had set up an office at the Leader's planetside residence and sent out messages to the Gens on Montfort's list of subjects, requesting their presence for an informal chat. She scheduled four people to come and see her that afternoon. She hadn't specified the subject of the conversation, thinking that anything she said might influence what they would be willing to tell her. Also, if she made the reason for the request too specific, her intent to root out the remaining Natural Movement saboteurs would be clear. Cariad was aware she was treading a tightrope: she had to try to discover any remaining threats to the colony, but at the same time she was terrified of alerting the terrorists and triggering another devastating attack.

If the situation were different, she would simply arrest all the suspects. But she knew the Gens would never accept such draconian action. If she started locking people up without an obvious justification it would be disastrous for the current fragile harmony.

The first three interviews seemed to go smoothly. Cariad asked the suspects about their experiences over the last few months, as if she was conducting a general checkup on the mood and morale of the colony. She also asked about the suspicious injuries that Montfort had reported as well as inquiring about other injuries the suspects had sustained, trying to find out if they had credible explanations. All three interviewees had related believable stories that explained their lesions. Cariad was fairly satisfied that none of them were lying. Also, when the interviews were over, none apparently realized Cariad's real intention behind her questions. They seemed pleased that their opinions had been sought and their experiences noted.

The next person on her list and the final person she planned to interview that afternoon was Cherry. Cariad had been surprised to see her name on the list. Cherry was the last Gen Cariad would have expected to be a Natural Movement saboteur, but then, she reminded herself, it was possible that none of the people on the list were terrorists.

What was more, Cherry had nearly died during the cave disaster. It was reasonable to expect that she would have been injured. That the woman had survived at all was something of a miracle. Ethan hadn't returned from his search for other survivors, so no other Gen who had been washed into the ocean had lived to tell the tale. And if Cherry was Ethan's friend, Cariad strongly doubted she would be allied with the Natural

Movement.

On the other hand, Ethan had said that Cherry and Garwin had been having an affair. Garwin's wife had been a terrorist. Was it too much of a coincidence?

Cariad walked to the door of her borrowed room in the Leader's offices, opened it, and saw Cherry sitting outside, gazing at her interface as she waited for her interview. Cariad greeted her and invited her in. Cherry gave her a sullen look before standing and following Cariad.

"I'm sorry to take you away from your work," Cariad said, wondering if that was the reason for the woman's bad mood. "What is it you do?"

"I'm a farmer," Cherry replied. Her sun-burnished skin testified to the fact. Her gaze was fixed hard on Cariad as she strode inside the room and sat down.

"I see," Cariad said. "Your employment status on your record is blank. I'll have it fixed."

"You do that," said Cherry. "Make sure you put my job in the little box. I'd hate my file to be incomplete. Is that it?" She stood up.

"No," said Cariad. "Of course not. I didn't ask you to come in to find out what job you do. That would be ridiculous."

"Would it? So many things around here are ridiculous. I find it hard to tell them apart."

Cariad paused and regarded the woman, trying to understand why she was so belligerent. Cariad had doubted she was a Natural Movement follower, but Cherry's hostile attitude was giving her doubts. Had she guessed why she'd been summoned? Was she trying to obscure the truth through acting aggressively?

Cariad decided to adopt a conciliatory attitude and see how Cherry reacted. If her problem was only a general resentment toward Woken she might be mollified. "Things have certainly been difficult ever since Arrival. It's been a trying time for everyone."

"But mostly the Gens," Cherry said.

"I'm not denying it," Cariad said. Of the three hundred and fifty-two deaths since arriving at Concordia, the Gens made up more than four-fifths of the total. "The Gens have borne the brunt of it."

Cherry's resentful attitude faded just a touch at Cariad's words. "You know Ethan, don't you?"

"I do," Cariad replied.

"Have you heard from him? Is he okay?"

"I haven't heard anything. He didn't want to stay in touch. As far as I know he's okay."

Cherry breathed a huge sigh. "Ethan's a good person."

Cariad nodded, her lips pressed tightly together. For some reason, Cherry's mention of Ethan had brought all Cariad's worries, fears, and sadness at missing her friend to the surface. Her emotion must have been apparent to Cherry as the resentment in her features faded a little further.

"So why am I here?" Cherry asked.

"I'm interviewing colonists about their experiences. I want to get a handle on how things are going. Find out how people are doing. How have you been since your accident?"

"You mean my near-drowning?" Cariad asked. "Why do you want to know?"

"I just said—"

"No. There's something else going on here. Why are you really questioning us?"

Cherry's stare was making Cariad uncomfortable. The interview wasn't going at all as the others had. She looked down to compose herself.

"Is this something to do with Twyla's sabotage?" Cherry asked.

Cariad looked up. "What makes you say that?"

"So it was her who did it."

"I didn't say that."

"You didn't deny it."

Cariad felt like she was the one being interviewed, or rather interrogated. "Okay, you got me. We're fairly certain it was Twyla. What do you know about her?"

Cherry had been leaning forward in her chair. She relaxed back into her seat. "Only that she was Garwin's wife and she taught kindy."

"That's all?"

"That's all. I hardly knew her."

"But... " Cariad hesitated to disclose that she knew about Cherry's affair with Garwin, but she figured it didn't matter now. "I heard that you and Garwin were in a relationship."

"We were. I started sleeping with him when I was nineteen."

"You were that young?" Cariad was surprised. Garwin was in his forties.

"Is it that shocking?" Cherry smiled wryly. "You Woken think you're so smart, don't you? You don't know half of what goes on in this colony. I wasn't the only person Garwin was sleeping with either."

"But he's so much older than you," Cariad said.

Woman-to-woman curiosity got the better of her. "Did you know he had other girlfriends? Didn't you mind?"

"I did know, and I didn't mind. I was only having fun, the same as he was. He said that Twyla didn't care and I believed him. Honestly, he didn't make a big secret of what he was doing. Unlike everything else he did."

"What did he do?"

"Disappear. For hours sometimes. And he would play people off one another. Everyone thought Garwin was their friend, but everyone knew of someone he didn't like."

"You don't make him sound very nice," remarked Cariad. Cherry's story didn't seem to be adding up. "If he was so fake, why did you stay with him for so long?"

Cherry shrugged. "I'm not one for serious commitments. All that romantic, sentimental stuff isn't for me. Garwin knew my attitude and he was happy to go along with it. The arrangement suited us both."

Cariad rubbed her temples. She wasn't sure where the interview was going. Was Cherry implicating Garwin as a Natural Movement follower? And if she was, was it to deflect suspicion from herself? Cariad decided to force the issue. "What are you telling me? You think Garwin might have been a saboteur too?" It was certainly possible. A terrible thought occurred to Cariad: had Garwin murdered Twyla and made it look like suicide to imply his wife's guilt and his own innocence?

"What's wrong?" Cherry asked. "Did I hit a

nerve? Garwin is under suspicion, isn't he? That's why he's aboard the *Mistral*. You're keeping him in confinement while you figure out if he's a member of the Natural Movement."

That was no big secret. Cariad was surprised Cherry wasn't sure of the fact. "That's right. We aren't sure that Garwin is innocent, so it's interesting to hear what you have to say about him."

"Well, I regret saying anything about him now. I don't think he's a saboteur. He worked too hard for Gen independence for that to be true. He just isn't very trustworthy."

"Okay," Cariad said. They were back to square one. It was no good, Cariad realized. Cherry was too smart to fool with subtle questioning. Cariad had no choice but to ask her outright what she needed to know. "Cherry, I have to ask you how you came by the abrasion on your hip."

"That scrape Dr. Montfort was so interested in? Is that the real reason why he wanted to examine everyone? He was looking for something that might link us to the Natural Movement?"

"Look, I can't tell you anything about that," Cariad replied. "Could you please answer my question?"

"No, I can't."

"Why? You were being very frank a moment ago."

Cherry said, "I'm not being evasive. I can't tell you how I hurt my hip because I don't remember. I'm covered in cuts and bruises from that fall from the cave and I don't know how I got any of them. I was kind of preoccupied at the time."

"Okay. That makes sense." Cariad felt deflated. She'd started the afternoon full of anticipation that she might make significant progress in the Natural Movement investigation but after interviewing four suspects she didn't feel she'd learned anything useful. Maybe she just wasn't cut out for the job. She was a scientist, not a detective.

"I think that's enough for now. Thanks for coming," she said to Cherry. "If you remember anything about Garwin that might be relevant, let me know."

"So I'm not a suspect anymore?" Cherry asked, standing up.

"I didn't say you were a suspect."

"No, but it's pretty obvious. You mean just because I scraped my leg when I fell into the ocean I'm suspected of setting off bombs?"

"I didn't say that either. As far as I'm concerned, everyone's a suspect until we find a reason to rule them out."

"Everyone except the Woken, you mean."

"I don't mean that at all."

"Huh," Cherry said dismissively. She strode to the door and went out.

In truth, Cariad hadn't strongly suspected the Woken. It was clear that the Gens had been infiltrated by the Natural Movement at the *Nova Fortuna's* departure, and that the cult had indoctrinated a number of Gens down the years of the ship's passage. Nothing Strongquist had found had implicated Woken involvement.

But Cariad's opinion had changed after hearing Rene's story. Now she wasn't so sure she could rule out her fellow scientists.

CHAPTER SIXTEEN

Ethan was wrapped in threads and they were pulling him down, down, down into the river. His eardrums and lungs felt like they would burst. It was pointless for him to cling onto life until the very end, he knew, yet he couldn't help it. A part of him continued to fight against inevitability.

Where were the threads taking him? To a gaping maw on the river bed where he would be eaten alive? Or would they squeeze him ever tighter and tighter, biting through his flesh, slicing him into pieces?

Panic forced his eyelids open. The river water was murky and stung his eyes. The current as well as the predatory threads was pulling him. He couldn't hold his breath any longer. A bubble of air forced its way out from his lungs. He fought the urge to breathe in. He was dizzy and sleepy. Calmness and serenity began to replace his fear.

It was a pity he had to die. He had so much to

live for, but then again, death came to everyone in the end. Ethan only wished he could have said goodbye to Cariad. She would never know what had happened to him. He hoped the colony would succeed and that she would live a long and happy life.

Another bubble of air slipped from his lips and was lost in the murkiness. He didn't have long now. Ethan was glad his death wouldn't be any worse than this. He felt peaceful and ready to go.

His head broke the surface. Shock made him gasp and he drew in deep lungfuls of sweet air. He had only a moment to wonder what was happening and take in a view of the wide, brown river and distant bank before the threads pulled him under again. Again, they dragged him so deep that the water pressed in on him.

The breath of air had given him new hope and vigor. He battled the enveloping threads, writhing and kicking against the tight bonds, but it was no use. He was so tightly wrapped he could barely move his limbs.

Just as Ethan thought he would die if he didn't breathe, his head popped above the surface again. He drew in air quickly. He had no idea what the threads were doing, but if a few more minutes of life were being offered to him, he would take them. This time the landscape had changed. He caught a glimpse of the arch-rooted plants with draping branches before he was pulled under once more.

The threads were dragging him at enormous speed. They had taken only minutes to travel a distance it had taken Ethan days to traverse.

As he edged perilously close to drowning for the

third time he slammed into a hard surface. With his remaining consciousness he wondered where he was. He hadn't expected to hit anything hard on the bottom of the river. He'd expected soft, slimy mud. Unless he'd impacted a wide, flat stone? But it hadn't felt like stone. The surface he was pressed against was smooth and regular.

The surface slid away. Ethan tumbled into a hole along with a deluge of water. The threads released him. Unable to stop himself, he took a breath and water flooded his throat and lungs. He coughed violently but his reflex reaction to coughing was to breathe in again.

To his profound surprise, the next breath he took was of air.

He continued to cough and retch in darkness. His feet were resting on a solid surface but he guessed he was chest-deep in water. His head, neck, and arms were somehow in a bubble of air at the bottom of the river. Ethan reached out but his fingers didn't make contact with any surface. The water was gurgling and gushing.

It was draining away. Ethan could feel the water moving downward. The level was dropping. It moved down to his stomach, then his hips, and then his thighs felt sodden and cold as the water left them. When it had drained as far as his ankles, the ground slid out from beneath his feet and he fell again. He hit another floor, landing hard and awkwardly. Ethan cried out as his ankle wrenched to one side and he fell heavily, one elbow taking his full weight.

The floor of this second chamber was covered in a thin layer of water about a couple of centimeters deep. Ethan continued to cough as his lungs tried to expel the remaining water that irritated them. His ankle and elbow sent out shooting bolts of pain. Where was he? Where had the threads taken him? Was he in some kind of storeroom, to be kept fresh until they were ready for him?

When his coughing finally eased, Ethan sat up on the watery ground. He remained in utter darkness. He couldn't even see his hand in front of his face. He was also soaking wet and so cold he trembled. But he was alive—for now.

Unwilling to trust his ankle with his weight, he crawled across the floor, trying to discover the boundaries of the place where the threads had deposited him. When he'd crawled about three or four meters, sloshing through the water that covered the floor, he met a solid vertical surface. Taking care to favor his uninjured leg, he stood up, sliding his hands up the wall and as far as he could reach over his head. He couldn't reach the ceiling.

Ethan continued his explorations along the wall and eventually discovered he was in a room about six meters square. A rushing sound came from all around, which he guessed had to be the river flowing past.

He was shaking with cold. He took off his shirt and pants, which seemed to be only draining the heat from his body, and wrung them out as forcefully as he could. He didn't have anywhere to hang them, so he put them on again, benefiting a little from the drier cloth. His boots were gone, apparently falling off at some point as the threads dragged him through the water.

Ethan went to a corner of the chamber and

stood, leaning against it, to avoid wetting his clothes again in the water on the floor. What now? He was shivering less than before, but that was about the only good thing about his situation. The threads were clearly keeping him confined for a purpose.

Then curiosity invaded his morbid speculations. He touched the wall again. The material didn't feel like natural stone, and it wasn't metal or plastic either. The chamber he was in was flat and square, as if it had been artificially manufactured. The threads had to possess some kind of intelligence to create the place.

Ethan also realized that the first room the threads had put him in was a kind of air lock, like he'd seen aboard the *Nova Fortuna.* Only here it was to transition between water and air, not between the vacuum of space and atmosphere inside the ship. The air lock was another sign of the threads' intelligence. Not only had they constructed a regularly shaped chamber, they understood that he needed air to live.

The realization that his captors were intelligent lit a tiny flame of hope in Ethan. If they possessed intelligence, perhaps the creatures could be reasoned with in some way.

He noticed that by some miracle, his recorder still hung around his neck. Thinking that it was extremely unlikely anyone would ever replay his words or look at the pictures he'd taken, he nevertheless felt compelled to continue to record his experiences. He turned on the device.

After relating his story of being captured by the threads, transported along the river, and deposited in the chamber, he went on, "From what I can tell about this place, the threads must be intelligent to create it and place me here. If they're intelligent, I guess they probably have some kind of language. Though I don't know how to communicate with them, or even where they are. I can't hear anything except the noise of the river water passing by outside. I remember seeing vids of aquatic animals on Earth but I'm not sure how they communicated. I think it might have been through electrical impulses or light. If that's the kind of language the threads use, I don't have a hope of talking to them and making them understand that humans are intelligent too. If they knew that, maybe they would let me go."

The pain from his ankle and elbow had reduced to a throbbing ache and his uncontrollable shivering had stopped. He still felt very cold, however, and he was hungry. Perhaps it was insane for him to hope the threads might release him. Maybe his only salvation lay in finding his own way out somehow. Ethan racked his brains for a way to escape.

Of course, if he did make it out of the chamber, he would be in the rushing current of the river and unable to swim, but he would figure out that part when he came to it. Whatever happened to him then was a preferable alternative to waiting to become dinner.

He began to feel along the walls again, hopping on his good leg, trying to find a seam or hole that he might try to widen. He had no tools other than his hands, but the activity gave him something to do.

Some time later, he stopped. He spoke into the recorder again. "I haven't managed to find any kind of break in the walls. The material of the wall seems manufactured or at least cut with some kind of instrument. The threads are a sentient species. This is worrying and the implications are wider than I thought at first. What might happen if they decide they don't like humans living in their world? Could they find a way to leave the water and attack the settlement?

"The threads aren't dumb like the sluglimpets. They might be able figure out how to get past an electric fence. And the threads are in two places on this continent and possibly elsewhere too. I don't know if the colony would survive an attempt from the threads to destroy it. I have to tell the others. I have to warn them. But I can't get out."

Ethan could bear the prospect of his own death but not of the other colonists. They had all been through so much. So many of them had died already. He couldn't allow Cariad to die from an attack by the threads. He had already failed Lauren and Dr. Crowley. He wasn't going to fail her too. He thumped a fist against the wall in frustration, forgetting his injured elbow. Pain juddered up to his shoulder, making him cry out and curse.

He struck the wall again, using his good arm this time. As if in response, a light flicked on and Ethan was drowned in beams. He covered his eyes for a moment while they adjusted. When he looked out again, squinting and blinking, he finally saw the room that confined him.

CHAPTER SEVENTEEN

Osias had invited Cariad along on the trip to survey the lake. She was glad to take a break from interviewing the Natural Movement suspects as she didn't seem to be getting anywhere. She needed to try a different approach but she wasn't sure what that should be.

Verney was bringing the portable scanner that Cariad had arranged to be sent down from the ship. He'd fixed it to the bottom of a flitter and linked it with the vehicle's computer system.

"Do you know the range of this thing?" Verney asked when Cariad joined him at the flitter shed. "I don't fancy going anywhere near that water."

"I'm not sure exactly," Cariad replied, "but it should be accurate to twenty or thirty meters I guess. We'll soon be able to tell from the readings if we need to go any lower."

Osias was at the shed too. They all climbed into the flitter and Verney flew them out of the settlement and down the road that led to the farming district and the lake. When they arrived, he adjusted the vehicle's altitude so that they were high above the lake. Cariad could see the low buildings of the settlement in the distance.

The lake was self-contained with no rivers or streams feeding it. Cariad guessed it was fed from an underground spring. The body of water was irregular. A long tongue stretched out at one end while the other was smoothly rounded. At its widest point, the lake was about three hundred meters across, so it wasn't large. Cariad hoped it didn't contain more than a handful of the predators.

Verney started up the scanner and the flitter's interface came to life. The screen was a moving melange of shapes and colors as they flew over the water. A key at the corner explained the meaning of the different hues. The land around the lake was dark-hued and therefore comparatively cool. The temperature of the lake water seemed unusually high to Cariad, but she wasn't sure what was a normal range.

Verney cursed. "What are those?"

Cariad had been focusing on the key, but at Verney's exclamation she gazed at the image of the area they were passing over. What she saw was the last thing she would have expected. The floor of the lake was covered in square and rectangular shapes. If she'd thought it possible, Cariad would have said that what she was seeing wasn't much different from their own settlement's buildings.

Osias asked, "Is that one of them?"

The scanner's infrared readings were showing a living creature passing along what could only be described as a thoroughfare. The organism seemed to consist mostly of long sinuous limbs stretched almost five meters according to the scale on the scanner.

Cariad, Osias, and Verney watched in horrified fascination as the creature reached a building, if that's what the structure was. Rather than entering it from the side, however, the creature climbed on top and went through a hole in the upper surface.

"How deep are those things?" Osias asked.

"The structures?" Cariad said, looking at the image key again. "The tops of them seem to be only one or two meters below the water surface."

As they flew farther over the lake, they discovered its entire bed was filled with the structures. The lake was also alive with the tentacled creatures. Then they saw something even more remarkable.

"What the hell is that?" Cariad exclaimed. The heat signatures in the water were going haywire. According to the key, the temperature under the water was hundreds of degrees centigrade. Cariad looked out of her window to the lake surface. It was smooth and still, reflecting the bright sunlight. The scanner was recording temperatures that should have made the water boil.

"Could it be volcanic water?" Osias asked. "I read about hot springs on Earth."

"No," Cariad replied. "No way. Look at it. If that was natural hot water, it would be spreading out. The water surface would be steaming, if not bubbling. Look at it. That heat looks like it's being created artificially."

"I hate to admit it," said Osias, "but I think you're right."

They were looking at bright spots of heat that quickly faded to a normal temperature, as if something was containing it. The scanner also showed the spreading limbs of thread creatures operating near the heat source.

The implications of what she was seeing sent Cariad's mind reeling.

Eradicating the organisms from the lake was a secondary consideration now. A "town" appeared to exist beneath the water. What they had all been assuming was local, predatory wildlife seemed to be sentient. Concordia was inhabited by intelligent, indigenous beings. The probes had failed to discover the fact because the creatures were aquatic, or perhaps the probes had found them but the information had been removed long ago by Natural Movement infiltrators.

The colonists were interlopers who had invaded an occupied planet.

***

Cariad sent the vid from the scanner up to the xenobiologists aboard the ship as soon as she returned to the settlement.

"How much are you going to tell people?" she asked Osias as they were discussing what to do at his Leader's residence.

"I haven't decided yet," Osias replied. "I have to tell them something. Verney was with us and saw everything. He won't keep quiet about it, but I wouldn't ask him to anyway. Gens are very sensitive to being shut out from important information right now. But I don't want everyone to panic either."

"I don't think that's likely, do you?" Cariad asked. "The threads have kept to themselves as long as people didn't stray too near the lake. I don't see any reason their behavior should suddenly change, providing we don't provoke them."

"I guess you're right," Osais said. He chewed his lip. Cariad pitied this young man who had the weight of human civilization's last hope on his shoulders, let alone the lives of around eighteen hundred men, women, and children depending on his decisions.

"I'm going up to the *Nova Fortuna* to speak to the xenobiologists about what we saw today," she said. "As soon as I find out anything useful, I'll let you know." She knew the scientists would want to speak to someone who had been at the lake when the scan took place. Osias would have enough on his plate dealing with the fall-out from the revelation about the thread creatures.

"Okay. Thanks."

"Osias," said Cariad. "You're doing a great job. The Gens have survived a hell of a lot so far. They can get through this too." The Leader thanked her again before she left.

Cariad had tried to sound more sanguine than she felt, hoping to buoy Osias' confidence. In truth, she was deeply disturbed by the notion of what seemed to be a society of intelligent beings sharing Concordia with them. Hypothetically, the fact that they were aquatic implied that the two sentient species on the planet could live peaceably, one occupying the land and the other inhabiting the waterways. Yet if human history had taught her anything, it was that intelligence brought with it the desire to explore, occupy, and exploit new territories. The few months that the colonists had lived on the planet had passed relatively peacefully but who knew what the future held? The threads had already demonstrated their belligerence on the young child and father they had killed.

Cariad had to wait over half an hour to catch the next scheduled shuttle and all the while she was occupied with worry. The last time she'd checked Ethan's flitter signal, it still hadn't moved. She couldn't help feeling that something was terribly wrong. She had a desperate urge to travel across the country to try to find him and check that he was okay.

But how could she leave the colony when it was in such a precarious state? She had barely begun her investigation into the Natural Movement and she wasn't at all satisfied that their threat to the colony was over. She'd left her techs to deal with the important task of restocking the gene pool by themselves for far too long. And now a third problem had emerged.

At least this was something she could safely leave to someone else to deal with. Xenobiology wasn't her field. Other expertise was required. She would tell the scientists what she'd seen and then go to see her techs for an update on how they were getting along.

As soon as Cariad disembarked from the shuttle aboard the *Nova Fortuna,* she went quickly by transit car to the xenobiology section. These Woken were the envy of the rest because their equipment had lain virtually untouched throughout the colony ship's long journey. Most of the others, like Cariad, had to work with ancient, worn apparatus.

She asked for admittance at the security panel. When the door slid open and she walked through into the lab, several sights greeted her. The first was a sluglimpet. The scientists had managed to trap one. The creature lay on its back on an examining table, held by straps made of a material that resisted the corrosive acid. It was still alive and its legs wriggled horribly. Though the creatures were Cariad's least-favorite animal, the sluglimpet's confinement seemed rather cruel.

Next to the sluglimpet was a man in a wheelchair. The revival process had left him paralyzed from the waist down. Cariad didn't know him very well.

It was the other person in the room who really caught her attention, however.

"Cariad."

Auburn-haired and covered in freckles, he looked exactly as he had when they'd wished each other good luck and parted one hundred and eighty four years previously. Kes. Montfort had revived Kes. Cariad felt a confusing rush of emotion: relief that her friend's revival had been successful and happiness at seeing him again, but also she also felt somewhat guilty.

Her friend walked around the examining table and its wriggling sluglimpet. He came over to her and wrapped her in his arms. "I missed you," he said.

Cariad hugged him back. "Missed me? How long have you been up and around?"

"I just started work today. I was one of the last to be revived, apparently."

Cariad laughed. "Then in your terms you only saw me a few weeks ago. But I've missed you too. I had no idea you were being revived. I wish Montfort had told me. I would have come to see you."

"Ah, I asked him not to say anything. People don't look their best, do they? All that flaking skin. You know what it's like. Vain of me, I know."

"I'm really pleased to see you didn't suffer any ill effects... Oh, sorry."

The xenobiologist in a wheelchair, who Cariad remembered was called Vasquez, said, "Don't worry about it. I'm quite used to it. But if you two could spare a moment from your joyful reunion, I believe you're here to discuss the scan readings from the lake?"

"Yes, that's right," Cariad said, her happiness at seeing her friend again quickly dissipating. "I take it you've had time to look at them closely. What do you think?"

"Well," Vasquez said, "professionally, I'm intrigued. However, personally, those images have left me feeling apprehensive, if not downright scared."

Cariad's mood fell further. "I was hoping you were going to tell me I was wrong."

"No," said Vasquez. "As far as I can guess from this admittedly scant evidence, I think these aquatic creatures may well be highly intelligent, and judging from their behavior they are not at all friendly."

CHAPTER EIGHTEEN

Although Ethan now had the benefit of light, he hadn't been able to find any possible way to escape the chamber. The walls were patterned with swirling grays and blacks that were not unlike the threads. The light shone down from the entire ceiling. It glowed softly like sunlight through water. Ethan guessed that though the beams had hurt his eyes at first, the light wasn't strong compared to daylight.

The ceiling was only just out of his reach. He couldn't see where it had opened to allow him to fall through. When he lifted up a hand to try to touch the glowing surface, stretching as high as he could, he noticed that the ceiling was emitting warmth as well as light. Below him, water covered the floor about a centimeter deep.

His situation was unfortunate but it could have been worse. Ethan guessed that he might be able to sleep in such a shallow layer of water without becoming too cold. Sleep was the last thing he wanted to do, however. What he wanted was to escape.

After searching thoroughly again, he'd discovered that the swirls that covered the walls and floor didn't hide any imperfections that he might work at to break through. He needed another way out.

As he tried desperately to think of a solution to his problem, Ethan realized that the light had come on just after he'd hit the wall of the chamber. Were the two actions connected? There was only one way to find out. He struck the wall again, hard, with his balled fist. His other hand was resting on the surface and he felt the vibration of his blow. When nothing happened, Ethan hit the wall again. Again, there was no result from his effort other than a smarting hand. For the third time, he thumped the wall. Nothing.

He gave up, concluding that the appearance of the light at the same time that he'd struck the wall before had been a coincidence. Ethan turned around to lean back on the surface and rest his hurt leg. Then he nearly jumped out of his skin.

The wall opposite had become transparent. Beyond it was a mass of threads, churning and roiling in the muddy river water. The sight was so disgusting, it made Ethan retch. He slid down the wall, hitting the floor with a thump. The creatures pulsated against the see-through wall, wriggling and heaving all the while.

If Ethan could have clawed his way out of the chamber and away from the creatures, he would have. He closed his eyes against the sight, wishing the light had never come on. His chill was leaving him and being replaced by an uncomfortable, humid sweatiness. He was nauseated. He opened one eye a crack. The horrible creatures were still there. What were they doing? Could they see him? They didn't seem to have any eyes. Could they sense his presence some other way?

He looked up at the light. That would be where the threads would enter the chamber to come for him. The hole in the ceiling would open, the river water would pour in and bring with it the dreadful threads. He closed his eyes again and wondered how long it would take.

***

Ethan had no way to tell how much time had passed, but he guessed that he had sat in the corner of his wet prison for an hour or longer while the threads writhed against the transparent wall. If they intended to enter the chamber to attack him, they were taking their time about it. Perhaps they were interested in observing him for a while. If the threads could construct a solid-walled cage, a ceiling that lit up, and a wall that turned from opaque to clear, the creatures might have guessed that he wasn't from their planet.

In that case, the threads might want to keep him alive. They would want to study him. Ethan gave a shudder as the full implication of his new understanding hit him. The Woken didn't study living Concordian creatures—the only living things aboard the *Nova Fortuna* were humans and a couple of insects that were bred for food—but Ethan had learned about animal experimentation that used to take place on Earth.

This new prospect was more terrifying to him than the idea of being eaten alive. If he were only prey to the thread creatures, he could hope for the end to come quickly. But if the threads wanted to experiment on him they would keep him alive as long as they could.

His only hope lay in getting away. There was no way out of his cell, but if the threads wanted to approach him, they would have to come inside at some point. That would be his chance and he would have to take it. He would have to be ready.

If only he had a weapon of some kind, even a knife. Then he might have felt more confident about attacking the slimy, squirming beasts. But all he had were his bare hands. They would have to do.

He watched the creatures, tension eating away at him. The constant sight of his captors and the murky, flowing water oppressed him heavily. Ethan got to his feet and hobbled toward the transparent wall, leaning against another wall for support as he went. The motions of the threads didn't seem to be affected by his slow, hesitant approach at first, but as he moved closer to them, the swirling and writhing increased.

The threads' appearance really did resemble the patterning on the walls of the chamber, Ethan confirmed as he drew nearer to them. The first time he'd seen them had been when they had tried to catch Cherry at the lake, but he'd been too distracted then in his effort to save his friend to take in many details about how they looked. The same was true of the occasions they'd attacked him, but now he could study them he could see their tentacle-like limbs were intricately patterned in many shades of black and gray.

The patterning was easiest to see when they briefly pressed their limbs against the transparent wall. As they moved away they became less distinct due to the muddiness of the water. There didn't seem to be any rhythm or order to their movements.

More time dragged past as Ethan gazed at the threads, their whirling almost hypnotizing him. The wall was close enough for him to reach out and touch it. He found he'd grown less appalled by the sight of the creatures. He lifted a hand. It wouldn't hurt to touch his side of the clear wall. He placed the tip of his index finger against the cool surface. Instantly, the agitation in the threads redoubled. They wriggled almost too quickly to observe as if in response to his gesture.

Ethan snatched away his hand, alarmed by the reaction of the threads. But it was too late. A whirring sound started up overhead. He'd triggered something.

He watched the ceiling, squinting against the light. The surface was vibrating very slightly. Were the threads opening the airlock? Were they coming in to get him? Ethan balled his hands into fists. Whatever they planned on doing to him he would fight them to the last breath in his body.

A section of the roof lifted and began to slide to one side. Water poured through it for a moment, adding another centimeter to the layer in the chamber. Then something else appeared. Not wriggling threads, but something bulky and dark.

The thing fell and hit the floor, splashing into the water and bursting apart. Ethan stared at the object in growing recognition, and overhead the whirring began again.

The hatch in the ceiling was closing. At the last second, Ethan realized the chance he had. He leapt onto the sodden mess that had been pushed into the chamber and reached up to the closing hole in the ceiling. But he sank into the soft, black object, and his ankle gave way. He couldn't reach high enough. His grasping fingers met nothing but air.

The hatch closed and Ethan fell. He sprawled on top of the threads' delivery. It had taken him a moment, but he had recognized it eventually. The lump was his food sack from the flitter, drenched and beginning to rot. He rolled off of it. Tugging the sack open, he reached inside and drew out a package. The contents were soaked in muddy river water and entirely spoiled and inedible.

As Ethan gazed forlornly at the wet, disintegrating mess, he came to a better understanding of the threads. They knew that he and the flitter were connected, and they perhaps guessed that what they had given him was his food. Were they intending to keep him alive and confined for a long time?

CHAPTER NINETEEN

After leaving the problem of the intelligent thread creatures in the lake with Vasquez and Kes—promising to meet up with Kes the following day—Cariad grabbed a take-away dinner from the refectory and went to her cabin, tired and sleepy. She'd been finding it hard to sleep in the strange room at the Leader's residence, partly because she was planetside. She'd gotten used to sleeping aboard ship. The faint vibration of the ship's engines was soothing.

Cariad comm'd Osias to update him on what Vasquez had said, then she ate her food. The next thing she did was check the position of Ethan's flitter signal. Checking the satellite report had become like an itch she had to scratch. Each time she looked it up, she hoped to see that the flitter had moved. Each time she'd been disappointed.

That night, however, she saw something worse than no movement. She saw something she hadn't imagined could happen. The signal was gone.

It wasn't possible. The devices that emitted the signals were virtually indestructible. They were intended to be used to locate the vehicles in case of an accident and were built to withstand extreme impacts, fire, immersion in deep water, and other extreme stresses. What could have happened to cause the signal to disappear? Cariad checked the report and checked it again. She requested a second report, this time encompassing all of Concordia. Ethan's flitter signal had entirely disappeared from the planet.

No matter how hard she searched or stared at the screen, the result was the same. She no longer knew where Ethan was or even if he was still alive. She felt like she should tell someone, but who could she tell? Concordia had no rescue services. The colony wasn't far from being in need of rescue itself. Ethan's expedition had been a personal choice, taken in full knowledge of the incredible risks involved.

Also, he hadn't asked permission to leave. At the time there hadn't been anyone for him to ask. Anahi had stepped down as Leader and a replacement hadn't been elected. And Ethan had taken a flitter for his own long-term use, which was technically illegal. The flitters belonged to the colony. They weren't for anyone to use as they wanted.

The settlement had been in such a state of upheaval after the flood at the caves, with the Guardians withdrawing and relations between the Gens and Woken in flux, Ethan had simply made his decision to check for survivors and then embark on a longer expedition, and slipped away.

If Cariad raised a hue and cry about the missing flitter signal, what would happen? Traveling into the wilds of Concordia, even as a group, was risky, and the colony numbers were already dangerously low. They couldn't afford to lose more people. She had a strong suspicion that Osias would forbid anyone to leave and try to find Ethan.

She was torn. She wanted to head out to the site of the last signal from the flitter, but should she? She was needed at the colony. Cassie and Florian were able assistants, but she wasn't sure they could manage the complexity of the DNA matching required to maintain the health of the settlement's gene pool. And she was heading up the Natural Movement investigation.

There was also the question of what she might find at the place where Ethan's flitter had disappeared. Whatever had happened to the vehicle had to be serious. What if the same thing happened to her flitter too?

Cariad wasn't the adventurous type. Her decision to participate in humanity's first deep space colony had been out of her usual character. The idea of traveling to wild, remote regions of Concordia scared her. She didn't have the skills to survive a night outdoors, let alone being stranded in the wilderness. Yet she couldn't ask anyone to accompany her if she did go. There were plenty who would—Ethan was universally liked—but it wouldn't be fair to risk even more lives to try to help him.

By the time a new day had begun aboard the *Nova Fortuna*, Cariad had hardly slept and was exhausted with worry. Each minute that passed felt like another minute lost that might have saved Ethan's life. What if he was hanging on somewhere, desperately hoping someone would arrive to help him? Cariad was haunted with images of finding his body minutes too late.

Yet she couldn't just up and leave, flying out alone into the back of beyond, could she?

Cariad hurried to the refectory. At that time in *Nova Fortuna's* ship's schedule, her assistants should have been eating breakfast. If she was going to make a rescue attempt, she would need to brief Cassie and Florian before she left.

Her gaze roamed the tables. Ever since the majority of the Gens had gone planetside after Arrival, the refectory had been much emptier and quieter, but Cariad couldn't see either of her techs eating breakfast. Maybe they'd gone to work early.

***

Cassie and Florian were in the lab, though they hadn't started work. Cassie was sitting on a stool and Florian was standing over her, showing her something on an interface. Cassie was laughing. She looked up as Cariad entered the room and Florian whipped the interface away guiltily.

"Hey," Cariad said, "it's fine. I'm not here to reprimand you. It isn't even time to begin work yet. What were you looking at?"

"Oh, it's kind of stupid," said Florian. "I just put together a vid of animals for Cassie."

"It's so funny," Cassie said. "He made subtitles for what they're saying to each other. Do you want to see it?"

"Another time maybe," said Cariad. "I'm here to tell you I have to go away again for a little while."

"What?" said Florian. "You say that like you've actually spent some time here."

"I know," Cariad said. "I'm really sorry."

"Where are you going?" Cassie asked.

"I can't say. I don't think I should be doing what I'm about to do. I want to ask you a favor. Could you cover for me?"

"Now I'm really intrigued," Florian said. "Are you going to let us in on the secret?"

"I would if it didn't mean I could be getting you into trouble. If this turns out badly, I don't want the blame to shift onto you two."

"This is like a drama vid," Cassie exclaimed. "It sounds so exciting. Can we come too?"

"No," Cariad replied. "Absolutely not. It took me all night to decide to go myself. And now that I have decided, I wish I'd left earlier. So I really have to go now. But if anyone comes around asking for me, could you act like I've just popped out and you don't know where I am?"

"Well the second part of that will be true," Florian said. "What do you think, Cassie? Should we lie for the boss?"

"I'm willing if you are," she replied, looking up at him.

Did she bat her eyelashes at him? Cariad had a feeling that Cassie and Florian would enjoy their time working together without her around.

"Go ahead, Cariad," Florian said. "Go deal with your clandestine intrigue. We'll cover your ass."

"Thanks," said Cariad. "I shouldn't be gone more than a day or two."

She walked quickly to her cabin. Though she was worried about Ethan, she was pleased about the romance between her techs. Relationships between the Gens and Woken were exactly what the colony needed. A generation of children from such pairings would do a lot to break down the barriers that had sprung up between the two sides.

In her room, Cariad checked the satellite signal once more, hoping that it might have returned, but there was still no sign of it. It had definitely disappeared. She pushed a warm jacket and a change of clothes into a bag. She had no idea what to take on such a journey. She didn't think Ethan had taken much more with him than food and water. But she didn't have the access to the supplies that he had. Aside from the regular meals provided at the refectory, only snacks were available aboard ship. She couldn't walk into the ship's stores and demand a week's supply of food. Even if the purser allowed the request, it would raise so many questions that someone in power might hear of her plan and prevent her from leaving. And as a Woken she had no access to the storerooms at the settlement. A request there would seem even stranger.

She would have to gather what snacks she could and hope that she could find Ethan. He had a good supply of food. Then again, his supply would be on the flitter, and the flitter had gone missing, so... Cariad shook her head. She would have to cross those bridges when she came to them.

She took a transit to the shuttle bay, where she boarded the next shuttle going planetside. She traveled to the surface regularly so her journey passed without attracting any attention. Her biggest obstacle was yet to be conquered—borrowing a flitter.

All the way to Verney's shed, Cariad tried to think of a logical reason why she might need to borrow one of the valuable vehicles. She couldn't think up a single one. She wasn't one of the scientists like Rene or Anahi who needed to go out into the surrounding fields to sample soil or crops. She wasn't a Gen farmer who lived outside the settlement. Neither was she a mechanic who might have to fix a broken down roadmaker.

As she approached Verney, her mind was a blank. He looked up at her curiously from his desk just inside the shed doors.

"I need a flitter," Cariad blurted, feeling hopeless.

Verney looked down at his interface screen. "I don't have any bookings for this morning." He looked at her expectantly, folding his hands on his lap and cocking his head.

"I didn't book one," said Cariad. "I... " She sighed. What choice did she have other than to come clean? "Ethan's gone missing. I want to try to find him."

Verney sat up. "Ethan's missing? Since when? I didn't hear anything about it."

"He went to do some exploring days ago. He has a flitter—"

"I know he has. I was waiting for him to bring it back. No wonder he hasn't been answering my messages. Where's he gone?"

"Deep into the continent. Alone. He took supplies along with him and didn't know when he would return."

"Well that isn't strictly allowed, you know."

"I know. But that's what he's done. I was tracking his flitter signal from the satellite feed but it's disappeared. I want to go after him."

"Well... " Verney rubbed his bald head. "I don't think I have the authority—"

"Neither do I," said Cariad. "And please don't try to get permission because I'm pretty sure the answer will be no. Neither the Leader nor anyone else who might permit the flitter use will agree to send another vehicle out when one has already been lost. But I have to try to find Ethan. I have to. Please, can you help me?"

Verney considered a moment before standing up. "You can take one. After everything Ethan's done for this colony, he doesn't deserve to be abandoned when he needs our help. There's some who would say that one of these vehicles is more important than a human life. I don't agree."

"Thank you," said Cariad. "Thank you so much."

"I'll have to make something up to put in the record," Verney went on. "But I have an idea. Wait here. I'll have to lock the shed, but I'll be back soon."

"Oh. Okay."

He went out and closed the wide shed doors, leaving Cariad alone under artificial light with the flitters, which filled half the bays. Had Verney been lying? Had he trapped her in there in order to have her arrested?

No. She was being ridiculous. There wasn't any need to lock her up just for trying to take a flitter. Her apprehension about her upcoming journey was making her jittery.

The shed doors opened, flooding the interior with sunlight. Cariad exhaled in relief as Verney entered alone. He was carrying a weapon. "I borrowed this for you from a farmer friend who I knew was in town. If you're going out alone into the wild, you'll need it."

"Thanks," Cariad said, taking the gun from him awkwardly. She had no idea how to fire it, but she would have time to figure that out on the long journey to Ethan's last known position.

Verney went over to the nearest flitter and unlocked it. Cariad joined him and climbed inside.

"They aren't hard to operate," Verney said. He showed her the controls. "The screen defaults to a local map and the flitter's position on it. Link your interface with the flitter's system here."

"Okay."

"They're nearly impossible to crash, too. Just remember to activate the auto-leveling if you're going over steep slopes, or the vehicle will tilt to follow the slope."

"Right," said Cariad. "I've got it." Now that the obstacle of obtaining a flitter had been overcome, she was eager to leave.

Verney stepped back. "She's all yours. I hope you find him. If we lose Ethan, it'll be a hard blow to the colony."

"I know. Thanks again." Cariad closed her door and started up the machine. She flew the flitter somewhat erratically out of the shed as she got used to the controls. On Earth, she'd made the effort to learn how to drive a car even though it was unnecessary, just for fun. Every motorized vehicle had been connected to a network that operated them safely and appropriately according to the traffic conditions. It was only preppers living off-grid far from civilized areas who needed to know how to drive cars. Cariad wondered how those survivalists had fared when their desires and fears had come true.

Once she was through the gates in the electric fence, she slid her interface into the slot on the flitter's control panel and uploaded the location of the last signal from Ethan's flitter. The spot was on the other side of a mountain range that cut diagonally across the center of the continent. A broad river swept away from the range and emptied into the ocean on the far coast. The dot that represented the most recent signal was right on the edge of the river.

Cariad input the position as the flitter's destination. The estimated time to arrival was sixteen hours traveling at maximum speed. To Cariad, it seemed incredibly slow, but the flitters hadn't been intended for long-distance travel. They were supposed to be used to traverse rough terrain around the first settlement. Faster modes of transport were expected to be built on site eventually, and the shuttles could be used until then at a pinch. Survival had been the priority, not jetting around the new world. If the colonists needed to move to another continent or perhaps one of the islands of the archipelago, they could always return everything to their ship and reposition the *Nova Fortuna* in orbit.

Cariad watched the terrain as it went past agonizingly slowly. The dot on the map didn't seem to be getting any closer. She wondered what had happened to Ethan's flitter. Had he crashed into the river? That didn't seem likely after what Verney had said. And though water in the system might wipe out the flitter's circuits, it didn't explain what had happened to the vehicle's transmitter.

The thought of never seeing Ethan again tugged at Cariad's heart. She'd been worried about him when he set off on his journey, but she hadn't believed that she would never see him again. It just hadn't seemed possible. Now, the impossible appeared to be turning into a reality.

She refused to believe it. Ethan was alive out there somewhere, and she would find him and bring him back to the settlement. She would bring him back home.

The day passed and the kilometers were gradually eaten away. Cariad grew tired and sore from sitting in the flitter for so long, but she didn't stop the machine. She felt she'd already delayed too long to respond to the loss of Ethan's signal. She didn't want to waste another moment.

Darkness fell, and still Cariad went on. The flitter's safety systems meant she didn't fear crashing into anything. The shadowy landscape flowed steadily past. Cariad had little interest in it, even though she was the first human being to set eyes on the land. Ethan had taken a different route, traveling down the coast. She only wanted to reach her destination as quickly as possible.

As the ground rose into foothills and then mountains, the air grew chill. Cariad put on the jacket she'd brought along. She'd eaten the last of her snacks hours ago and now only had water to calm her growling stomach. Hungry and cold, she finally fell asleep lying across the seats, hoping that the following day would bring the sight of her dear friend's face.

During the night, bitter cold awoke her. She sat up, shivering. Outside, the stars were brightly illuminating the snowy white slopes of the mountains' peaks. The flitter was traversing a high pass. Cariad pulled all her remaining clothes out of her bag and put them on. She wrapped a jersey around her head to try to retain some body heat. Feeling a little warmer, she fell again into a restless sleep.

When the sun rose, the flitter had crossed the mountain range and was traveling through the foothills on the other side. Cariad saw the beginnings of hundreds of streams that fed into the great river, which was a broad band of silver. In another few hours, she would be at the spot where Ethan's flitter had stopped transmitting.

She was headachey and faint with hunger, but eventually the feeling disappeared. Cariad drank water and tried to think positively. She imagined Ethan's delight when he saw that she'd come to rescue him. She wondered what he would tell her on the way back to the settlement, and what things he'd seen and discovered on his travels.

He would be alive. She was sure of it. He had to be.

CHAPTER TWENTY

Ethan regarded the disgusting, sodden sludge that comprised his river-soaked packets of food. At least clean water wasn't an immediate problem. The supply bag contained his small water tank that remained intact. Yet he'd grown so hungry he knew he would have to try to eat too.

He dug a wet packet out from the mess. Its original contents had been dried algae, and the stuff seemed the least affected by the water. The algae was supposed to be rehydrated before you ate it anyway. Ethan dipped his fingers into the green goo and lifted some to his mouth.

He didn't much like algae when it was at its best, let alone when it had spent days soaking in dirty water. He swallowed the slimy stuff without chewing it, grimacing as it slipped—cold and glutinous—down his throat. At first he didn't feel too bad, but although his stomach's reaction wasn't immediate, it was violent. He was in the middle of attempting to eat another mouthful when the first one he'd swallowed returned, erupting from his throat almost before he knew what was happening. Ethan crouched on all fours as he vomited up the algae. Even when no more remained in his stomach he continued to retch, bringing up sour bile.

His vomit splashed into the thin layer of water on the floor and began to dissolve and spread out. Ethan edged away in disgust, crawling to the other side of the chamber.

He guessed he had been confined at least a night and a day, though the lack of natural light made it difficult for him to perceive the passage of time. He was either too deep below the water surface for sunlight to penetrate, or the water was too murky. The threads that gyrated at the transparent wall were illuminated by the light from inside his cell.

As the hours had passed, the creatures had observed him continually without respite—if observing him was what they were doing. It could be a coincidence that they happened to be outside the clear wall, but Ethan thought it unlikely.

"What do you want from me?" he asked the whirling tentacles. They'd given him food, so they wanted to keep him alive, but for what? He stood up. His ankle hurt less now. He limped across to the clear wall. "What do you want?" He touched the surface, causing the threads to whirl faster. After the first response when he'd touched the wall, Ethan had done the same thing over and over again, but the threads hadn't deviated from their reaction of moving faster.

His feelings of revulsion and fear about the creatures had entirely gone. He'd gotten used to them and now only felt curious when he watched them.

Ethan yawned and sat down, resting his forehead against the wall. All the time he'd been in the chamber he'd only managed to take short naps, sitting against a corner of his chamber. He hadn't been able to fall asleep on the wet floor while the light constantly shined from above and while he was under constant observation. He also worried about the air in the chamber. The room was watertight and so it had to be airtight too. How long would the oxygen last? He had no idea. He didn't think he was running out of air, but then he didn't know how that would feel.

Maybe that was another reason he was so tired. Maybe he'd used up most of the oxygen.

Ethan slid his hand over the surface of the transparent wall and watched the tentacles as they constantly brushed it and moved away. An idea struck. Did the thread creatures communicate by moving their tentacles? Perhaps they were trying to speak to him.

Ethan traced a figure with his fingers on the smooth surface. He couldn't move as fast as the threads, but his movement might communicate something to them. He tried moving both hands, mimicking the whirl of the threads, though much more slowly. He watched them carefully.

His motions had no effect he could discern.

"Let me out," he said to them, hopelessly. "Let me go. Why are you keeping me here?"

Without any warning, the floor dropped, jarring

Ethan as he dropped with it. The distance it fell wasn't far. Maybe just a few centimeters. Between the bottom of the wall and the floor was a dark gap. Ethan was about to reach inside when water sprayed out so forcefully it pushed him away from the wall and across the floor. The vomit that lay in a wide pool was washed away.

Then, as suddenly as it had dropped, the floor rose. The threads had washed the floor clean, but that was it. Ethan remained trapped.

He forced his tired, hungry brain to concentrate. If the threads were intelligent, which he guessed they had to be, then they probably had some way to talk to each other. Unless he wanted to live out his remaining days or hours trapped in a disgusting pit beneath a river, Ethan had to try to learn how to communicate with them. The goal seemed impossible. On the other hand, he had no urgent appointments to keep.

Ethan tried waving his hands around at the threads, without result. He then tried moving his body too but that had the same zero effect. He wondered what else he could try.

As he racked his brains, Ethan thought back to the two events that had occurred since he entered the chamber: the moment the light in the ceiling had turned on, and when the wall had become transparent. Just prior to each event he had hit a wall. Ethan turned to look at the threads whirling outside his cell. As they moved, they were pressing their tentacles against the surface. Could it be that they communicated by moving water? He guessed they might sense currents and ripples on their skin. That seemed to make sense. Human ears picked up vibrations in the air, but the threads were aquatic animals. Water was like air to them.

Ethan returned to the transparent wall, formed a fist, and struck it. As he did so, he felt the wall give way a little under his hand. The material felt different from the other walls, which were solid and unyielding. The clear wall felt springy. Ethan was so preoccupied by the different sensation that it took him a moment to notice the effect of his blow. The threads had gone. After hours or days of their ceaseless movement, they had disappeared. Only the murky river water was visible from his cell, sweeping past sediment and plant debris.

Finally, he had a result. He'd done something to affect the creatures who had captured him. Though what it meant, he couldn't tell. He touched the transparent wall again, pushing it and testing its flexibility. He wondered why he hadn't noticed that before. Maybe he'd been too preoccupied with watching the creatures.

But where had the threads gone? Had he frightened them away? The previous times he'd struck a wall, they'd given him light and revealed themselves. By the same logic, something positive should have occurred when he hit a wall for the third time. He had to try again.

Ethan hit the wall and waited. Nothing. He tried once more. Still no result occurred. But as he moved to strike the wall once more, Ethan stepped back in fear. A gigantic thread creature thrust against the transparent surface. The thing was so massive it looked as though it could envelop and crush the entire chamber.

Ethan swallowed. What had he done? Had he

summoned this terrifying animal by hitting the wall? Had it been waiting all this time for its tasty snack to make a move? The creature was swirling slowly and sinuously, its long, thick threads pressed so firmly on the flat surface they were squashed and their intricate patterns distorted.

Was the giant thread creature trying to talk to him? He placed a hand on the wall. At first, he couldn't detect any movement, but when he closed his eyes and concentrated, he could feel the wall quivering. The creature was creating the effect, but if it was trying to communicate Ethan didn't have any idea what the message was.

He closed his eyes again and concentrated. He wanted to try to discover if there was any kind of pattern to the vibration. He remained in the same position for long minutes, straining with all the sensitivity he possessed to feel any nuances in the vibrations.

Finally, he gave up. He walked away from the wall in frustration. Maybe he had figured out the threads' method of communication, but the information was useless if he couldn't perceive their meaning. He was a human being. Vision and hearing were his strongest senses, not touch. And he lived in air. He guessed that the threads possessed a sense that "heard" the movement of water, just as his ears picked up sound waves.

The massive thread creature continued to press itself against the wall, as if intent on communicating with him.

"It's no good," Ethan told it. "I can't hear you." He pointed to his ears then shrugged, which he knew was ridiculous. Of course the creature wouldn't understand his gesture. It might not even be able to see, and yet... The threads had been able to discern that *he* could see, otherwise they wouldn't have constructed a transparent wall or given him light. They also seemed to know he was intelligent. They'd been guiding his actions by rewarding him when he performed the "correct" action.

He wondered if the times when the threads had tried to drag Cherry into the lake or himself into the river, they'd only been trying to bring a human into their watery domain? If that was the case, what their ultimate purpose might be, Ethan couldn't divine. Although the threads might not be predatory, they were keeping him captive. If their intentions were harmless they had a strange way of showing it.

Whatever reason the threads might have for their actions, Ethan had to get out. He couldn't live on spoiled food and limited water, and the oxygen in the cell would run out at some point. His only hope lay in convincing the threads to let him go. He returned his attention to the wall and the huge thread creature.

They would have to begin with the basics. Ethan couldn't remember learning to speak but he thought that babies and toddlers started out by naming things. Would that work here? He thought back to his earliest days at kindy. He remembered doing a lot of counting and learning about numbers. The idea seemed promising.

Ethan struck the wall once. He held up a finger and said, "One." He didn't think the creature could hear him—it just felt good to hear a human voice, even his own. He struck the wall twice, held up two fingers and said, "Two." He repeated the procedure for *three*. Would the creature understand the pattern?

He placed a hand gently on the wall, shut his eyes, and concentrated. Was it his imagination or did he feel the wall bow inward very slightly three times? He struck the wall three times again then touched it and waited. The sensation of the surface bending inward was so marginal, he wasn't sure he could actually feel it at all.

He wished the creature would give a stronger response, if that was what was happening. Then it occurred to Ethan that if the creatures communicated through vibrations in the water, they were probably much more sensitive to touch than humans were. Maybe his blows against the wall were like the loudest roar.

He tried tapping the wall three times, then felt for a response. This time, he was positive the wall did move. The giant thread creature *was* repeating his message back to him, and it was matching the strength of his communications too. He was finally communicating with his captors.

What should he do next? Ethan's mind whirred like the tentacles of a thread creature, trying to think up a plan for building on his discovery. Repeating numbers back and forth with the threads was a gigantic leap ahead, but numbers wouldn't allow him to demand that they set him free or tell them he needed fresh air and clean food and water.

As he pondered the problem, watching the massive thread organism, Ethan became aware that his foot was aching. His boots had come off while he was being dragged through the river. He lifted the aching foot to look at its bare sole and saw a cut he hadn't noticed before. The skin around it was puffy and wrinkled from long immersion in the water on the floor and the lips of the cut were swollen and inflamed. It seemed to be infected.

If he'd been aboard the ship, he would have gone to the medical bay, but there in the chamber he had nothing to treat the cut. He wasn't sure what happened to infections that went untreated but he guessed it wasn't good.

Looking at the slowly writhing thread creature outside his cell, Ethan realized that the need for him to learn how to communicate with ii might have become even more urgent.

CHAPTER TWENTY-ONE

As the hours and then minutes counted down to the flitter's arrival at its destination, Cariad's positive thinking was slowly transforming. What if Ethan wasn't to be found? Where and how long would she look? Or what if he was injured and dying or trapped somewhere and she couldn't rescue him?

Hope and trepidation fought within her as the final minutes passed and the massive river drew nearer. She was was flying above a forest of umbrella-shaped plants with high roots. Cariad spotted the dark gray sand of the river's shore. She peered at it. She couldn't see a flitter or Ethan, but perhaps she wasn't close enough.

The dark gray strip grew wider but no matter how intently Cariad looked, the boxy shape of a flitter didn't come into view. But then, why would it, she reasoned. The vehicle's signal had disappeared. For that to happen she guessed the flitter had to have been severely damaged. She shouldn't expect to see it.

Perhaps it had crashed into the water. If it had, Ethan might have made it out in time and swum to the shore—except that none of the Gens could swim.

She'd arrived. The river's shoreline spread out underneath her. Cariad landed her flitter and stepped out onto the bare, smooth sand. It didn't show any signs of disturbance.

***

Cariad searched and called Ethan's name, walking along the river bank in both directions. Hours passed and she grew light-headed with hunger and fatigue. She couldn't see or hear the slightest sign of him. She even went as deep as she dared go into the vegetation. But the only footprints she saw were her own. Nothing seemed to exist to indicate that Ethan or his flitter had been at the place. Cariad had even double checked on her interface that she had the right spot, but there couldn't be any doubt about it.

She paused in her search at last and leaned on her vehicle, gazing absently at her footprints in the sand. The evidence of her meanderings deeply saddened her. If *she* had left so much clear evidence of her presence, Ethan should have done the same. But everywhere she'd been the silt had been smooth. Not even the local wildlife had disturbed it.

As the time had passed, Cariad's emotions had progressed from deep disappointment to anxiety to fear and despair. What had happened to her friend? She couldn't figure it out. Flitters had enough stored energy to last for months of continual use. Ethan shouldn't have found himself suddenly without power as he flew over the river. According to what Strongquist had said, it seemed unlikely that Ethan's flitter had broken down. Like the *Nova Fortuna's* shuttles, they were Earth-manufactured. The flitters hadn't been put together from kits by the settlement mechanics. They would have been thoroughly tested before being loaded onto the ship. And none of the other flitters had shown any faults.

A darker thought occurred to Cariad. Had Ethan decided to end it all and deliberately flown the flitter into the river? No. Even if he'd given up on life, the flitter's safety mechanism would have kicked in and prevented it. She couldn't believe that Ethan would do such a thing anyway.

Cariad climbed into her vehicle and started it up. She would be able to cover more ground by flying than on foot. If Ethan had left the site where his flitter had gone down he could be kilometers away. She lowered the window so she could call his name as she went along.

More hours passed while Cariad flew long distances up and down the river bank and deep into the vegetated areas. She even flew right over the river to search the bank on the other side. Finally, as the sun began to set, Cariad returned to the original site where Ethan's flitter signal had been lost. The place was exactly as she had left it.

In the remaining light, she resumed walking and calling her friend's name. She continued until she was stumbling with tiredness and ravenous with hunger. She had shouted herself hoarse. In the end, she was forced to stop. It was no use. Ethan wasn't there.

Cariad watched the ruffled river water sweep past in the darkness as she gravely accepted the obvious conclusion. Clearly, some kind of disaster had befallen her friend. Only something devastating could have destroyed the flitter's transmitter, and if Ethan had survived he would not make it back to the settlement without his vehicle.

Whatever had happened to Ethan, it didn't look like she would ever see him again.

Cariad hugged herself and hung her head, finally giving in to the likelihood that Ethan was gone. Her chest grew tight, a hard lump formed in her throat, and fat tears spilled from her eyes, dripping onto her crossed arms. She liked Ethan so much. No. She loved him. And now it looked like she would never see him again.

As Cariad stood on the wet riverbank, accepting and grieving Ethan's loss, she was thrown back to a scene from her past that haunted her—that would haunt her to the end of her days. Once more, she was standing on the steps of the cryopreservation center with her family, knowing she would never see or hear from them again, like she was standing on the edge of her grave and saying goodbye before she stepped in.

Now that she'd lost Ethan, the scar of her grief and guilt about leaving her family behind was torn open afresh. She shook with sobs. Regret overwhelmed her. Why had she joined the *Nova*

Fortuna Project? How could she have been so cruel to the people who loved her?

What wouldn't she give to go back in time and cancel her application to the project? But now she was stuck there, responsibility for the colony's success weighing heavy on her shoulders, with little to look forward to except a lifetime of regrets.

Then she grew angry at Ethan. Why hadn't he stayed at the settlement? He could have found a way to overcome his problems there. Instead, he'd abandoned them. And now he was gone.

Some time later, when Cariad had sobbed herself dry, she realized that it was deep night. The river was darkly reflecting the stars but apart from that the scene hadn't changed. The water flowed past and the strange, stringy domes of vegetation faintly swayed in the light breeze. Concordia continued on, impervious to her sorrow.

Cariad wiped her face with her sleeve and climbed into the flitter. She took a final look at the river that had probably swallowed Ethan before programming her vehicle to return to the settlement. The flitter lifted, turned, and flew in the direction of the mountains, hulking blackly in the starlight.

Hunger gnawed at Cariad, but her melancholy and anguish affected her worse. With Ethan's loss everything had changed. She knew she would struggle to summon the willpower and desire to carry on in her work. She felt like her decision to join the *Nova Fortuna* Project was a giant mistake. Perhaps the entire colonization attempt was a mistake. Maybe it would fail and they would all die painful, drawn-out deaths from starvation, or fall victim to the sluglimpets or other indigenous predators like the thread creatures.

Cariad curled up on the flitter seat, one arm folded over her empty belly, the other forming a rest for her throbbing head. After some time, she slept.

At some point during the night she woke long enough to cover herself up against the cold. When she woke again, it was just before dawn and the flitter had reached the foothills on the other side of the mountains. The air was warm again. Cariad sat up and removed the extra clothes.

In spite of her low emotional state, her stomach protested its prolonged emptiness. She drank some water to quieten it. Checking the control screen, she saw she would arrive at the settlement at about mid-afternoon. Cariad rested her forehead against the window and looked out sightlessly. She had a hollowness inside her that had little to do with hunger.

Her mind wandered back to the scab it loved to pick at. She remembered going into the cryopreservation center after saying goodbye to her family. Meredith Crowley had comforted her as they waited together to be sedated prior to being prepared for their cryo chambers. Cariad hadn't always seen eye-to-eye with her fellow scientist on issues surrounding the project, but that hadn't diminished her respect and regard for the older woman. Meredith had gently held her as her guilt took over from her resolve to participate in the project. She'd told Cariad that if she backed out she would regret it for the rest of her days.

Meredith had been right, of course. The truth

and wisdom of her colleague's words had given Cariad the strength to see it through. How she wished the poor woman hadn't died so horribly in the First Night Attack. What a loss to the colony that had been.

Cariad sat up straight and rubbed her neck, which had developed a crick from sleeping awkwardly overnight. She reflected on what Meredith had said to her that day and how it had changed her perspective.

This project is bigger than all of us, the older woman had said. *It's bigger than all two thousand two hundred people embarking on the voyage, it's bigger than the thousands more consigned to living out their lives aboard a starship without their consent—it's bigger than the ship itself. You're the best geneticist we could ask for, Cariad. You've dedicated years to the task of sending humans out to the stars. Do you think it would be right for you to step down and let a lesser-qualified person to go in your place? Humanity's entire evolution has brought us to this point. It wouldn't be right for you to turn away now. Your family loves you, but the* Nova Fortuna *needs you.*

It had been Meredith's words that had originally gotten her over her guilt and sense of loss, Cariad remembered. Up until then she'd been thinking of herself as an individual and beating herself up over how her actions affected others. But that wasn't why she was there.

Cariad understood she had to go on. She couldn't allow her grief to overwhelm her. She wasn't on Concordia for herself: she was there for the colony, and she would do her damnedest to bring it back from the brink of disaster.

Her new sense of resolve didn't make her any happier but she found she was a little calmer. She checked the ETA again. She had two hours to go. It was enough time to gather herself and make plans for everything she needed to do when she got back. She picked up the clothes she'd covered herself with during the night, which were scattered all over the place, and put them away in her bag before tidying up other small bits and pieces.

With her improved composure her hunger returned with a vengeance but not even crumbs remained of the snacks she'd brought along. Drinking some more water made no difference to her aching stomach. There was nothing for her to do but try to ignore the pain.

The final part of Cariad's journey dragged on intolerably. When she finally caught sight of the settlement's electric fence and single-story houses, it felt like a benefaction. The flitter automatically navigated to the entry point in the fence. She was waved through before being carried along to the flitter shed, where Verney was sitting and eating his lunch.

Cariad flew the flitter into a bay and climbed out, feeling as though she'd been gone half a lifetime. Verney's expectant expression fell when it was clear she brought no passengers with her.

"You didn't find him?" he asked.

Cariad shook her head, tears threatening. "I looked all day. I couldn't find any trace of him. Not a sign."

"We'll have to send out a search party," said

Verney. "There'll be plenty of volunteers. That man has a lot of friends."

"I wish we could do that but I don't think it'll ever be allowed. The flitters are too precious for us to use up their energy searching for one man who could be anywhere on the entire continent. All we have is his final position, and I searched the area thoroughly. There wasn't a single indication that anyone had been there."

"Doesn't matter," said Verney. "I'll speak to Osias."

"Okay," Cariad said. "I hope you get somewhere. If you do receive permission to mount a search, let me know. I'll come along." Verney's action would mean he would have to tell Osias what she'd done, but she didn't really care.

Verney gazed at her closely. "You look terrible. What happened to you out there?"

"Nothing," Cariad replied. "I'm just upset about Ethan and I haven't eaten for a while."

"Well your second problem's easily fixed." Verney picked up the remains of his lunch and handed them to Cariad.

She munched the half-sandwich gratefully.

"Shame the first problem isn't so easy to solve," Verney continued.

After gulping a mouthful of sandwich, Cariad said, "Thanks for letting me take a flitter. I don't know what I would have done otherwise."

"You're welcome," said Verney. "I'm going to shut up the shed now to go speak to the Leader."

Cariad said, "And I'm going to the *Nova Fortuna*. I have a few things to do."

CHAPTER TWENTY-TWO

"The giant thread creature never seems to rest or sleep," Ethan said into the recorder, "so I can work with it whenever I want. Yet I'm not making much headway. We repeat numbers at each other and I think I've taught it a pattern of touches that I use to represent my name. What I did was, I put my hand on my chest and tapped out the pattern I made up. The thread creature repeated the pattern, but then it touched the end of one tentacle to the frilled hole at its center and tapped out a different pattern. I guessed that it was telling me its name in return.

"I wasn't sure if we understood each other so I did some tests. I repeated the pattern I thought it was using to refer to itself, which is *soft-soft-soft-hard-hard* pause *hard,* and the organism pointed at itself every time. It seemed to be testing me too, pressing the pattern for my name on the wall, and I would touch my chest. I think that shows the creature probably understands we're talking about names. I don't want to repeat the creature's name pattern in these recordings, so I'm going to call it Quinn. I don't know why, but the name seems to fit."

Ethan turned off the recorder, choosing not to go into more detail about the state of affairs in the chamber. He was hungrier than ever and his foot was growing more painful, and communicating anything beyond numbers and names with Quinn was difficult almost beyond belief. Ethan's main problem was that he had very few objects to use as teaching tools, and words like "algae" or "bag" weren't particularly useful. What he wanted to tell Quinn was that his food was bad and the chamber floor was too wet, but he had no edible food or clean and dry cell to show as a comparison. He'd lifted his foot up to the thread creature and tried to teach it the words "hurt" and "pain." Though the creature repeated the patterns correctly, it used the same patterns when Ethan held up his other foot, indicating it thought he was saying "foot," which was understandable.

One thing that Ethan did have plenty of was water—something that Quinn would be very familiar with. Ethan decided to try to teach the creature a pattern that meant "water." He dipped his hand into the shallow pool he was forced to sit in, lifted his hand and let the water drop from his fingers. He tapped a new pattern on the wall. *Hard-soft-hard* pause *soft-hard*.

Hard-soft-hard pause *soft-hard*, came Quinn's message back. The creature had copied it perfectly as always, but what had it understood as the meaning? As a test Ethan held up his other hand, which was dry. Quinn pressed the wall. *Hard-soft-hard* pause *soft-hard*.

No. Ethan shook his head, though he knew the gesture was meaningless to the creature. Ethan lifted up a wet hand to allow water to drip from it again and pointed to the drops before repeating the message to Quinn. The reply came. *Hard-soft-hard* pause *soft-hard*. Ethan lifted a dry hand. Quinn said, *Hard-soft-hard* pause *soft-hard*.

No! Ethan shook his head vigorously. To his surprise, Quinn waggled a tentacle in response. Ethan laughed. It was an unexpected response. He shook his head for a third time and was rewarded with a shaken tentacle. Excited, Ethan repeated the gesture and when his action was mirrored, he laughed again, louder. He seemed to have made a breakthrough.

His elation quickly dissipated, however. He'd just confused the entire process of trying to teach Quinn a pattern for the word "water." Who knew what the creature thought was going on?

"Okay," Ethan said. "We're going to begin again from the top." Instead of using his hand to drip water, Ethan squeezed an empty food packet, pointed at the drips, and tapped out the pattern. There was a long pause before Quinn repeated the pattern back. Was he trying to figure it out? Had he understood? Ethan stood up and wrung out the tail of his shirt, once again pointing at the drops. This time when Quinn repeated the pattern to him, he did it without hesitation.

To check that they now had a word for water, Ethan wiped his hand dry and held it up. He felt the wall and waited for Quinn's response. This time, none came.

Yes! They seemed to be making progress again. In spite of his dire state, Ethan grinned. He felt he'd achieved something important, even if he never made it out of the cell. He was the first human to communicate with a Concordian native. He wished he could tell Cariad about it.

Seizing the opportunity to build on the interaction, Ethan nodded vigorously. Quinn waggled his tentacle in response, but Ethan was sure the creature moved in the same way he had before when he'd mimicked Ethan shaking his head. That wasn't right.

If they were to understand each other, having words or gestures to mean "correct" and "incorrect" was vital. Ethan thought about the problem for a while until he thought he might have figured out a way to establish these two words. First, he pressed the wall to convey the word "water," then dripped water from his hand. He nodded firmly several times. Next, he repeated the pattern for "water" then held up a dry hand. This time, he shook his head clearly from side to side.

Quinn seemed to think about this for a bit. All of his tentacles except the one he used for communicating with Ethan constantly writhed, but they seemed to slow down a little. The single motionless tentacle that hung behind the transparent wall waved gently from side to side and then up and down.

Ethan repeated what he'd done previously with a dripping hand followed by the pattern for "water" and nodding his head, and a dry hand followed by "water" and shaking his head. Once more, Quinn hesitatingly moved his tentacle on the vertical then horizontal plane.

It was time for a comprehension test. Ethan held up a dripping hand but this time he pressed the wall four times, hard. He hadn't said "water." He'd only said "four." His chest tight, he waited for Quinn's reply. After a few moments it came. The creature gently wafted his tentacle from side to side. *No.*

"You got it," Ethan exclaimed, jumping to his feet. "You did it, Quinn. You great scary water monster. You did it!"

Quinn didn't react well to Ethan's outburst. He scooted away until he was lost to sight in the murky water.

"Hey," Ethan shouted. "Come back! I'm sorry." He peered into the muddy, rushing current but there wasn't even the tip of a tentacle to be seen. He slumped down to the floor.

He'd inadvertently ruined everything, just when he'd been making some progress. Had he frightened Quinn away or had he left for another reason? It was so hard to tell. Maybe the movement of suddenly jumping up conveyed something bad in Quinn's language. Or maybe it was only that human bodies and the way they moved was so odd to the thread creatures Quinn had felt suddenly disgusted or menaced.

Ethan scooted over to the corner and rested against the opaque wall. He felt odd about Quinn leaving. After hours and days of wishing the thread creatures would stop their endless undulations outside his cell, Ethan found he missed Quinn's presence.

In fact, he found he hadn't felt so lonely all the time that he'd been traveling across the continent. Perhaps he'd been too interested in his adventure, or maybe the memories of Lauren and Dr. Crowley that had been crowding his head had kept him company. Now that he was trapped in a chamber with the very real prospect of a horrible death looming over him, Ethan wanted to be with other living things, even if it were an only alien organism and all they could say to each other was "water," "yes," and "no."

Ethan's forehead was resting on the transparent wall. He felt a slight bump and when he looked up, he saw a tentacle pushed against the wall near his head. Quinn had returned.

Careful not to move too suddenly, Ethan only nodded carefully. He hoped the movement conveyed his appreciation that Quinn was back. Wafting a tentacle gracefully upward and downward, Quinn seemed to echo the sentiment.

Ethan sat up. He had a lot of hard work ahead if he was going to create some more words in this new language that he and his tentacled partner were inventing. It might be the only way he was going to survive.

CHAPTER TWENTY-THREE

On her way through the settlement to the shuttle field, Cariad passed by one of the newly opened stores. It was a bakery, and the scent of freshly baked bread that wafted from it sent Cariad's stomach into spasms. The half sandwich Verney had given her had barely put a dent in her hunger. She opened the door and went inside.

The sight of the interior of the bakery sent nostalgia rushing through Cariad. The place had been modeled in the style of stores she used to shop at on Earth, except that a person was there to serve. In Cariad's time, the store's system would read the customer's embedded chip as they entered and registered whatever they took with them when they left.

Most of the shelves were empty but the island in the center of the shop was piled high with bread. A wave of remembrance and wistful longing for the Earth of her time washed over Cariad. A man holding the hand of a toddler was being served at the counter, and both he and the server stared at her.

"Can I help you?" the server asked, in the tone of someone inquiring after her mental health.

"I... I... " Cariad gathered herself together. "You're selling bread?"

"That's right," said the server. "Baked this morning. It's still warm."

Cariad's stomach gave another lurch. "Can I buy a loaf?"

The server said, "I don't know. Have you been fitted with a chip?"

"Ah. No, I haven't." As a Woken, Cariad wasn't yet officially part of the settlement's economy. "The credit system has started up?"

"Yes," the server replied. "So unless you have a chip or one of the old cash vouchers... "

"Okay." Cariad looked longingly at the bread. "Where did the flour come from?"

"From the ship. The wheat crop won't be harvested for a while yet."

"Of course. It smells wonderful." Cariad's mouth was watering. Then she felt guilty for thinking about food when Ethan was probably dead.

"Oh for stars' sake," said the man with the child. "Give her a loaf. I'll pay."

The server's eyebrows lifted. "Are you sure?"

"Yes," the man replied. "Why not? I have to spend my creds on something. There's not much else to buy yet."

"Thanks," said Cariad, "but I couldn't. I guess it must be really expensive."

"That doesn't matter," said the man. "I

remember you, I think. You're that Woken who helped Ethan during the First Night Attack. Take the bread as thanks."

The server was slipping a loaf into a plaspaper bag. "I wouldn't turn it down if I were you. That pile is all we'll have until we receive another flour delivery from the ship." He handed Cariad the filled bag.

She held it to her chest, appreciating the softness and warmth. "Thank you."

As Cariad walked to the shuttle field, she broke off pieces of the loaf and ate them. The bread tasted delicious. Even aboard the ship bread was a rare luxury. Wheat wasn't grown on a large scale because it wasn't as nutritious or productive as other crops raised in the limited space of the agricultural area.

Eating the bread warmed Cariad's heart too. The introduction of the credit economy was an indication of progress in the colony, and the Gen man's offer had been kind despite his gruffness.

Cariad was nearly at the shuttle field when her interface chirped. She'd turned it off while she'd gone on her trip to find Ethan, and upon her return she'd seen several messages from people who had been looking for her, including Kes. Guiltily, she'd recalled agreeing to meet up with him the day that she'd left the settlement. Her worry over what had happened to Ethan meant she'd entirely forgotten about the arrangement. She would have to comm him later to apologize. In the meantime, a live comm request had arrived. Cariad sighed. She expected it would be from Osias. She guessed she would have to answer for her actions sooner or later. But when she checked it was Addleson aboard the *Mistral* who wanted to speak to her.

"Cariad," Addleson said. "Where did you get to? Everyone's been looking for you all over."

"It's a long story. Too long to explain in a comm."

"Hmm, well, I was wondering if you were going to speak to Garwin again. We'll keep him here as long as you like, of course, but... "

"I understand. I'll be over to speak to him again soon."

"Okay. Pop in and say hi when you come over, won't you? I'd love to hear a long story. To be honest, captaining a ship that isn't going anywhere gets a little tedious after a while."

"I'll do that."

"Oh, and Aubriot's been asking for you. Hence the big search."

"Aubriot? What does he want?"

"No idea. He's been loafing around here annoying everyone."

"Right. I'll speak to him when I have time."

After saying goodbye to Addleson, Cariad was about to put her interface away when it chirped again. She hurriedly checked to see who it was this time, hoping it wasn't anyone important. The shuttle to the *Nova Fortuna* was just about to leave.

It was the Leader.

"Verney told me what you did, Cariad," said Osias. "Officially, I don't approve. Unofficially, I think it was extraordinarily brave of you. Either way, Ethan's death is a great loss."

"I don't know that he's gone for sure," Cariad

said. "I didn't find a body. I didn't see any sign of him."

Osias' expression was solemn. "I know. Verney explained. I had to turn down his request to send out a search party."

Cariad pitied the man. He was very young to have to make these life-and-death decisions. "It's okay. I understand why."

"The colony's survival is my priority. I can't risk others' lives when there's so little hope."

"I know, and Ethan wouldn't want you to. He told me so when he set out. He knew the risks." Though what she was saying was true, Cariad felt almost treacherous. A part of her just didn't want to let go of the hope that Ethan was still alive. In a way she was glad that it was Osias who was making the call, and not her.

Osias asked, "What are your plans now?"

"I just have to check in with my techs, then I'm back on the Natural Movement investigation. I'm going to focus on a subsection of the current suspects."

***

When she arrived on the *Nova Fortuna*, Cariad went directly to the Fertilization Labs. Predictably, her two techs were hard at work. They had seeded the remaining gestation bags with the newly developing embryos, they told her.

"And they all took again?" Cariad asked.

"One hundred percent success rate," Cassie replied.

"I knew I could rely on you two."

The techs beamed in response to her praise.

"From what I can tell," said Cariad, "the cat got

out of the bag that I wasn't around."

Florian flushed a little. "Yes. That was my fault."

Cassie chuckled. "Every time someone came in looking for you, he would tell them a different story. After the fourth or fifth visitor, the stories became more and more outlandish." She put a hand over her mouth and giggled. "He told one person—was it Anahi?—that you'd gone back to Earth aboard the *Mistral* to buy cheese, and he told someone else that you were mining for gold in… where was it?"

"Timbuktu," Florian said, shame-faced. "I couldn't resist. Sorry."

Cariad rolled her eyes. "Remind me not to ask you to do anything other than create new life in the future."

"To be fair," Florian replied, "that's probably about all I can be trusted with."

"It's okay," Cariad said. "It doesn't matter. People were bound to figure out I wasn't around soon enough, and I'm back now. But I came to tell you that you're going to be working without me quite a bit in the future. I'm going to be busy with other things. But I know you'll do a great job. If you ever need me, I'll only be a comm away. Are you okay with that?"

A subtle glance passed between the two techs. Cariad had the impression they would be very happy to be working together without a third wheel hanging around.

"We're fine," Cassie said. "The tricky part is over. It's plain coasting from now on… or something."

"Plain sailing," Florian said.

"Great," Cariad said and took her leave of the young couple.

The next person she had to visit wasn't far away. The Fertilization Labs were sited next to the soil biology area, which was why Florian had commandeered two of their rooms to convert into additional gestation facilities.

Cariad pressed the door security for the soil labs. Rene buzzed her in. She was working alone.

"So you're finally back from your clandestine assignment?" Rene said. "Where were you? I guessed that Florian's story about you deciding to become the first person to sail single-handedly to the next continent wasn't entirely true."

When Cariad told Rene where she'd been, the woman's face fell. "Oh, Cariad, I'm so sorry. Poor Ethan."

"Yes." Cariad took a breath. "Rene, the reason I'm here is because I wanted to talk to you some more about that injury you had that you can't explain."

"Okay, but maybe you should take a little time off after your trip. I don't mean to be rude but you look awful. Like you haven't slept for a week."

Her comment caused Cariad to realize how bone-tired she was. Yet she was determined to press on with rooting out any remaining Natural Movement members as quickly as she could.

"To be honest, I don't feel too good," Cariad replied. "Thanks for your concern. Anyway, I was thinking about your injury. If it wasn't due to an accident—which seems likely, or you would remember it—then the obvious answer is that someone did it to you."

"Do you think so? But I would remember that too, wouldn't I?"

"Not necessarily. Not if you were unconscious."

"But then the pain would wake me up."

"Maybe the person who did it sedated you."

Rene frowned. "I don't know. That seems even less likely than hurting myself then forgetting about it. I mean, this person would have to have done it when I was alone, and I'm only ever alone when I'm in my cabin."

"Yes," Cariad said. "I thought about that too. They would have had to break through the ship's security to get inside."

"Exactly. And who would be able to do that? The techs back on Earth designed the ship's system. It's impenetrable."

"I know." Implications were beginning to pile up in Cariad's head.

"Cariad," said Rene, "I don't understand where you're going with this."

"I'm not sure where this is leading me yet either," said Cariad, but she was almost certain about one thing: at least one terrorist remained alive.

CHAPTER TWENTY-FOUR

Time was running out for Ethan. His foot was swelling up and the pain from it disturbed his sleep. The wound was red and puffy and a white, gloopy liquid oozed from it. It didn't look good at all. What would happen if he didn't receive medical treatment? On the *Nova Fortuna* the doctor would have given him a shot and covered the wound in healing gel. Ethan wasn't sure happened to infections that weren't treated but whatever it was, it was happening to his foot.

Also, after his early success at creating a mutual, touch-based language with Quinn, progress had stalled. The patterns they'd agreed on included those for their own names and for numbers, water, food, yes and no (and, by extension, correct and incorrect) and parts of their bodies. Ethan now knew that *soft pause soft-hard-soft* stood for tentacle, and the pattern for the hole at the center of the thread organisms' bodies was *soft pause hard-hard-hard*. He'd also taught Quinn patterns for major parts of his own anatomy, though the creature appeared to struggle to understand the difference between "eye" and "head," and he'd wanted to assign each of Ethan's fingers a different touch pattern.

Most importantly, after many demonstrations, Ethan had taught Quinn a pattern that meant "open." When he was as sure as he could be that the creature understood his meaning, Ethan had tried to show that he wanted Quinn to open his cell, to no effect. It had been a tenuous hope. He doubted that the room had been created for any purpose other than to confine him, and Quinn wouldn't be so stupid as to open the exit just because he was asked. Maybe he didn't have the authority to do it, Ethan had mused, wondering about thread society.

He sat in the corner of his cell, nursing his aching foot, contemplating the fact that the conversation that he needed to have with Quinn, which involved him persuading the thread creatures to let him go, was weeks or months or perhaps years away. It might even prove impossible to reach that level of communication. Although he'd finally found food that was still edible in his pack and he had water for a few more days, Ethan couldn't afford to spend much more time learning to communicate with his captors. The wound on his foot wasn't going to get better by itself. He was worried that sooner or later it might kill him.

If Quinn wasn't going to let Ethan go free when he asked, he would have to force his way out somehow. But the chamber's walls were tough and he had nothing strong or sharp to cut the material. Even if he had, Quinn would undoubtedly guess what he was up to long before he succeeded. Ethan hadn't experienced punishment from the thread creatures yet, and he didn't want to find out what they would do if they caught him trying to escape. One disturbing possibility had crossed his mind: the creatures had so many tentacles they might consider his losing one or two of his own a mild form of discipline.

Any escape attempt Ethan made had to be fast and it had to be one hundred percent successful. He wouldn't get another chance.

Quinn was outside the cell as always, waving his tentacles around apparently randomly, though for all Ethan knew the creature could have been explaining quantum physics. In fact, he was probably asking Ethan to return to the wall to continue their lessons, but he was in too much pain, too tired, and too despondent to pursue the extremely difficult and long-winded task.

Ethan closed his eyes, though that seemed to intensify the pain from his foot. He thought of the other Gens back at the settlement who were getting on with the task of colonization. He thought of Cariad and Cherry, and of Garwin. Had Cariad discovered whether Garwin was a Natural Movement follower? He wondered how the colony was getting along and if Cherry was finding it too much trouble to farm his land as well as her own.

His thoughts returned to Cariad. He usually tried to not think about her because when he did, the pain of missing her was so great it was almost as bad as the grief he felt over Lauren's and Dr.

Crowley's deaths. He felt he would do anything and everything to see her again.

And with that thought, a possible answer to his problem popped into his mind. He worked out the steps, then scooted across the floor to the transparent wall. For his plan to work, Ethan had to make Quinn understand that the word "more."

Then he realized he would not only have to convey the concept of "more" but also the concept of "I want." He'd already tried to convey the idea of wanting for hours without success. How could he explain the meaning of something that he couldn't show or demonstrate? Quinn couldn't read a look of longing or hunger on Ethan's face. He probably wasn't paying attention to Ethan's face at all. The threads did all their communicating with their limbs.

Ethan heaved a sigh and looked up at Quinn's whirling tentacles. "Well, *more* shouldn't be too hard, should it?" Wearily, he pulled over a few random soggy food packages to show his companion.

After beginning with one food package and adding others to the pile, followed by touching the wall in a set pattern over and over again, Ethan was reasonably convinced that Quinn understood the pattern to mean "more."

"I want" was much more difficult. After a long while of trying Ethan remained uncertain that Quinn really knew what he meant. It was also possible that the creature had interpreted his meaning as "take something and pretend to eat it."

Finally, when Ethan thought he had a slim chance of success with the sentence he wanted to convey to Quinn, he pushed aside the mound of food packages. Before he began, Ethan rehearsed the touch patterns in his mind. A mistake might lead to hours more confusion. When he was sure he was ready and Quinn was waiting with a tentacle resting against the other side of the wall, Ethan pressed out his message: "I want - more - food."

A pause followed while Quinn lifted his tentacle away from the wall then replaced it. Hadn't he understood the message? Ethan tried again. "I want more food."

Quinn pressed his answer, "Yes." But he didn't leave the wall. Ethan had expected him to go away if he'd understood, but the thread creature remained in position with a tentacle resting on the transparent surface. Ethan tried for a third time. "I want more food."

"Yes," came the answer. What did Quinn mean? Was he saying that he understood the message? Or was he agreeing that Ethan did want more food but that it didn't mean it was Quinn's responsibility to go and get him some? Either interpretation was entirely possible, and probably more besides. Ethan had no way of knowing what Quinn meant by his "Yes."

Perhaps Ethan hadn't been successful in conveying the ideas of "more" or "I want" after all. Whatever it was that had gone wrong, his attempt seemed to have failed. Ethan slumped against the wall, trying to shut out the pain radiating up from his foot.

He could feel Quinn's messages through his shoulder, but he didn't have the energy or the willpower to make the effort to interpret them. It looked like he would never make it out of the cell, never return to the settlement, never see Cariad again.

As the soft and hard pressures with pauses continued, Ethan wondered what Quinn made of his experimental subject. Was he concerned by its stillness? Was he trying to trigger it into a new performance? The thread monster would have to be disappointed. His entertainment was over for the day, if it was daytime. For all Ethan knew it could be the middle of the night.

He would have liked to have seen the surface of Concordia once more. Perhaps a view of the gigantic river in the starlight, or of the ocean beyond the caves. He would have counted himself lucky if he could have only seen the settlement. The single-story pre-fabricated homes, stores, warehouses, and workrooms would have been a better sight than the four walls of his prison and his alien overseer.

Ethan must have lost consciousness for the next thing he knew a noise startled him awake. He opened his eyes and hauled himself up from the floor where he'd slipped down to lie in the water. Pain lanced from his foot, making him gasp. The swelling had risen above his ankle. His foot had turned dusky.

The noise that had woken him repeated. A loud thump and clatter came from behind him. Ethan swiveled around. The roof hatch was opening. A pile of items had fallen through, wet with river water. All of them were from the flitter.

Ethan's heart soared. For a moment even the

pain from his foot was forgotten as he slid over toward the heap. There weren't any food packets among the various objects. Of course there weren't. The thread monsters had correctly identified and brought him all his food supplies in his first delivery. He'd been relying on the hope that the creatures wouldn't be sure what might or might not be human food so that when he asked for more, they would bring him the other contents of the flitter. They probably guessed there was something else in there that he needed to survive.

The creatures had been correct. For Ethan to live he had to escape, and to escape he needed... He plunged a hand into the pile of saturated blankets, clothes, and other items of equipment. Like a light in the darkness, he felt the touch of something hard, cold, and smooth. He grasped the butt and extracted it from the pile.

The Guardian weapon that Cariad had pressured him to take at the last minute was about to prove very useful.

CHAPTER TWENTY-FIVE

After gleaning little in the way of useful information from her first round of interviews of Natural Movement suspects, Cariad was ready to move onto the next stage. As she sat in her office in the Leader's building at the settlement, Kes comm'd her, wanting to meet up, but she explained she was much too busy. She closed the comm, aware that she hadn't told Kes the entire truth, but that would have to wait until she had time to see him face to face.

She brought up the files she needed and input the cross reference search. At the same moment, Aubriot burst in. "So you *are* here! I thought your team were covering up for you again when they said you were planetside. Why have you been ignoring me? I must have comm'd you fifteen times."

Cariad said, "I don't know about you, but I was brought up to knock, ring, or otherwise announce my presence when I wanted to see someone, and not to barge in like a cow in a barn."

Ignoring her rebuke, Aubriot sauntered over and took the seat opposite Cariad, casually hooking one of his knees over the arm. "I came to tell you what we need to do about those aliens in the lake that you found."

"Aliens? They aren't aliens," said Cariad.

"Aren't they?" Aubriot unhooked his knee and sat up. "You mean we brought them with us from Earth? Rubbish."

"No," Cariad replied. "I don't mean that at all. The creatures in the lake aren't aliens because they're indigenous. On Concordia, *we're* the aliens."

"Pff." Aubriot flapped a hand dismissively. "Don't split hairs. You know what I mean. Anyway, I thought up the perfect solution."

"Really?" Cariad closed her interface screen and folded her arms. "Go ahead. I'm all ears." She couldn't imagine what someone like Aubriot might think was an acceptable solution to the problem of a lake full of sentient predators right in the middle of their farming district. Or maybe she could.

"It's simple," Aubriot said, "I'm surprised no one's done it already. The *Mistral* is armed. Why not just—"

"Blow up the lake from orbit?" Cariad finished for him. "How did I know you were going to say that? Well, thanks for your helpful suggestion. Now if you don't mind, I have a lot of work to do."

"So that's already the plan, right?" Aubriot

asked. "Someone thought of it before me. We're gonna nuke the lake."

"No, we aren't going to use the *Mistral's* weapons to destroy the life in the lake or anywhere else on this planet. No one else suggested the idea, and I'm guessing that's because no one else is quite so stupid."

"Huh? What?" Aubriot's expression was contorted with confusion. Cariad wondered if it was the first time anyone had ever insulted him to his face and he was struggling to grasp the concept. The penny seemed to drop and his features darkened. "Now wait a minute! Where do you get off calling me stupid? My idea's perfectly sensible. A single pulse from the *Mistral* would vaporize a lake in less than a second. Then farmers can carry on growing their crops without fear of gigantic squid breaking into their homes at night to eat them."

Cariad's mouth dropped open. "Who told you that? I never heard anything so ridiculous."

"I don't remember," Aubriot replied. "Everyone's saying it. So, like I said, we need to take these aliens out pronto before more people die."

"For the last time," Cariad said between her teeth, "they aren't... Oh, never mind. Look, maybe what no one's told you is that these creatures are almost certainly highly intelligent. From what we can tell they're controlling some kind of heat production process under water."

"If they're intelligent, that's all the more reason to strike first," Aubriot said. "The best defense is —"

"Offense. Yes, I've heard that saying. But I don't think you've really considered the implications if we attack them."

"What's to consider?" Aubriot asked. "We take them out. End of story. Problem solved."

"No. Problem not solved. Problem most likely increased by several orders of magnitude. If these creatures are intelligent and we destroy a whole lake full of them, what do you think's going to happen next?"

Aubriot looked blank.

Cariad said, "Do you honestly think that the organisms in the lake are the only ones that exist on the entire planet? Is that really how you think nature works?"

"All right," Aubriot replied. "I get it. So you're saying there might be more of them? Okay. I'm not an idiot. But so what? If we demonstrate a show of force now... Show them what we're capable of... That's going to stop them from attacking us. All the more reason to nuke the lake now."

"I wish you'd stop saying *nuke the lake*, like anyone would be so dumb as to fire an actual nuclear warhead right into the middle of our farming district. As far as I'm aware, the *Mistral* doesn't even carry nuclear weapons."

"Picky, aren't you? Nuke, blast, annihilate, what difference does it make? I still say we take the water bugs out of the equation now, and I'm not hearing any good reasons why we shouldn't." Aubriot sat back in his chair, looking smug.

Cariad had a feeling that he wasn't as intent on pushing through with his suggestion as he made out to be. Instead, he seemed to be quite enjoying their argument. She reflected that Aubriot probably didn't have many—or any—friends or social contact.

She sighed. "If more thread organisms are living in other parts of the planet, which I don't doubt at all, and we blow up hundreds or perhaps thousands of their relatives in the lake, they aren't going to react well. We might suddenly find ourselves at war, and apart from the fact that's the diametrically opposite reason for us being here, we can't afford to have any more colonists dying young. I've done the calculations. Assuming restocking the gene pool goes to plan, we'll only narrowly escape inbreeding further down the generations. We're at our limit. Even if we wanted to go to war, which we don't, we just can't risk it."

"Don't you think you're being a bit unrealistic?"

"No. I don't."

"But these predators live in water," Aubriot said, "and, in case you haven't noticed, we breathe air. How are they even going to try and fight back? Besides, they started it. They've attacked three people and killed two. If these squid things are intelligent, that's all the more reason to show them their actions won't be tolerated. Why should we let those deaths go unpunished? Think about that poor kid and its dad. Don't you care? Don't you think they deserve justice?"

"Oh, please." The irony of Aubriot spouting off about sympathy and justice was laughable. "Of course I care. Probably a lot more than you. It's hard to just accept those deaths and do nothing. But I still don't think that blowing up the lake is the answer, especially when it might spark a reign of terror. Anyway, the people who were attacked strayed near the lake, which the creatures probably view as their territory. It could be that they were only acting instinctively."

"Which kind of goes against your argument that they're intelligent," Aubriot said, his eyes hooded.

Cariad suddenly felt like she'd been playing a game of chess and now she was in check. "If the thread creatures aren't intelligent, that's even more reason to *not* blow them up. You can't blame an animal for doing what comes naturally to it. Have you forgotten the Mandate? We aren't here to ride roughshod over the place. The *Nova Fortuna* Project isn't supposed to be a reiteration of colonizations on Earth. Razing the landscape and destroying the local wildlife aren't on the agenda, no matter how intelligent a species might be. Now, I have a lot of work to do. So, drop it, okay?"

"Already have, as a matter of fact," Aubriot said, looking even smugger.

"What? Then why are you even here?"

"I've just been in to see Osias. He's got the veto on whatever happens in the colony and he was quick to shoot me down. I have to say, you had better arguments, though."

Cariad let out a huff of frustration. "If you're only here to waste my time, please leave. I have much more important things to do."

"Yeah," Aubriot said as if an idea had just occurred to him. "So what is it you're doing anyway?"

"I can't tell you."

Aubriot rolled his eyes. "You really are shit at

this, aren't you? Let me guess. You're investigating the Natural Movement terrorists."

"No, I'm... " Realizing there was little point in denying it, Cariad sighed and asked, "How did you know?"

"I heard you were supposedly interviewing people about their "experiences" in the colony, and I thought, how likely is it that the woman who's responsible for one of the most vital aspects of the colonization is going to waste her time on that bullshit? By the way, I think everyone else has probably figured that out too. So, you think that nutter who blew up the caves wasn't the last of them?"

"I can't talk to you about it. Now, please. I need to work."

"What if I said I could help?"

How characteristically Aubriot, Cariad thought. The man would never demean himself enough to actually ask anything of anyone. If he couldn't demand, he would suggest. Then if the answer was no, he hadn't lost face from receiving an outright refusal. "I would say thanks but no thanks."

"And why might that be?"

Cariad was surprised. The question gave an opening for potential criticism. This was a side of Aubriot she'd never seen. What was going on under that self-assured, arrogant surface? Perhaps the man's experience of living on Concordia was falling below his expectations. After all, he wasn't like the rest of the Woken, who were all scientists with defined roles. And he wasn't a Gen, working to build a functioning community. He was a floater with no vocation or purpose. And the gulf between

Aubriot's luxurious, wheeling and dealing existence on Earth and his current life was vast. Cariad felt the tiniest shred of pity for him.

"The investigation is confidential," said Cariad. "That's why. Only I and one or two others know the details and that's how it has to be. Any leak of information could tip off a saboteur and prevent me from catching them."

"You think I can't keep a secret?" Aubriot exploded with laughter. "Sweetheart, you've never been in business, have you? Do you really think I could have amassed my trillions if I let slip about sensitive information?"

He had a point. "Still," Cariad said, "until I've ruled you out, you're technically under suspicion too. I can't let potential suspects in on the investigation."

"I'm a suspect? I wasn't even revived for most of the attacks. And of all the colonists on this planet I'm the least likely to be a Natural Movement follower. I mean, think about it. You think I'd finance the project so I could destroy it?"

Cariad felt like she was in check again, only this time it was beginning to feel like check mate. "Well... " She was out of objections.

Her sense of defeat must have shown because Aubriot said, "Sweet! Tell me what you've got so far." He brought his chair around to Cariad's side of the desk and opened her interface screen.

She knew she'd been bamboozled but she didn't know a way out of it. In other words, Aubriot was back on form. With some reluctance, Cariad told him about the Natural Movement tattoo that the Guardians had found on Twyla's body and

Montfort's examination of all the colonists for similar tattoos, or evidence that indicated a tattoo might have been removed. She also explained that she'd interviewed the people on a list of possibilities that Montfort had drawn up.

When she'd finished, Aubriot said, "Got it. What are you doing now?"

"I was just cross-matching the names of people I interviewed with Twyla's class lists over her career as a kindy teacher. The saboteur of the First Night Attack was a kindy teacher too, so I'm also looking at her former students."

"Right. Did you find any matches between the people taught by the saboteurs and Montfort's list?"

"I'd only just input the search when you came in."

"So what does it say?" Aubriot leaned into her as he reached over to scan the screen. Cariad tried to push back but he was far stronger. "Hmm... Just one. What do we know about her?"

"Well if you'd let me see who it is... "

Aubriot shifted away to allow Cariad access to the screen. When she saw the name, her heart sank. She didn't like the woman, but she still didn't think she could be a Natural Movement follower. Yet Aubriot was correct. The search had brought up only one match: Cherry.

CHAPTER TWENTY-SIX

The Guardian weapon had been thoroughly soaked in river water for days. If it no longer worked, Ethan didn't know what he would do, but he finally had a chance to escape and he was going to take it. He grabbed the weapon from the pile of his belongings. His foot was so painful he couldn't put even the slightest weight on it, so he hopped to a corner of his chamber. He would use the weapon to cut a hole wide enough for him to get out.

He hadn't forgotten the small fact that he couldn't swim, but he would just have to try his best to get to the river bank somehow. If he drowned in the attempt it would be a better death than the one he currently faced.

Leaning on one wall for balance, Ethan rested the butt of the weapon in the crook of his shoulder. If he succeeded in burning a hole in the tough material of the wall, the water that poured through it would be a torrent. He would have to force his way out against the pressure of the water and if that was impossible he would have to wait until it filled the chamber.

He pressed the trigger. An arc of light flew from the weapon, hitting the wall and sinking through it. A jet of water spurted out. The weapon still worked despite its long soaking. The Guardian technology had come through for him. He cut a slit in the wall, turning the water jet into an arc. Ethan was immediately soaked head to toe.

To fire a constant beam, he kept his finger on the trigger. Water was pouring from the line he was cutting, fizzing and steaming in the heat. Water was already rising in the cell. Ethan didn't waste time glancing over at Quinn to see the creature's reaction.

Ethan only had to create a hole that he could fit through, and he was nearly half done. The fountain of water erupting from the gap made it hard for him to hold the beam steady, and he struggled to remain upright. He was already unbalanced from standing on one leg. The water in the chamber continued to rise.

Would a tentacle poke through the hole and try to stop him? Were thread creatures waiting for him on the other side? The beam from the Guardian's weapon was heating the water it touched, and the tide in his cell that had risen to Ethan's thighs was uncomfortably hot. He hoped that might be sufficient deterrent to keep the threads away.

He was three-quarters of the way through cutting the hole and the water emerging from it was a deluge. It was hard for him to see where to direct the beam to cut the remaining quarter-circle. The water immediately next to the cut surface boiled and steamed.

If both of Ethan's feet had been unhurt, he could have tried to kick out the hole before he completed the circle, but his injured foot made that impossible. He was also waist-deep in water and nearly floating. Still, he decided, he could try to pull the flap inward. The water pressure was already bending it toward him. He released the trigger of his weapon and slung it across his back on its strap. He poked his fingers through the gap he'd burned, then grabbed and pulled at the hot material.

That was all it took.

The flap broke free and water flooded in, sweeping Ethan up and carrying him across the chamber on a wave. As he felt himself sink beneath the surface he took a gulp of air. He had to get to the hole. Ethan kicked his legs like he'd seen swimmers do on vids, hoping to propel himself forward, but the force of water entering the hole made his attempts futile.

The water was also murky. Opening his eyes was painful and when he managed it he could see little except brown silt. His lungs were also becoming painful, and his injured foot felt like it was being stabbed with hundreds of knives. Ethan soon lost his sense of direction.

If he could only find the hole. If he could only get through, the river current would bear him away from his prison. He might not make it to the surface, but at least he would die free.

Ethan reached ahead blindly. He guessed that

the rising water would have lifted him above the level of the hole, so he angled his body down and kicked again. The agony from his bad foot almost made him cry out, but he knew the first lungful of water he breathed in would be the end of him. He refused to die in a cage. With an enormous effort he kicked again.

His fingertips brushed something rough. By some miracle he'd found the edge of the hole. He kicked for a third time and wildly grabbed. He had it. The ragged edge he'd burned was under his hand. The chamber had to be nearly full of water because he felt hardly any pressure from water entering through the hole. His lungs were screaming for air. He found the other side of the hole, grasped the edges in each hand, and pulled himself through.

Immediately, he was swept into the cool rush of the river water. He'd done it. He'd escaped the thread creatures' prison. He was free.

CHAPTER TWENTY-SEVEN

When Cariad had asked Cherry to come back for another interview, she refused and then didn't answer any further comms. Cariad was forced to take a flitter and the two compliance enforcement officers appointed by Osias to bring in the headstrong Gen. Aubriot had insisted on coming along too.

The enforcement officer who flew the vehicle was a woman called Mariko. The other officer was a man called Arden. Cariad didn't know the criteria Osias had set out that qualified the two of them for their new jobs. When the Manual had been written, it had been assumed that conflicts would be peaceably settled through discussion and consensus. No one had thought that the colony would require policing, at least not until the colonization was one or two generations down the line.

Cariad was sitting next to Aubriot in the back

seat of the flitter while the two compliance enforcement officers sat up front.

"Wait. Where does this woman live?" Aubriot asked as the flitter passed through the gates of the electric fence that surrounded the settlement.

"Cherry's farm is next to Ethan's," Cariad replied. "She took it over after he left. We might have to find someone to take both farms on now."

"I didn't realize we'd be going all the way out there," Aubriot said. "Is it far?"

"Half an hour or so," Cariad replied. "You'll get to see that lake you were so keen to nuke."

Aubriot nodded but didn't reply. He was looking uncharacteristically pensive.

Cariad asked, "Is this your first time outside the settlement?"

"Yeah, it is."

She watched him out of the corner of her eye. Was it possible that the confident, arrogant Aubriot was feeling nervous?

"They only come out at night, you know," she said.

Aubriot turned toward her sharply. "What only come out at night?"

"The predators that got into the camp on the First Night Attack. They're nocturnal. We won't see any during daylight, so there's no need to be afraid."

"Who said I was afraid?" Aubriot shot.

"No one. I was only explaining in case you were wondering."

Aubriot scowled and returned his gaze to the landscape.

On Cariad's previous visit to the farming

district, she'd been too worried about the victims who had been dragged into the lake to pay much attention to her surroundings. That day, faced with the solemn and regrettable task of taking Cherry in for questioning against her will, Cariad was glad of the momentary distraction.

The landscape had changed considerably since the time she'd gone with Ethan to see his farm. Then, using a flitter had been a necessity. Vegetation had covered the ground all the way out to the land allotted for the farming district. Now, a roadmaker had paved the entire route, making it accessible to the wheeled vehicles brought on the *Nova Fortuna,* which made Cariad question why they were using a flitter at all. It had become a habit to use the flying craft. She would have to speak to Osias about measures to curb their use.

The tall fern-like plants that surrounded the settlement gave way to the shorter vegetation that marked the beginning of the farming district. They soon passed a field full of tall green shoots. The colony's first crops were growing strongly. Little on the planet seemed to be interested in eating or otherwise harming the Earth crops, which was perhaps a predictable outcome of evolution. Whatever organisms and viruses had evolved on Concordia hadn't been exposed to plants from Earth up until that moment. Osias had told her of some disturbances in fields of root crops where they hadn't been able to identify the pest, but the effect was localized and minor.

They were well inside the farming district before they reached Cherry's house.

"That's the one," Mariko said, pointing to a

square, single story building in the distance. It was identical to all the other pre-fabricated farmhouses but Mariko knew the location from the flitter's guidance system. The vehicle glided down the lane that led to the building.

Cariad couldn't shake a guilty feeling about forcing Cherry to come in and be interviewed. It was tantamount to arresting her. Also, Cherry was Ethan's friend and Cariad also didn't think he would have been so blind as to not notice something not right about her. He'd spotted it in Twyla. And there was the fact that Cherry had very nearly died at the flooding of the caves. It seemed unlikely that Twyla would have killed another follower. Yet perhaps she hadn't known Cherry was there, or maybe it had only been the death wish of the movement playing out.

"So what do you plan on doing with this woman when you've got her?" Aubriot asked.

"Question her, of course."

"Hmpf." Aubriot lifted a lip in a sneer and looked out across Cherry's fields.

"What does that mean?" Cariad asked, silently regretting taking the bait.

"You're a scientist. You might know everything there is to know about your specialism, but most of you are clueless about human nature. Face it. You're not exactly cut out to be an interrogator, are you?"

"Maybe not," Cariad replied evenly. "But I'm as good as anyone else, and someone has to do it."

"You're correct on the second," Aubriot said, "wrong on the first."

"Oh really? I'm not as good as anyone else? Who

do you think would be better?" she asked, simultaneously guessing Aubriot's answer.

"Isn't it obvious? I could do a better job at getting the truth out of someone than anyone else on this planet or floating above it. Blindfolded, deafened, and with both hands tied behind my back."

Cariad relished the mental image Aubriot's words conjured up. "I wouldn't be too sure of myself if I were you. Brow-beating and threats yield poor results as interrogation tactics."

Aubriot seemed about to launch into a tirade, but then thought better of it. "I wasn't talking about having a go at her. I'm not thick. Do you think I did so well in business by bulldozing my way through negotiations?"

Cariad actually thought that a large part of Aubriot's success was due to the massive wealth he'd inherited, but she diplomatically decided not to voice her true opinion. If Aubriot could curb his natural responses for the sake of civility, so could she. "To be honest, I don't know. I don't know anything about business negotiations."

Visibly pleased at the rare, almost-compliment from her, Aubriot said, "There's a lot to it, but a technique every successful businessman uses to get the deal he wants is to make the other person feel like they're benefiting from the agreement too. Another important skill is to be able to read people. In some ways, it's a lot like playing poker. You can't give anything away, but at the same time you have to be able to guess what everyone else is thinking."

They pulled up outside Cherry's farmhouse. It

was mid-afternoon, and Cariad guessed that the woman would probably be out at work in her fields. It might take some time to find her. They all exited the flitter.

"What do you say?" Aubriot asked.

"You mean about whether you can be there when I question Cherry?"

"Yes."

"I guess so. But the minute you do something to jeopardize the interview, out you go."

There was a creak from up ahead. Cherry had come out onto her porch. Her weapon butt rested on her shoulder and the muzzle was pointed directly at them.

"You're assuming I agree to be interviewed," she said.

An awkward pause later—Mariko and Arden seemed suddenly confused about what exactly they were supposed to do—Cariad said, "I'm sorry. I have to ask you to come back with me to the settlement."

"You have to *ask* me?" Cherry laughed. "If you're here to ask me, why have you brought the colony's latest bullies along? And what's the fallen tycoon doing here? What you really mean is, you're ordering me to go with you. Isn't that right? Why dress it up? You and the other Woken really can't stand it to have us Gens doing what we like, can you? Ethan's gone. Garwin's under arrest. I knew I'd be targeted sooner or later. I'm only surprised it took you so long."

"I don't like to do this either, Cherry," said Cariad, hating the whiny tone in her voice. But she really was sorry. "But you have to come back with us. I have to talk to you about your involvement with the Natural Movement."

"Huh. That's the cover for taking me in, is it? Couldn't you have thought of something more convincing? Do you really think the Gens will believe I could be a saboteur?"

"They'll believe it if you don't come with us quietly," Aubriot said.

Cherry had been staring down Cariad, but her gaze flicked to the financier. "No Gen would ever think that of me."

"I wouldn't be so sure," Aubriot said. "People love to gossip, and the nastier the rumor the better. There's gonna be someone who'll say you put up a fight because you've got something to hide. No smoke without fire, you know. But if you come with us now, without a fight, that'll show everyone you're clean."

Aubriot's argument seemed to have an effect. Cherry frowned and hesitated to respond.

For the first time ever, Cariad found herself impressed by Aubriot.

Then Cherry said, "Yeah, like I care what people think." She swung her gaze back to Cariad, and with hatred written on her features, she lifted her weapon to fire.

Mariko and Arden finally sprang into action. Before Cherry could get out a shot, they felled her with stunning pulse rounds. Aubriot climbed the steps to the farmhouse porch, lifted up Cherry's small body, and carried her to the flitter.

CHAPTER TWENTY-EIGHT

When Ethan came around, he was lying in the dark. It took him a few moments to remember what he'd been doing before he lost consciousness. He'd escaped from the thread creatures! He'd cut a hole in the cell wall with the Guardian weapon and got out into the river.

He sat up and hollered as pain shot out from his foot. After a while, the waves of agony subsided enough for him to think. Where was he? The ground was flat, hard, and smooth. If he'd made it to the riverbank, he should have been sitting on sand. Was it nighttime? He couldn't see any stars, and the air was still. Not a puff of breeze stirred. He could hear the river, though. The rushing sound seemed to be all around him. Had he made it to an island?

Then, through his pain-fogged mind, the truth hit him. He wasn't on an island. He was inside some kind of artificial structure. A terrible dread grew in his stomach, almost paralyzing his thoughts. He couldn't believe it. It couldn't be. Not after all his efforts.

The floor he was sitting on slid out from beneath him. He fell and hit a second floor hard. The jolt turned his foot into a ball of fiery agony and for some time all he could do was endure the pain and hope that it would lessen.

When Ethan could open his eyes at last, what he saw sent a wave of horror crashing over him. He was back in the chamber. It was cleaner than it had been—the river water that had flowed in through the hole had washed out all the debris of Ethan's time in there—but it was unmistakably the same place.

Dismay overcame him. He closed his eyes. After all that he'd gone through, all that he'd suffered to escape, he was back where he'd started. He must have only gone a short distance in the river before the thread creatures captured him again. They'd put him in the water lock above the cell while they drained the chamber and repaired the wall. Then they had dropped him into it again.

He was facing the three opaque walls. The transparent wall was behind him. Was Quinn there, waiting to speak to him? Ethan couldn't bring himself to turn around and look. When he'd escaped, he'd been prepared to die in the attempt. Now it looked like even that privilege would not be allowed. The thread organisms were determined to keep their experimental animal in captivity forever.

For a long time, Ethan didn't move. He lay on the floor. He didn't think he had the willpower to ever move again. He couldn't even bring himself to report what had happened into his recorder. His world was four walls and a globe of pain centered on his foot. If he'd had a knife, he imagined it would have hurt less to cut off his leg than to experience the suffering the appendage was causing him.

If there had been another option than to lie there and passively accept his fate, Ethan would have taken it, pain-wracked and near death as he was. But no more options were open to him. The thread creatures would never give him the weapon again, and without it there was no way out of the chamber unless his captors granted it. And the thread organisms had already demonstrated how little they were willing to let him go.

His fate was set. His supplies were gone, which meant he had no water. He would last another few days, then that would be it. There was no point in him even moving from where he was. There was no point in doing anything anymore.

Yet, despite everything, he found that he just couldn't give up.

Very slowly and with great care, Ethan sat up. His head swam and he was nauseated though his stomach was an empty hole. Propping himself on his arms, he looked over his shoulder. Quinn was there at the clear wall. Or Ethan guessed it was Quinn. It looked like him. The creature held a tentacle to the wall as if ready to begin a new attempt at communication. It probably was Quinn.

Gently, Ethan swiveled around to face the wall. "Why won't you leave me alone? I don't want to talk to you. You've killed me. I'm going to die here, and it's your fault. Why have you done this to me?"

Of course, Quinn offered no reply other than to hold his tentacle against the surface, ready to communicate. Despair and anger held Ethan motionless, unwilling to give the creature another moment of his attention. Then something else prompted him to move. Curiosity? Tedium? Loneliness? He began to make the slow, painful journey over to the wall.

Centimeter by centimeter Ethan dragged himself across the wet floor until he finally reached his destination. Leaning on the wall for support, he lifted a hand to feel Quinn's signal. He felt the pattern, *No.*

A pause.

No.

Ethan waited. The touch pattern was repeated a third time. *No.*

No, he mustn't try to escape? That seemed to be what Quinn was saying. Ethan rested his forehead against the wall. Was that simple message what he'd gone to the effort of dragging himself over for? Then again, what else should he have expected? Little more could have been communicated. Between them, they had a vocabulary of just a few words.

The wall moved slightly. Quinn wasn't repeating the same message. He was saying something different.

The wall flexed twice. *Hard-hard.* That was easy. *Two.* Quinn was telling him, *Two.* Two what?

Ethan repeated the touch pattern. Quinn confirmed it. *Two.* But then he communicated something else. It took Ethan a moment to recognize the message. It was one of the words he'd taught Quinn to trick him into bringing him his weapon. *More.* Quinn pressed the wall again. *Two more.*

Ethan's heart froze. Had the thread creatures caught two more colonists? Were they bringing them to his chamber? But, no, that was impossible. The settlement was hours away by flitter and no one else would have come to the river. They had no reason to. Quinn couldn't mean two more people. So what did he mean?

CHAPTER TWENTY-NINE

If looks could kill, Cariad would have been dead and buried and Cherry would be dancing on her grave. The aggrieved Gen sat opposite Cariad in her interview room in the government building. The compliance enforcement officers had insisted on putting her in handcuffs. Cariad hadn't even known that Mariko and Arden *had* handcuffs, but apparently the devices had been designed and roughly manufactured according to examples an engineer had seen in vids. Cariad had the impression that Mariko and Arden only wanted to try out their new toys.

Cherry had been disgusted when, as she came around from being stunned, the manacles were snapped into place around her wrists. *"Really?"* she'd spat at Mariko, who'd at least possessed enough integrity to look a little ashamed. Cariad had been about to tell the officer to remove the cuffs, but Aubriot, who was sitting beside Cariad, had frowned and given a slight shake of his head. She'd been swayed by his opinion. At Cherry's farmhouse, Aubriot had demonstrated that he had good insight into human nature. He'd almost persuaded Cherry to come with them peacefully, which, given the woman's feisty character, was quite an achievement.

Cariad didn't know what purpose it would serve to restrain Cherry, but she was willing to take Aubriot's suggestion on faith for the moment.

"Are you going to tell me why I'm here?" Cherry asked. "You're all insane. I've never had anything to do with the Natural Movement. I never even heard of them until after the First Night Attack. I don't want to destroy this place. Why would I? It's my home. It's all the Gens' home, if only you'd leave us in peace to live in it."

Cariad said, "You might say none of the Gens would ever want to destroy the colony, but that isn't true. The saboteur in the First Night Attack was a Gen, and we're almost certain Twyla was responsible for the disaster at the caves."

Cherry's expression of sullen fury softened with curiosity. "And this all has something to do with that injury on my leg you were asking me about?"

Cariad didn't respond. She'd questioned Cherry about her suspicious abrasion earlier and gotten nowhere. Now Cariad needed to discover whether Cherry had been indoctrinated into the Natural Movement while being taught at kindergarten by Twyla.

Cherry moved to fold her arms but was prevented by the handcuffs. She scowled and barked, "Isn't anyone here going to tell me anything?"

"We're waiting to hear what you have to tell us," Aubriot said, smiling enigmatically.

It was a sneaky move, but Cariad could see Aubriot's tactic. Someone with a guilty conscience might feel compelled to spill the beans into the vacuum he was creating. She doubted that the technique would have worked on experienced criminals back on Earth, but the Gens were probably more easy to fool than even ordinary Earth citizens.

Yet Cherry was either too smart to be taken in by Aubriot's bluff or she really was innocent because she didn't bite. "Tell you what exactly? Wait, forget that. What I really want to know is, on whose authority did you stun me and drag me from my home, and who's given you permission to keep me here? I thought we'd seen an end to suppression of Gens' rights when the Guardians deactivated. What makes you think it's okay to treat me like this? Who do you think you are? You're only a Woken," she said, looking at Cariad. "You're some kind of ex-big shot," she went on, referring to Aubriot. "And you two are just Gens who are in love with the idea of bossing people around." Cherry turned to Mariko and Arden with a sharp look. "I'm not going to forget this, you know," she added before returning her angry gaze to Cariad.

Mariko looked as though she was regretting her decision to cuff Cherry.

"What if I said you're here because you were taught by Twyla?" Cariad asked.

"I'd assume you're trying to find out if she

involved me in the Natural Movement too."

"Do you remember being taught by her?" Aubriot asked.

"Hardly. It was a long time ago. What I don't understand is, why have you come after me in particular? Twyla must have had hundreds of Gens pass through her kindy class. Why pick me out?"

"Maybe we're going to interview all her ex-students," Cariad replied.

"But you had to start somewhere, and unless I've missed out on some gossip, I'm the only one you hauled in so far. I wasn't the first kid Twyla taught, so you aren't moving in chronological order. I can't think of anything else that would distinguish me from the others, except... It's something to do with my injury, isn't it? That was what you wanted to talk to me about before. I scraped my leg when I fell from the cliffs and I was taught by Twyla. That's what sets me apart."

The workings of the Gen's mind impressed Cariad. On another world, in a different life, she would have made a good scientist. But Cariad couldn't give away the fact that Cherry had hit almost perfectly on the reason for her arrest and questioning. The only thing she hadn't guessed about was Twyla's tattoo.

More than ever, Cariad felt that Cherry was innocent, but she couldn't just let the young Gen farmer walk free on the basis of a gut feeling. Besides, Cherry was the only suspect she had. Cariad looked to Aubriot for ideas. His brows were knitted and he was resting his lips on a folded forefinger, deep in thought. When his mind was occupied on a problem and he wasn't bulldozing everyone around him, the man was almost bearable.

Aubriot leaned forward, resting his elbows on his knees. "What do you remember about being taught by Twyla?"

"Not a lot. It was twenty years ago after all."

"But you do remember some things," Aubriot suggested.

"Bits and pieces. I remember being so engrossed once when Twyla was reading a story that I peed my pants. Is that the kind of thing you want to know?"

"No," Cariad said. "But do you remember the story? What did it involve?"

"Hmm... If I remember rightly, it was about how technology and science ruined the lives of everyone on Earth, but that when they changed their bad ways and began to live in a natural state, they were happy and could grow flowers again."

"Really?" Cariad asked.

"No, of course not," Cherry replied. "Though that's what you were hoping I would say, isn't it? Believe me, if I was a Natural Movement follower, I would never tell you how I'd been indoctrinated. That would be incredibly stupid."

Cariad sighed. "So what do you remember?"

"I don't know. Just the usual stuff you would expect. I was only four or five years old. After I left her class, I didn't have anything to do with her. If she was going to convert me to the cause she would have kept in touch, don't you think? From then until she killed herself, all I really knew about her was that she was Garwin's wife."

"I wanna talk to you outside," Aubriot said to

Cariad, rising from his seat.

Though she was annoyed at his bossy manner, she followed him into the corridor. When the door to the room was closed, Aubriot said, "I don't think she has anything to do with this."

"What makes you say that?"

"I can usually tell when someone's covering something up. Either she's a very good liar or she's being straight with us. She's angry as hell about being brought in and questioned, but I'm pretty sure she isn't trying to pull the wool over our eyes."

Cariad's initial reaction to Aubriot's words was relief. His opinion chimed in with her own feelings. But she was also frustrated. What could she do next? Twyla was dead and the remaining people who might have worn the Natural Movement tattoo had no link to Twyla or the first saboteur.

The door to the room flew open but was quickly slammed shut. The sounds of a scuffle came from behind it, followed by shouting. Cariad quickly opened the door again. Cherry was on her feet and struggling with Mariko and Arden.

"Let me go! You have no right to keep me here. Let me leave!"

Mariko and Arden could barely hold onto the woman as she twisted and turned to extract herself from their grip. She bit Arden, who responded by slapping her and shoving her into her seat. Cherry leapt up and tried to kick him. Mariko pounced on her.

"That's enough," Cariad shouted. "Stop it."

But her words had no effect. Cherry was furious and there was no restraining her. Mariko was trying to reach for her weapon. Cariad didn't know what to do. The situation was way out of control.

Cherry's face was contorted with rage and wisps of hair clung to her sweaty forehead. "Let me go! Why are you targeting me? It isn't fair. I haven't done anything. Go talk to the other people on your list. Or your precious Woken doctor. Why aren't you interrogating him? You're protecting your own just like you always do."

"Wait," Cariad shouted. "Stop. What did you say? Are you talking about Montfort? What does he have to do with this?"

Cherry stopped struggling. With a vicious look she replied, "He's got a mark on his hip too. Did you bring him in for questioning? No. I didn't think so."

CHAPTER THIRTY

Ethan was burning up. His lower leg was grossly swollen and stank. He was so hot he could barely think. He also needed water desperately. He'd sucked up the river water that had lain in a thin layer over the floor and now his prison was bare. He didn't know how much time had passed since his recapture.

The meaning of Quinn's message of *Two more* still eluded him and he was too sick—too near death, he realized—to try to figure it out anymore. His idea of developing a way to communicate with his captors had been stupid. Even if he'd managed to speak to the threads clearly, they would never have let him go. They must be able to see the difficulties he was in, yet they still held on to him. He was only an observation subject to them. They were curious but they held no sympathy toward him whatsoever.

So what was the point of trying to speak with

Quinn? Ethan's efforts only gave the threads more information—information that they might try to use against the colonists.

No. He would not speak to Quinn again. Instead, he would spend his last hours remembering all the good moments in his life, and he would leave one final message in case his recorder was ever found.

Ethan tried to ignore the pain in his leg as he cast his mind back over his life. He recalled his first memories of playing with his friends in his home room, of meeting Lauren at Main Park when they were both kindergartners, of endless boredom at school, learning about Earth and their great purpose in life as Gens of the *Nova Fortuna* Project. He remembered the momentous changes as Arrival Day had approached, like the revival of the first Woken and the lifting of the prohibition on natural reproduction. His great friendship with Dr. Crowley had begun not long afterward.

Then, after Arrival, all the settlers' hopes and anticipation had turned to sourness and despair as the Natural Movement's sabotages tore into the colony and warring factions formed. Ethan wondered how different things might have been if terrorists hadn't dogged the colonization and if the Guardians had never appeared. By now, he would have been tending his farm with Lauren. Perhaps they would be awaiting the arrival of their first child.

Though he'd had misgivings about such a life, from his current perspective it looked blissful.

Still, he'd gotten to know Cariad, and their growing friendship had helped him through the hard times. He turned on his recorder, the only thing remaining to him apart from the clothes he wore.

Ethan recorded an account of his attempt to escape his captivity and went on to explain how he'd found himself back in the chamber. He also described his physical condition. He didn't go into detail about the outcome he expected. That was obvious.

He paused as he wondered what else to say. All of his journey across the continent and the things he'd observed had been recorded. He'd also outlined his experiences in his prison and his attempts to communicate with the threads. What else was left? In the face of his imminent end, it all seemed unimportant. There was only one thing he wanted known to whoever might find his recording: "Tell Cariad I loved her."

CHAPTER THIRTY-ONE

It had taken Cariad some time to figure out what to do about Cherry's revelation. The moment the words had left the Gen's lips, certain facts from the investigation suddenly began to make more sense. When Strongquist had pointed out to Cariad that only someone who had an understanding of the structure of a shuttle could have placed a bomb right next to the fuel tank, she'd suspected the saboteur was a Gen who worked on or in the spacecraft. None of the other Gens were familiar with shuttles—the *Nova Fortuna's* had been mothballed the entire trip. But all the Woken were at least vaguely familiar with standard shuttle structure after flying in them many times on Earth.

And then there was the fact that the saboteurs' bombs were made from chemicals refined out of fertilizer. The process wouldn't have been too hard for a Woken, who were all trained scientists. There was also Rene's odd experience. Cariad had suspected that her friend was being set up, but a high level of expertise would have been required to break into her cabin, sedate her, injure her, and administer a pain killer that would prevent her from noticing the wound until later.

The final damning evidence centered on Montfort's history. He hadn't worked on the *Nova Fortuna* Project. He'd applied to come along as a cryonic revival specialist. Although he wasn't unfriendly, none of the other Woken knew him in the way most of them knew each other after years of working together non-stop.

Cariad's first impulse had been to confront Bob Montfort face to face and ask him if what Cherry reported was true. A physical examination might prove it if the doctor still bore a scar from his injury. But if Montfort really was a Natural Movement follower he might not be the only one, and closing the net around him could prompt a co-conspirator to do something drastic. It made more sense to tread softly. Cariad needed another way to confirm Cherry's words, then the doctor could be watched. Perhaps he might lead them to other saboteurs.

She'd decided in the end to approach Alasdair. She knew the medic pretty well and trusted him. Of course, it was possible that he also belonged to the Natural Movement but she had to take that chance.

Both Montfort and Alasdair had returned to the *Nova Fortuna* after completing their examination of all the colonists for signs of the Natural Movement tattoo, though Alasdair hadn't known that was what they were looking for. And so the next day Cariad took the shuttle up to the ship.

Cherry remained in custody at the Leader's offices, much to her outrage. Cariad hated to confine her but she might tell others what they'd talked about and word might get back to Montfort. The Gen hated the Woken so much Cariad couldn't trust her.

As she sat aboard the shuttle, she went over the plausibility of Cherry's statements. The Gen had said she had a fling with the doctor while he was planetside. That was how she'd seen the mark on him. Knowing Cherry's penchant for older men and no-strings-attached relationships, Cariad thought that part of the farmer's story was entirely plausible.

And if she had slept with Montfort, she would have had the opportunity to see markings on his body that weren't usually visible. After Cariad had questioned her about the abrasion she'd sustained in her fall from the caves, Cherry would have remembered seeing a mark on Montfort.

When Montfort had examined Cariad, it hadn't even occurred to her to ask him if he'd included himself in the process. Every single colonist had to be checked for the Natural Movement tattoo or a sign that one might have been removed. Montfort and Alasdair were no exception. But who had examined them? Before leaving the surface, Cariad had asked the Gen doctors at the settlement hospital, but they couldn't give an answer.

It seemed that if the Woken doctor and his Gen medic had been examined at all, they must have examined each other. So she had to speak to Alasdair.

When Cariad disembarked the shuttle aboard the *Nova Fortuna*, she didn't go directly to the medical center, however. She had no good reason to go there and she didn't want to alert Montfort that she was speaking to Alasdair. He might guess why.

She needed to speak to the medic without Montfort's knowledge. While she tried to figure out how she would do that, she headed to the Fertilization Labs to see how Cassie and Florian were getting along.

"Cariad," Cassie exclaimed as Cariad went inside the lab. "We were wondering when you might be back. What's happening planetside? Do you want to see the fetuses? They're all growing nicely."

"That's great." Cariad sat on a lab stool. "Thanks for holding the fort while I was away. I'm still busy, though. I don't know when I'll be back here full time."

Florian said, "Don't worry about it. Do you want some fake coffee? I was about to make us some."

"Yes, please." Even the *Nova Fortuna's* excuse for coffee was welcome in her current anxious state.

"Is everything okay?" Cassie asked. "We've been getting on with all the work without any problems. I would have comm'd you if we had any issues. You don't have anything to worry about."

"Oh, I'm sure you have, Cassie. You and Florian do a fantastic job. I don't have any concerns on that account. I have bigger problems than that right now."

Florian put a steaming mug in front of her.

"Anything we can help you with?"

Cariad looked at the young Woken properly for the first time. He had an odd look on his face, like he was keeping a secret. Cariad turned to Cassie, who was suppressing a grin. "Is there something I'm missing? Something you want to tell me?"

The two techs laughed and grinned ear to ear. "You tell her, Cassie," Florian said.

"No, you." Cassie nudged him gently with her elbow.

"Okay." Florian cleared his throat, folded his hand in front of him, and said proudly, "Cassie and I are getting married."

"You are?" Cariad strode over to the young couple and enveloped them both in a hug. "I'm so happy for both of you."

"Careful," Florian laughed. "There's someone who's a little fragile at the moment."

"What?" Cariad released the couple and stepped back. "Is one of you sick?" Then she noticed Cassie was blushing. "Oh, stars, are you pregnant?"

Florian put an arm around Cassie and kissed the top of her head. "We are."

"Oh my... " said Cariad. "That's... fast! And amazing. Congratulations. Oh... I think I'm going to cry." And she did. The tears welled up and overflowed like a waterfall spilling down her face. It was as though the happy news had brought all her worry, grief, and anxiety into focus. Though she was trying her best to move on, she missed Ethan dreadfully.

She cried so much, Cassie put an arm around her shoulders. "It's okay, you know. It isn't that amazing. This kind of thing happens all the time."

"Yes," Florian added. "But it turns out creating new life naturally is a lot more fun than doing it in the lab."

Cassie batted him. "Cariad, what's wrong?"

She wiped her eyes. "I can't tell you why, but I need to speak to Alasdair without Dr. Montfort knowing. I'm not sure how to do it. I can't go to the medical center—Montfort would want to know what was wrong with me. And I can't risk comming Alasdair either in case he tells Montfort."

"Huh?" Cassie said. "This is very weird. Are you sure you haven't been eating psychotropic Concordian plants?"

"Believe me," Cariad said, "I'm not deluded. I've never been more serious. When this all comes out, you'll understand."

"Oh well, if you want to talk to Alasdair, that's easy," Cassie said. She lifted the back of her hand to her forehead. "I suddenly feel faint. I think I need immediate medical attention."

"You're a genius, Cassie," Florian said. He lifted his comm button. "Medical center? Cassie isn't feeling great. Could Alasdair pop over to take her blood pressure? I don't think it's anything serious, but it wouldn't hurt to check her over."

"What would I do without you two?" Cariad asked.

Alasdair arrived within minutes carrying his equipment. "What's up, Cassie?" he asked as he came into the lab. "Feeling dizzy?"

"No, I'm fine," Cassie replied. "Cariad wants to talk to you."

"What?"

"And we're leaving work early today," Florian

said.

"Good luck," said Cassie as they went out.

"What's going on?" Alasdair asked, putting his scanner down on the lab bench.

Cariad took a breath. "It's about Montfort. I need to ask you about some things."

"Oh?"

"Yes. Let's sit down." When they were both settled on stools, Cariad continued. "You remember when you and Dr. Montfort had to check everyone for signs of a suspected skin disease?"

"Do I? That took us forever. And then after all that we didn't find anything. Total waste of time."

"Yeah. So I guess you were both checked too?"

"Of course. The doctor nearly forgot but I reminded him. That would be ironic, wouldn't it? If we were suffering from the disease we were checking everyone else for."

"You say Montfort almost forgot to have himself checked?"

"Yes. He's usually very thorough but we were both overworked at the time. Why are you asking me all this? Has the disease broken out after all? You should be talking to the doctor, not me."

"Alasdair, this isn't about the skin disease. It's about Montfort and it's important that he never knows about this conversation. I can't tell you why, but please trust me. Can you do that?"

The young medic frowned but then shrugged. "Okay."

"You said you had to remind Montfort that you should both be checked too. So who checked you?"

"We checked each other. The settlement doctors

were too busy dealing with the patients from the cave disaster. It was a little embarrassing, frankly. But then it was done and we came back to the ship."

"Right. When you examined the doctor, did you see anything unusual?" Cariad didn't want to lead Alasdair by suggesting anything if she could help it. If he remembered seeing something significant without her prompting him, his response would be more reliable. She held her breath.

"No," Alasdair said. "The doctor didn't show any symptoms of a skin disease. At first I thought he might have something—I could see a lesion of some kind on his hip—but he said it was a birthmark."

CHAPTER THIRTY-TWO

"Can you imagine what it must have felt like to learn that the secret to faster-than-light travel had finally been discovered, but that you were still fated to live out your life in this stinking cesspit? That your fellow scientists and engineers were actually planning to build an entire fucking starship but not let anyone travel on it? Can you imagine just how much that would mess with your *mind*?" Steen glared at the camera so fiercely Cariad hoped for a return of Mina, the woman who had calmed him down the previous time he'd worked himself into a rage.

She was in her cabin, spending the quiet shift aboard the *Nova Fortuna* while she tried to figure out what to do about Montfort. It seemed obvious that he belonged to the Natural Movement. It would explain his evasiveness about allowing Alasdair to see his "birthmark," and so many other facts she'd discovered.

What a terrible coincidence it would be if the

very person she'd asked to check the colonists for the Natural Movement tattoo was a member himself. One thing she could be sure about: if she was right, Montfort would not have implicated any co-conspirators in the list of suspects he'd given her. They all had to be innocent—including Cherry. Just as soon as she could, Cariad would have to apologize to the woman and let her go.

.Had Montfort hurt Rene to implicate her because he knew the evidence from the bomb attacks implied that one of the saboteurs was a Woken? If so, he'd made a mistake in picking one of Cariad's close friends, whom she would be least likely to suspect.

Cariad hadn't told anyone else about her suspicions. She was concerned that if Montfort had managed to break through security to enter Rene's cabin, he might also be able to monitor the comm channels. She would have to tell Osias and Aubriot in person. In the meantime, she needed to come up with a way to confirm Montfort's guilt for sure and to catch any co-conspirators too, if possible. But the answer to her problem had eluded her. Tired and confused, Cariad had decided to watch some more of the holo that explained the origin and purpose of the Guardians.

"You know what?" Steen continued. "If those damn digital archaeologists hadn't uncovered the Natural Movement plot, things could have been a lot different. We might have put in all this work for ourselves! How about that? We couldn't have built a colony ship like the legendary, one-and-only, *Nova Fortuna!* But we could have made something else—something that would have allowed us to see a little of the galaxy before we died. It wouldn't have been much but it would have been better than eking out a miserable existence here."

Steen moved closer to the camera until his face almost filled the screen. "When I die, no one's going to remember me. No one writes histories of great scientists anymore. Hell, hardly anyone *writes*. Everything I've discovered, all the work I've done, it will all be forgotten." His face twisted as fury gripped him again. "Do you think anyone else could have uploaded the remnants of human minds into those androids?! Could he have?" He jabbed with a finger to an unseen person. "Or her? Or him? No! It was me." He thrust his finger at his chest. "It was me who finally figured it out. And for what? To protect some people I never met from some other people I never met? So what? What do I care whether you live or die?"

"That's enough," exclaimed a voice from offscreen. Steen turned and Mina came into view. "Stop it, won't you? Just stop."

"Fine," Steen spat. "Finish it yourself." He stalked away, leaving Mina staring after him.

She faced the camera and gave a half smile, partly apologetic, partly embarrassed. "Steen gets a little hot-headed at times." She composed herself for a moment, then said, "He's right. He did upload the androids' minds. We spent years trying to figure out how to do it. We almost gave up. We were going to use artificial intelligence. But you would have spotted that the androids weren't human right away. All the lengths we went to in order to give them that realistic, natural appearance would have gone to waste. You wouldn't ever have allowed them any control in the colony." Mina frowned.

"I hope you don't mind that we did that. We talked about it for such a long time—all the years that we needed to prepare. Everything took so long: first we had to source the materials, then we had to source the machines to manufacture the things we needed to build the ship and all that went into it. You have no idea of the lengths we went to. If you're a revived scientist, you'll know what went into the *Nova Fortuna* Project. Well, we couldn't just comm someone and ask for whatever we needed. Nowadays, comm systems are practically non-existent. Anyway, we did it in the end. But the effort that went into building the *Mistral*, the commitment it took, meant we weren't prepared to take any chances. You see, we sacrificed everything for this. We gave up our own hopes of ever leaving Earth. We had to make sure it was worth it.

"We decided to make the androids seem human so that you would believe them, listen to them, and obey them, if necessary. No offense, but we thought that the Generational Colonists might be quite naive and simple. Six generations of only as much education as was available on the ship and no real life experience? If none of the cryosuspended scientists were successfully revived, the Generational Colonists might be able to survive, but could they defend themselves against terrorist attacks?

"We couldn't take the chance that they might not accept or listen to the androids we were sending to protect them. We had to make them masquerade as humans from a technologically advanced Earth. But please believe me when I tell you they're there to help. They'll deal with anything that threatens the survival of the colony and although their minds are human, they are programmed to give their lives for you. We made it so."

Steen reappeared. "I have more I want to say."

Mina rolled her eyes. "Be my guest. But keep it civil, okay? The people who'll see this haven't done anything to deserve your anger."

Cariad turned off the holo. She could listen to another of Steen's rants when she felt up to enduring it. For that moment, she had more important things to think about. She turned out the light and went to sleep.

***

As she left her cabin the next day, Cariad met Kes, who was coming to see her. Guilt immediately swept Cariad. She'd lost count of the number of comms from him that she'd ignored. She realized that she hadn't seen or spoken to him since meeting him at the xenozoologist lab for the first and only time after he'd been revived.

He held out his arms to her, and she forgot her guilt and awkwardness. They hugged. Cariad relaxed into the hug. She felt like she hadn't been hugged in a long time. When she looked up at her friend, he said, "What's up, Cariad? I know you're busy. We all are. But this isn't like you."

"I'm so sorry, Kes. I should have made time to talk to you sooner. But you have to understand, I was revived two years before you. Things are different for me. It's been a long time since I last

295

saw you and I've been through a lot."

He released her from his grasp. "So you're telling me you've moved on? That your feelings aren't the same as they were back on Earth?" Kes was earnest but spoke gently.

"I guess I am," Cariad replied, her guilt returning in a flash. "That must seem harsh, I know."

"Well, for me it's only been a few weeks since I last saw you," said Kes. "I know we were never really serious—who had time for relationships back then? But I thought that once we were out here, starting a new life, we might try to build on what we had. We never really discussed it, but... "

Cariad winced. "I think I felt the same way, back then."

"But not now?"

"I don't feel the same now, no." Cariad waited for the inevitable question.

"You met someone, right?"

There it was.

When Cariad didn't reply, Kes raised both his hands, palms outward. "Hey, I'm not going to stand in your way. I'm happy for you. Really."

"He died."

"Oh... Whoa. Cariad, I'm so sorry." Kes rubbed his forehead. "And here I've been, hounding you..."

"You couldn't have known. Please don't feel bad."

"Come here." Kes held out his arms and they hugged again. Kes whispered into her ear, "You know I'm here for you, right? Just as a friend."

Cariad nodded, trying not to cry, thinking she didn't deserve him—that she should have explained herself sooner. She sniffed and released her hold on Kes, standing back. "I have a lot to do right now, but when things are calmer, maybe we can meet and I can catch you up on everything that's been happening."

"Vasquez has already told me plenty about what's been going on. I can hardly believe you guys are still going. But I'll look forward to hearing your stories too."

"Okay. By the way, did you find out any more about the thread creatures in the lake?"

"We did. We've been analyzing the scan you performed and we've completed two more of our own. The species is highly intelligent. No doubt about it. We've seen them draw down atmosphere from the surface, presumably to use for processes that require gaseous oxygen. And we've observed the same control of heat that your scan picked up. We haven't attempted to capture a specimen—if the fila are intelligent, that isn't likely to go down well."

"The fila?"

"We named them *Fila cherryensia*. Fila is Latin for threads and we added cherryensia in honor of the first person they tried to catch."

Cariad laughed.

"Does that sound funny? It's standard for naming new species, apart from the catching people part. You must know that."

"I wasn't laughing at the name. I'm not sure how the person you named them after will react, that's all."

"She should be honored. Her name will live on forever now."

"Hopefully all our names will live on forever." Cariad was reminded of Steen's bitter remarks.

"Is something wrong?" Kes asked.

"No, I was just thinking of something."

"I don't want to add to your woes," said Kes, "but another idea occurred to me: the lake is small compared to other bodies of water on the planet. We don't have any reason to suppose that the habitation we discovered is anything more than an unimportant little collection of fila residences, like a village or hamlet. It's more than likely that there are vast fila metropolises in oceans and major rivers."

"Uh, I thought you said you didn't want to add to my woes. Actually, that thought had crossed my mind. I really have to go, Kes. I'll comm you as soon as I can. I promise. And thank you for being so understanding."

"It's no problem. I hope whatever it is that's so urgent is fixed soon."

"Me too," Cariad replied. She left Kes and hurried to the bay, where the *Mistral's* shuttle was awaiting her.

CHAPTER THIRTY-THREE

Garwin was looking better than he had the last time Cariad had seen him, which felt like a long time ago. Though his hair was grayer than ever, he'd filled out a little and had lost his despairing look. Should she speak to Osias about setting him free? It seemed extremely unlikely that he had anything to do with the Natural Movement.

He'd been lying on his bunk reading an interface when Cariad went into his cabin. He put the screen down and sat up. "Cariad. It's good to see you. Sit down."

"How are you doing? You seem better."

"I do feel better, thanks. Cooped up here, I've had plenty of time on my hands to go over everything. You know, it's odd, but I still miss Twyla a lot, though I'm getting a bit more used to the fact that she's gone."

This remark threw Cariad into a moment of confusion. It was hard to reconcile the idea of

Garwin's deep love for his deceased wife with the fact that the woman was a mass murderer. Then there was also Cariad's own grief for Ethan, which was still raw, and—she couldn't help but feel—more justified.

"Don't get me wrong," Garwin said. "I accept what Twyla was and I'll be forever ashamed of what she did, but I miss the image I had of her, if that makes any sense. And the real Twyla... I pity her. All those years she lived with me, she could never be honest or open about what she really thought. She was probably deeply indoctrinated too and hated the life she was forced to live and everything it represented. And then the murders... Maybe she convinced herself that she was doing a favor for all those people she killed. Or maybe not. I've had plenty of time to try to understand it but I still don't and I don't think I ever will. Yet on some level I still miss her, and we can't change our feelings, can we?"

"I guess not," Cariad replied, though she was no closer to understanding Garwin's feelings than he was himself. "It sounds like you've been going over your years with Twyla a lot. But I didn't hear from you so I suppose you didn't remember anything that might help us."

"I'm very sorry but I didn't. The Natural Movement must have been good at covering their tracks. I couldn't think of anything Twyla did apart from what I told you before. She did sometimes disappear but I never questioned her. It didn't seem fair considering the fact that I often did the same."

"Okay. Can you tell me, did she have any

contact with Dr. Montfort?"

"The Woken doctor?" Garwin frowned, then his face brightened. "Yes, I do remember something to do with him, but she only saw him once as far as I can recall. It was before Arrival Day. She told me the doctor had invited all the kindy teachers to a session on first aid. She went along and came back a few hours later. That was it."

"She never saw him again as far as you were aware?"

"No. But like I said, neither of us pried too deeply into the other's business."

Cariad wondered if the first aid session had been the moment Montfort made contact with his co-conspirators for the first time—the kindy teachers who were the most recent iteration of Natural Movement members, last in a line stretching back to Frederick Aparicio. How had the doctor identified them? What pretext had he used to check for their tattoos? Or had he drugged them? How had he felt when he discovered that the cult's plan to seed the *Nova Fortuna* with its filth had succeeded?

"Is Dr. Montfort a Natural Movement follower?" Garwin asked.

"I can't tell you anything about the investigation. I'm sorry."

"I never thought that one of them might be a Woken. That kind of changes things, doesn't it?"

"What do you mean?"

"You can't blame the Gens for everything anymore."

"Oh Garwin, can't you please stop with this stuff? It doesn't help, you know. You're as bad as

Cherry. As long as you keep hating us, it just makes things worse."

"You've seen Cherry recently? How's she doing?"

"She's... " Cariad decided not to tell Garwin about his lover's current situation. It was hardly a defense against his low opinion of the Woken. "She's fine."

Garwin smiled. "Say hi to her from me if you see her again, won't you?"

"I will."

ALERT ALERT. All crew to battle stations. All crew to battle stations.

The announcement had come over the *Mistral's* intercom. Cariad and Garwin stared at each other.

"What's that about?" Cariad asked. "Have the crew been having drills?"

"No. This is the first time I've heard that announcement. Do you think the ship is about to be attacked?"

"I'm going to speak to Addleson." Cariad stood up to leave.

"Wait," Garwin said. "What should I do? I can't just stay here."

"You're going to have to for the moment." Cariad ran out. She felt bad locking Garwin in his cabin when the ship might be under attack but she didn't have time to figure out a better option. She ran through the corridors to the bridge.

Addleson swung around to see her as she went in. The usually relaxed, affable Gen was pale and tense.

"What's going on?" Cariad asked. "Tell me this is just a practice run."

"It is," Addleson replied. "Though it's a much-needed one. Come here and I'll show you the reason."

He was leaning over the console of one of the scanner operators. Cariad joined him and looked at the screen but she couldn't interpret it. All she could see was a mass of lines, dots, and vectors.

Addleson pointed to a dot that didn't look much different from the others. "We've been continuing the Guardians' work of mapping the local starscape. Everything we've found has been a natural astronomical body. Not this. It isn't in orbit around anything. And it isn't a comet."

"That doesn't make it a starship, though," Cariad said.

"The scanner read its composition about ten minutes ago. It's made of a variety of metals—refined metals."

"Oh no."

"And it's a regular shape: a crescent. And then there's also the direction it's moving, which appears to be from the planetary system where the Guardians detected signs of sentient life, and right toward us."

"Damn. How long until it reaches us?"

"That's the other thing. It's traveling incredibly fast. It'll be here in roughly four days, give or take a few hours depending on how quickly it slows down, assuming it *is* us it's heading for. But as the thing's aiming directly at us... " He paused and took a breath. "You get what I mean."

"Four days?" Cariad echoed. "What are you going to do?"

"We only just discovered what we might be

dealing with, but of course I'm going to do whatever I can. We have a good understanding of the *Mistral's* weaponry now, and I'll continue to drill the crew. We'll be prepared by the time the alien ship arrives."

Though Addleson sounded confident, his eyes said to Cariad, *I have no idea what I'm doing here.*

"Perhaps they aren't planning on attacking us," she said.

"That's to be hoped for, but we have to prepare for that scenario."

"Yes." Cariad didn't want to say anything to Addleson in front of his crew, but she knew what he was thinking. He was only someone who had been trained to fly a colony ship. He wasn't military. He'd probably never even fired a gun. If the approaching vessel was hostile, the *Mistral's* pilot was seriously out of his depth. But he was all they had.

CHAPTER THIRTY-FOUR

Water was creeping into Ethan's prison cell. He was thirsty, but he was too weak and ill to turn over to drink it. He was lying on his back, the ever-present, ceiling-wide light shining in his eyes whenever he opened them, which wasn't often. Mostly, he drifted in and out of consciousness, much preferring the times when he wasn't awake, when dreams invaded his mind and he experienced a brief respite from the all-encompassing throb of pain from his leg.

But the water had woken him. It was cold and it was soaking into his shirt and pants and the hair on the back of his head. He vaguely wondered if the threads had finally realized he was dying and they were going to fill the chamber to drown him and put him out of his misery.

Despite everything, he didn't want to die. More than ever, he wanted to return to the settlement and Cariad, but he lacked the strength to fight anymore. His fate had been sealed the moment that he received the cut to his foot, only he hadn't known it then. All his efforts to communicate with the threads and to escape had been a waste of time. Even if he had achieved those things, he would still have died somewhere out in the wilderness, alone, finally succumbing to the infection he'd contracted days previously. Or had it been weeks? He'd lost track of time.

The water continued to seep in, arriving through a gap between the walls and the floor. It was a hair crack, not the wide space through which the threads had forced jets of water to clean out the cell.

Ethan lay still as the water crept up his body. He turned his head to study it. The liquid was slightly murky—river water. Should he sit up? It would only delay the inevitable and he wasn't sure if he was able to.

The light went out.

It was the first time Ethan had been in darkness since the threads had recaptured him after his escape. He was immediately disoriented. The solid black all around seemed to press in on him. His hands splayed out, gripping the floor, seeking reassurance in its firm levelness. Some sense of his orientation returned and his breathing slowed a little.

The water continue to rise. As it covered more of his body he grew colder, though the chill brought a small amount of relief from the pain of his foot. The water crept up over his ears, distorting his hearing. His breathing sounded loud and he also heard a shifting, groaning noise like a large object moving. Was it the sound of his chamber opening to allow the river water in?

Ethan wished the creatures would leave him alone to die in peace.

From somewhere, he found the energy to brace himself against the floor with his hands and push himself slowly upright. The gradual filling of his cell with river water was dreadful. Though it would have been easier to lie still and accept that the end had finally come, brute instinct forced Ethan to fight for a few more minutes of life.

He moved backward, sliding through the rising water, until his back hit a wall. There, slowly and with great difficulty, he managed to eventually rise to his feet. By this time the water was up to his knees. Had he remained lying down it would have covered his face.

Leaning against the wall, balanced on one leg while lifting the other gingerly off the floor, Ethan wondered if he should make one final recording—a last report on what was happening to him. He decided against it. He couldn't imagine that his words would do anything other than horrify whoever listened to them.

In case he changed his mind in his final moments, he lifted the recorder off his neck and tossed it across the chamber. The device thunked against the opposite wall and splashed into the water.

The floor dropped from beneath his feet. Ethan fell into the water, cursing. More of it had flushed suddenly into the chamber and Ethan found himself almost sinking into the new depth. After some moments of struggle when he hit his infected foot against the floor more than once, his grasping hands finally found the wall and his good foot made contact. He could stand upright once more.

Something brushed his leg. The touch was so light Ethan almost thought he imagined it, but his previous encounters with threads that dragged him into the river remained too vivid in his memory. He knew exactly what that touch meant. The thread creatures had come for him. That was why they'd dropped the chamber floor—so they could enter the chamber.

Though he knew the gesture was useless, Ethan reached down and grasped the tendril that was winding around his ankle. He pulled at it, but its grip only tightened. The sensation wasn't painful yet. Ethan wondered what the threads had in mind.

He tugged at the tentacle with two hands, though it was hard to reach it and keep his face out of the water. Another thread arrived, writhing over his arms and hands, and another. They spiraled around and up his leg. They twisted over his arms. He could feel their delicate touch on his waist. There was nothing he could do to stop them.

A lightning bolt of pain shot out from his infected foot. The threads had that too. Agony blinding his mind, Ethan fought. Thinking was impossible. He could only react. Then he was under the water. The threads were all over him. Their probing tips slid across every part of his body.

Ethan's head bobbed above the water. He drew in deep lungfuls of air and yelled out his pain. The threads were drawing tighter around his infected leg. His agony peaked higher. Dimly, he heard himself screaming.

Then he knew no more.

CHAPTER THIRTY-FIVE

Cariad was on her way from the shuttle field to Osias' office when a woman stopped her in the street.

"Is it true?" the woman asked.

"Is what true?" Cariad countered, stalling. She didn't know how much the Leader wanted the colonists to know about the approaching unidentified starship.

"Is it true we're going to be attacked by aliens?" The woman grabbed Cariad's arm. "Are we are all going to die?"

"Please let go of me," said Cariad. "I'm going to speak to the Leader. I'm sure he'll make an announcement soon."

Her face collapsing in despair, the woman released her grip on Cariad. "So it is true. After everything we've been through, it's all going to be for nothing."

She seemed to be speaking to herself rather

than responding to Cariad's words. Cariad left her quickly before she could ask her anything else.

Osias' office was busy with people who wanted answers to similar questions. Clearly, Addleson hadn't managed to prevent the *Mistral's* crew from comming the settlement with the news. Osias had wisely installed a secretary in his outer office and the man was dealing with the agitated, anxious visitors calmly and efficiently, asking them to take a ticket and wait their turn.

When he saw Cariad arrive, however, he waved her over. "You can go straight in."

"Hey," someone protested. "She only just got here. I've been waiting ages."

"She has a prior appointment," said the secretary.

Cariad went through into the inner office, where she found Osias on a live comm. He was speaking to Addleson, who was giving him an update on the data they had on the alien ship. Osias motioned for Cariad to sit down.

"Thanks," he said to Addleson. "As soon as you find out anything else, let me know." He closed the comm, rubbed his face with both hands, and let out a sigh. "Just when I think we're getting back on track, making some progress, something else happens."

"This might not be the disaster everyone's thinking it is," Cariad said. "We don't know for sure that it's a starship. We're in a relatively unexplored region of space. We don't know what's out there. The scanners could be picking up a new type of astronomical object. And if it is some kind of spacecraft, it might not belong to an alien race.

Perhaps it's another ship sent from Earth after the *Mistral*." Cariad was trying to be optimistic, but she knew her suggestions were unlikely to hold weight, especially considering what she'd learned from watching Steen and Mina's holo.

"And if it is an alien craft," Osias said, "maybe they don't want to kill us."

"Exactly."

Osias sighed again. "Yet we have to respond as if we're about to be attacked. We can't wait until we're under bombardment before we take precautions to protect ourselves. That would be foolish."

He was right, of course. "Have you decided what those precautions entail?" Cariad asked.

"No, I haven't. Strangely enough, my experience as a mechanic didn't prepare me for warfare with alien races." Osias' tone was bitter.

It was the first time Cariad had heard him speak in such a way. He was clearly feeling out of his depth and overwhelmed. "Osias, whatever you decide, people will stand behind you. No one is expecting you to work miracles."

"That's lucky, because I happen to be all out of them right now."

"If this ship does attack," Cariad said, "the *Mistral* can provide some defense, but we need to protect the rest of the population as best we can. Though I'm not sure how to go about it. We don't know what weapons might be used against us."

"I'm also not sure what to do about everyone aboard the *Nova Fortuna*," said Osias. "Is it going to be safer for them to remain on the ship or come down to the surface?"

"I don't know. The *Nova Fortuna* is one massive target and it hardly carries any weaponry. It's also very slow to maneuver. I think it might be best to evacuate it. Planetside, we're harder to hit, especially if people are spread out and well hidden."

"That's what I was thinking. The settlement's another prime target. I'll have to move everyone out, but where do I send them? Anywhere outside an electric fence isn't safe after dark."

Cariad's chest tightened. She'd forgotten about the sluglimpets.

The door to Osias' office flew open.

"No, I won't wait," Aubriot yelled at Osias' secretary as he strode into the room.

The secretary was right behind him. "I'm sorry," he said to Osias. "I tried to tell him."

"It's okay." Osias turned to Aubriot. "If you're going to force your way in, the least you can do is close the door."

It was the secretary who closed it, however, while Aubriot walked to Osias' desk and sat down next to Cariad. "One of you is going to tell me what's going on. And no bullshitting. I had enough of that from your bouncer, Osias. What's this alien ship everyone's talking about?"

Osias looked exasperated. "You tell him," he said to Cariad.

"A few hours ago, the *Mistral's* scanners picked up an unidentified object heading directly toward Concordia. From its composition, the object seems to have been manufactured."

"So it *is* an alien ship," said Aubriot.

"Unless it's from Earth," Cariad said, "that

seems to be a valid conclusion."

"Fuck."

"Well put," said Osias.

"What are you going to tell everyone?" Cariad asked the Leader.

"The truth, of course."

"Aren't you worried that people will panic?"

"They'll panic for sure," Osias replied. "It's the only reasonable reaction in the circumstances. They'll panic, then I'll tell them what to do, and then they'll calm down and do it."

Cariad smiled. This sounded more like the pragmatic, resourceful Osias she knew. "Sounds like a good plan."

"Thanks," Osias said. "I just thought of it. Now I only need to work on the details."

"How long till the ship gets here?" asked Aubriot.

Cariad replied, "About four days."

"Bomb shelters," Aubriot announced. "You need to get everyone to dig bomb shelters, but outside the settlement. Go deep enough underground and it won't make a lot of difference what they throw at us."

"That won't work," Cariad said. "Outside the settlement is sluglimpet territory. The only other safe place is the farming district, and the aliens will probably be able to recognize the signs of activity there, too, making it another obvious target."

"Simple," said Aubriot. "Dig tunnels from inside the settlement to bomb shelters outside. The sluglimpets don't burrow, do they?"

"I don't think so," Cariad replied, making a

mental note to ask Kes.

"Then the only way for them into the shelters will be through the settlement. As long as the electric fence holds, everyone will be safe. If the fence goes, they wouldn't have been safe anyway."

It was a brutal way of looking at it but true nonetheless. As Aubriot seemed to have all the answers Cariad asked, "What about the *Nova Fortuna*? Do you think we should evacuate it?"

"It's a bloody sitting duck. Of course we have to evacuate it."

That meant the one hundred and twenty-three fetuses that Cassie and Florian had created would have to be abandoned. If the ship was attacked, any disruption to the sensitive gestation systems could result in their deaths. With no one available to correct imbalances or make repairs, one hundred and twenty-three lives would be lost before they'd even begun. Yet Aubriot was correct. Everyone aboard had to come down to the surface in case the *Nova Fortuna* was attacked.

"Right," Aubriot said. "I'll head up to the *Mistral*."

"Why?" Osias asked. "What are you planning on doing up there?"

"Help with the defense. I reckon I know weapon systems pretty well and I love battle tactics. One of my favorite hobbies."

Aubriot was energized and back on form. Making decisions. Bossing everyone around. Most of the time, it was extremely annoying. For once, Cariad appreciated this side of him. As he went to leave, she said, "Aubriot, wait a second. What do you think about the Guardians? Do you think we should wake them up?"

For the first time since he'd entered the room, Aubriot seemed stumped for an answer. "I don't know about that. Creepy bastards. I didn't have much of a chance to get to know them. I'll leave that one up to you two."

CHAPTER THIRTY-SIX

Florian was being serious for once. His earnest face looked out at Cariad from the interface screen. "No," he said. "No way. I'm not leaving them."

"I know how you feel," Cariad said, "but I wasn't asking you a question. I'm telling you. You and Cassie must evacuate. Get the next shuttle down here. You can stay in someone's spare room until the bomb shelters are built."

"Cariad," Florian replied, "I know you're my boss and you can fire me if you like, but I'm not leaving a hundred and twenty-three babies to fend for themselves while the *Nova Fortuna* is under attack. The ship's massive. It's very unlikely it could be destroyed, but if it receives a hit the gestation systems could go haywire or even shut down. You know as well as I do that all it would take would be one little alteration to the temperature or nutrients or oxygen and that would be it. Someone has to be here to keep the systems working. I'm not having the deaths of over a hundred babies on my hands."

"They aren't babies," Cariad said. "They're... " She thought of the little fetuses inside their gestation sacs. "Okay, they're babies. I know I'm asking a lot, but we can start again. We can replace them. We can't replace you. Please, Florian. Please, come down to the surface where you'll be safer."

"I'm sorry, Cariad."

She paused. The truth was, she would have done exactly the same as her tech if she were in his position. She swallowed. "Okay. I understand. I have a better solution. I'll come up there and take over from you. I don't want you to risk your life. Cassie needs you."

"I'm going to have to say no again," Florian replied. "You're our genetic specialist. The colony needs you more than it needs me."

"And I'm not abandoning Florian anyway," Cassie piped up. Her face squeezed in next to Florian's on Cariad's screen.

"What?" Florian said. "No. You have to go down, Cassie."

"You think I'd leave you to look after these babies all by yourself? If you're staying, so am I. I won't hear another word about it."

Florian looked his future wife in the eyes and turned to Cariad. "I guess that's it, then. Don't worry, Cariad. From what I heard, no one even knows if this thing that's heading for us is actually a starship, let alone if it plans on attacking. It's a lot of panic about nothing if you ask me."

"Exactly," said Cassie. "There's no point in risking the babies' lives on the remote chance of something bad happening. You know the system's so old now it needs regular checks. We can't do that from the surface."

"Besides," Florian said, "someone has to keep Geisen company."

"She's decided to stay too?" Cariad asked.

"Well," replied Floran, "if we are attacked the *Nova Fortuna* will need its pilot, and to be honest I think Geisen sees herself as more like the captain of the ship."

"Great," Cariad said sarcastically, though she could see the sense in the pilot's decision. With no one at the helm, the colony ship really would be the sitting duck Aubriot had stated. "I hope you're right that this is all a false alarm. I couldn't bear it if anything happened to either of you. And so much of our essential equipment is up there. If anything does happen to the ship, the colony's sunk."

"Honestly, nothing's going to happen," Cassie said. "I'm sure of it. By the way, what's going on with Dr. Montfort? The rumor is, two Gens arrived and arrested him. Is that true?"

"Yes, it is. The settlement has two compliance enforcement officers now—"

"We have cops?" interrupted Florian, incredulous.

"Yes, I guess that's what they are," replied Cariad.

"Is this something to do with you wanting to speak to Alasdair without Dr. Montfort knowing about it?" Cassie asked.

"Yes, it is to do with that. I'll tell you both all

about it when I can but we have more pressing issues to deal with at the moment. I can't force you to evacuate, but would you please reconsider your decision to stay on the ship? I don't want to lose those babies either, but you're more important. If the worst happens I'll lose the babies *and* two people I care about very much."

"Awww," Cassie said. "We love you too, Cariad. Don't worry about us. We'll be fine. But you take care down there, won't you? Stay away from those horrible sluglimpets."

"I will." Cariad closed the comm.

She was spending the night in her borrowed bedroom at the Leader's residence, tired and sore after a day spent helping to dig the tunnels and bomb shelters. The speed and efficiency with which the colonists worked had impressed her deeply. When they had a job to do, the Gens were resourceful and relentless, and they had no shortage of the engineering and building skills required for the project. Still, they were going to be hard pushed to complete the underground structures within the timeframe, even though they were only creating nothing more complex than hollowed-out spaces several meters below ground. Cariad sincerely hoped that her techs were right and the enormous effort was unneeded.

Work was going on around the clock and Cariad had eight hours in which to rest and sleep before her next shift began. Yet she knew sleep would not come easily to her. Though she accepted Florian and Cassie's decision she was extremely worried about them. And another concern plagued her. No decision had been made about the Guardians.

Should they wake them up?

In the holo from Earth, Mina had said the androids would protect the colony at all costs, but the Guardians' behavior had shown how dangerously this imperative played out in reality. The Guardians could be ruthless if they thought someone threatened the colony's success. Could they be trusted to only act against alien attackers? What might happen if they thought a colonist made a bad tactical decision during a battle? Would they try to remove that person from the scene of action, and how would they go about doing it?

A major point to consider was the fact that Aubriot was now aboard the *Mistral*. He was working with Addleson to optimize the ship's defensive capabilities. The Guardians had judged Aubriot to be a threat previously, would they come to the same conclusion the second time around?

Cariad realized that she hadn't watched the final part of the holo made by the Guardians' creators. Perhaps that might hold the answer to her dilemma. She had copied her personal files to the settlement's system the last time she'd been planetside, so it was simple to start up the holo at the point where she'd paused it.

Steen appeared above the display unit. Cariad had forgotten that Mina had handed over to him at that point in the holo. The young man seemed to have calmed down somewhat, however. Cariad hoped he would manage to refrain from ranting for this last section of the recording.

"There isn't a lot more to tell you," the young man said, a look of defeat in his eyes. "The specs for the ship and the androids are in the database.

This holo is more about us speaking to you face to face, I guess. We wanted to explain what we'd done and why, just so that you'd understand." He paused and stuck his hands in his pockets. "I have no idea who I'm speaking to right now or even if this holo will ever be played. Maybe we got something wrong and the *Mistral* won't make it to its destination. Or the Natural Movement succeeded in destroying the *Nova Fortuna* en route. Maybe this whole thing is an utter waste of everyone's time. But in case someone does watch this, I want to say, we're both human, right? We have that connection. And that's what our effort has been about. For us, our life's work is over. Once the *Mistral* departs, we'll have to find another reason to exist. It will all be on you. I hope you manage to keep the flame alive. We tried our best to help you.

"Maybe one day, your far-off descendants will manage to reach the same pinnacle of scientific achievement we reached when, under the most adverse of conditions, we built our rescue ship and our rescuers. I hope so. I'll never know, but I hope one day this will all have been worth it."

Steen gazed into the camera. It was like he was in the room looking right at Cariad, though in reality he was probably long dead.

"Good luck," he said.

The holo ended. Steen disappeared and Cariad was alone once more. That was it. She had watched the entire thing, but it had left her with nothing except a feeling of emptiness.

One day, she might have the leisure to ponder Steen and Mina's words. But right then she could only wish that she'd learned something that would tell her if they should reactivate the Guardians.

CHAPTER THIRTY-SEVEN

A man with a thick beard was looking into Ethan's eyes. Ethan sat bolt upright, knocking the man out of the way. Then the pain from his leg hit. He roared. He grabbed his foot but it wasn't there. It was gone. His eyes popping, Ethan found himself staring at a stump that ended half way down his lower leg. His foot had been amputated.

"Wh... Wh...," he gasped. "Stars, where's my foot? Where's my foot? What have they done to me?"

A voice to one side said, "I-I'm sorry. That's how you were when you arrived."

It was the bearded man. He'd scooted away from Ethan and was sitting scrunched up, hugging his legs in the corner of the chamber.

Ethan swung around, taking in his surroundings He was still in the threads' prison. Except he wasn't. This one was smaller, and... Ethan stared. A little girl was standing in the same corner as the man, her back pressed against the wall. She was rigid with fear.

"Sorry," Ethan breathed. "I'm so sorry." He lifted a hand toward the girl but she shrank in response to the gesture. "I won't hurt you. Ahhhh... my leg." Ethan subsided into silence, lost in the aching throb emanating from his severed limb.

The threads had cut off part of his lower leg. That was what why they'd entered his chamber. That was the pain he'd felt before he blacked out. His foot was gone forever. Blinking back tears of agony and shock, Ethan stared at his stump. The skin was pink and tender where it had been pulled over the wound. The edges of the cut were stuck tightly together though he couldn't see what was holding them in place.

"It looks like a good job to me," said the man.

"What?"

"Your operation," the man replied. "If it's any consolation, it looks like they did a good job. I'm sure the pain will ease with time. As it heals."

Ethan could barely comprehend the man's words. Why had the threads cut off his leg? Had they known it was diseased? Had they been trying to save his life?

Who were this man and this girl the threads were also holding prisoner?

"You're Ethan, aren't you?" asked the man. "I recognize you."

Ethan tried to ignore the pain he was suffering. "I am." He studied the man. He looked familiar. Ethan tried to imagine him without his beard.

"You won't know me," the man said. "I'm just a farmer. Name's Rudra. And this is my daughter

Ganika." He pulled the girl into his arms.

"Ganika," Ethan said, grimacing against the pain. "I'm sorry I frightened you."

"Don't worry," said Rudra. "She's a tough little thing. She's been through a lot and she's survived. Haven't you, sweetie?"

The little girl had buried her face in her father's neck. She gave Ethan a shy look then turned away from him again.

As well as Rudra and Ganika, Ethan noticed a third thing in this new chamber. Next to him lay a transparent, hollow, cocoon-shaped object. It had a slit down the center which was open. Ethan touched the strange receptacle. The material it was made from was like jelly but also resistant and smooth.

"That's what you arrived in," Rudra said.

"I was inside this?"

"I got you out a few minutes ago, before you woke up."

Ethan ran a hand along the outer surface of the receptacle. It was wet. He'd traveled through water. The threads had brought him here through waterways to be with the other humans they'd captured.

A realization hit. *Two more.* That was what Quinn had been trying to tell him—the threads had two more people in captivity, like him. Had Quinn been trying to say the threads wanted to take him to the others of his kind?

"I do remember you," Ethan said to Rudra as images from the past popped into his mind. "You were at the farmers' dorms during the first weeks of the settlement."

"That's right. I was there waiting for my allotment and for my wife to join me with Ganika. After that I was too busy working on my farm to see much of other people except my little family."

"How did you and your daughter end up here?" Ethan asked. "What happened to you? Wait. Are we in the lake in the farming district?"

"Yes." Rudra went on to tell Ethan that little Ganika had strayed too close to the lake shore and that the threads had captured her, and then they'd captured him when he'd tried to rescue his daughter.

The effects of his amputation made it hard for Ethan to concentrate, but from what he could understand, Rudra and Ganika had been confined in their chamber for weeks, probably longer than Ethan had himself.

Rudra explained that they'd survived eating raw vegetable roots that the threads had gathered from the fields for them and drinking water that was squirted inside at regular intervals. As had happened with Ethan's chamber, the threads cleaned it by flooding the floor then draining the water away.

"You don't have a transparent wall?" asked Ethan, noticing for the first time that all the walls were opaque.

"No," Rudra replied. "So you were in a cell like this one but yours had a clear wall?"

Now it was Ethan's turn to explain. As he told his story, he reflected that it was a good thing that the threads hadn't elected to reveal themselves to Rudra and his daughter. The little girl would have been utterly terrified.

When Ethan reached that part of his narrative where he'd cut open a wall in his chamber with the Guardians' weapon, Rudra's eyes lit up. "You managed to escape?"

"Yes, but the threads recaptured me immediately. I don't remember how exactly, but I ended up right back where I'd started. My leg had grown so painful by then I was barely aware of what was happening."

"It looks like the creatures solved that problem for you," said Rudra.

Ethan regarded his stump once more. Though it was incredibly painful, Rudra was right. His grotesquely swollen foot and ankle were gone and only healthy flesh remained. His leg had been literally killing him and the threads had prevented it from completing the job.

They'd also apparently transferred him hundreds of kilometers from the river to the lake. How had they managed it?

"How did I get into your cell?" he asked Rudra.

"The floor dropped and you were pushed in. I could see you inside the sack and as soon as the water receded I pulled you out."

Did an underground river or spring flow into the lake? Was that how the threads had brought him there? Ethan hadn't really thought about it but the lake water had to come from somewhere.

"I wonder why they brought me here?" Ethan asked, half to himself.

"I've been wondering that too," Rudra said. "They must want us all together for some reason. Or perhaps it's only for tidiness." He smiled wryly.

"It must have been hard for you," said Ethan,

"to be trapped here for so long with your daughter. How have you managed to carry on?"

"I've certainly had my dark moments. If I'd been alone, I might have tried to find a way to end it. But I couldn't leave Ganika, and I could never bear to hurt her to take her with me. So I carried on because I had to. I didn't have a choice. And with some imagination we've helped the time pass. I made this for Ganika." Rudra pointed at a dried up object that his daughter was holding.

After a moment, Ethan saw that it was a root roughly fashioned into a doll. Ganika crushed the toy to her chest and kissed it, then she walked slowly over to Ethan and held it out to him.

"Thank you." Ethan took the proffered gift. "What's its name?"

"Her name's Rooty," Ganika replied.

"Rooty," said Ethan. "Of course. It's a very good name for a root."

"She isn't a root. She's a little girl, like me."

"Of course. I see that now. Ahhh… " A fresh wave of pain washed over Ethan. He handed back the doll and closed his eyes.

When the pain had subsided and he could open his eyes again, Ganika was back with her father, sitting in his lap and playing with Rooty.

Ethan wondered if the threads intended for him to live out the rest of his days trapped in a small room with another man and his daughter. They clearly wanted to keep him alive for a reason. And they thought the attempt at communication was a failure because they'd placed him in a cell without a transparent wall.

With no possible means of escape, a life of

captivity seemed inevitable. And what would happen when he and Rudra grew old or sick and died? Would Ganika be forced to endure decades by herself, with no memory of another kind of life and other people outside? The future for all of them seemed to tragic to contemplate.

A burst of noise came from somewhere. It was so loud, Ethan clamped his hands to his ears. He looked around, trying to find the source, but none was visible. He caught Rudra's look of shared puzzlement. Ganika started crying.

The noise repeated. It was harsh and not like anything Ethan had ever heard before. Ganika was wailing and stamping her feet. Her father was trying to comfort her while not removing his hands from his ears.

Once more, an identical noise sounded, but this time it was a little quieter. This third iteration also sparked a tingle of familiarity in Ethan's mind. When the fourth repetition sounded it was quieter still, though Ethan still didn't risk removing his hands from his ears.

The fifth burst of noise decreased another notch in volume. Ethan dropped his hands. What was the pattern he was hearing in the sound?

"No," Ganika shouted. She held up her doll to the ceiling. "Rooty says you're very bad!"

On the sixth repetition Ethan heard it, and so did Rudra. Their gazes met, wide with shock.

Rudra said, "Is that—"

Another burst of sound. Except it wasn't sound. It was words. They were so distorted they were almost unrecognizable, but at the same time Ethan thought he could just make them out. Something was saying, "Out. Be careful."

CHAPTER THIRTY-EIGHT

Montfort's eyes were hooded and he didn't return Cariad's look as he was escorted toward her in the bunker. She saw that Mariko and Arden had finally found a justified use for their handcuffs.

Osias had given the order to construct a small cell within the shelter to hold the doctor. The man's guilt hadn't been clearly established but Osias had wanted to confine him until after the crisis of the arrival of the alien ship had passed.

But judging from the way that Montfort wouldn't meet Cariad's gaze, he was guilty as hell. She could hardly believe that this sullen, angry man and the doctor she'd worked with in reviving the cryonically suspended colonists, and who had helped her recover from her broken arm after the stadium bombing, were one and the same person.

Cariad walked into the comm room, which lay opposite the cell where Montfort was to be confined. The compliance enforcement officers put the doctor into the cell and locked the door. Cariad was relieved that she seemed to have uncovered at least one genuine Natural Movement terrorist and that Cherry had been set free as soon as Montfort had been arrested.

The bomb shelter consisted of a series of rooms, each of which held around forty people. The rooms were linked by tunnels that led from a main tunnel running down from an entrance within the electric fence of the settlement. Some Gen engineers had wanted to build more than one entrance, arguing that if it was destroyed, the entire population would be trapped.

But there had simply been no time. Instead, the Gens had stored digging equipment below ground so that they could dig their way out if their exit was blocked off. That would mean emerging into sluglimpet territory, but that couldn't be helped. They would just have to avoid going out there at nighttime. Unfortunately, the alien ship was due to arrive that night.

The shelter rooms were stocked with food and water and lidded buckets for sanitation. It was the best that could be done in the time available. The engineers had prioritized reducing the risk of collapse and installing fans to supply air from the surface, though they could be shut down if the atmosphere outside grew too hot. Everything else was secondary. A simple comm system running on wires connected the bunkers to the surface and then to the *Mistral* and the *Nova Fortuna*.

Montfort's cell was the only room that had a door. It was a simple one made of bars of plastiwood. Cariad could see the doctor from where she sat in the comm room in front of interfaces displaying live feeds from the settlement and the ships. Mariko stood guard outside the cell.

The doctor was slumped on the floor, his head on his knees. He didn't look like he intended to try to escape. After all, where could he go? Reaching the surface and leaving the settlement wouldn't help him. Even if the approaching aliens didn't attack, he couldn't survive by himself out there.

Cariad returned her attention to the interfaces. There wasn't a lot to see on the screen that showed the settlement. The streets were empty and the streetlights had been turned off so all that was visible were black, shadowy outlines of buildings against a brilliantly starry sky.

The bridge of the *Mistral* was a total contrast. It was busy with intense activity and loud with shouts detailing data on the alien ship and orders given by Addleson. The pilot seemed to have risen to the challenge of orchestrating his ship's response to the potential threat. Aubriot sat at a console that Cariad assumed controlled the *Mistral's* weapons. She didn't doubt that the financier had also bent Addleson's ear with advice on battle tactics.

Another interface displayed the exterior of the *Mistral*. Concordia hung below the starship a dark globe. To one side of the screen the *Nova Fortuna* could be seen, its spindle encircled by the massive wheel that had been Cariad's home, suspended and awake, for nearly two centuries.

Cariad thought of Cassie and Florian aboard the nearly empty ship, faithfully caring for the tiny lives that were in their hands. The *Nova Fortuna's* feed didn't show her techs. It only showed Geisen in her pilot's cabin, alone and tense as she prepared for whatever might happen.

Cariad typed a message to Addleson asking for an update. She didn't want to distract him by requesting a live comm. He answered immediately, however: "Cariad. Is Osias there?"

"No, he's still outside with the engineers. They wanted to make some final adjustments to the entrance doors. What's happening up there?"

"Bad news, we think. The ship's approaching much faster than we thought it would. We added more time for braking to the calculations than it apparently needs. Of course, that could mean that it doesn't intend to stop when it reaches us, but that doesn't seem likely. Its course hasn't altered."

"It's still on course for Concordia?"

"Yes. It's on a collision course with the *Mistral,* in fact. They seem to know we're more dangerous than the *Nova Fortuna*." The man's face was tense with worry.

"What's the ETA now?"

"Anything between an hour and ten minutes."

"Ten minutes!"

"Yes. The speed that ship's approaching, it doesn't look like it intends to pay us a friendly visit. You guys better seal yourselves in."

Cariad cursed. She comm'd Osias.

"Yes?"

"Addleson said they underestimated the arrival time of the ship. It could be here any minute. You need to get inside. Now."

"Okay. Got it."

Cariad comm'd Cassie next. "You two get into your crash seats, okay?" Cariad had insisted that the seats were to be installed in the reproduction section.

"But it isn't time yet," Cassie replied.

"Yes it is. Do it now. Please."

"Okay. I'll tell Florian. Take care down there."

"We will."

Cariad's skin prickled. She looked over to Bob Montfort's cell and found that he was staring at her. He had a weird, crazy look in his eyes.

"Your judgment is finally coming," he said. "We told you what you were doing was wrong but you wouldn't believe us. You puffed yourself up on the pride of your achievements. Your arrogance blinded you to the truth. You refused to bow down and now you're all going to pay. All your efforts, all your schemes, all your labor and suffering will come to *nothing*." He spat the final word, a look of triumph spreading over his features.

Cariad had no time to respond to Montfort's manic nonsense. She tore her gaze from him and went out into the tunnel, intending to run down to the main entrance and make sure Osias was in and the doors were sealed.

It was as she was running that the first attack came.

Though she was deep underground, the shock of the impact on the surface made her stumble and fall. The slim hope she'd carried in her heart that they were in no danger was snuffed out. She got to her feet and continued to run. But then shouts and the sounds of a scuffle came down the tunnel from behind her.

Still running, Cariad glanced over her shoulder. Mariko struggling with a man outside Montfort's cell. It was a Gen but Cariad didn't recognize him. She couldn't figure out what he was trying to do at first, then she realized he was trying to help Montfort escape. He had to be a co-conspirator.

Cariad began to run back to help Mariko, but another impact struck. Once more, she ended up on her hands and knees. She lifted her head to see Mariko knocked to the ground. The man had the keys to Montfort's cell door. He was opening it. Montfort emerged. What were they planning to do? And how could Cariad stop them?

She raced toward the two men, who were heading her way. "Stop! Stop them! Somebody help. Montfort's escaped." Mariko was lying insensible on the tunnel floor. Montfort and his rescuer were bearing down on Cariad, showing no sign of slowing.

They were upon her. She braced for impact but the two men only ran past her and away up the tunnel toward the entrance.

Cariad followed, speeding up to try to catch them. What were they going to do? They couldn't achieve anything while the settlement was under bombardment. Were they going to try to keep the entrance doors open, endangering everyone sheltering in the bunker?

An icy hand clutched Cariad's heart. Had Montfort's co-conspirator rigged something to blow up the shelter? Nearly every single man, woman, and child was present in the place, including most of the people who were usually aboard the *Nova Fortuna*. Even the last of the Woken to be revived were down there, including Kes. If there was ever a time to inflict the worst damage possible to the colony, this was it.

Fear spurred Cariad on. She had to catch Montfort and the other Natural Movement saboteur and stop them. She was nearly at the entrance. The engineers who had been putting the final touches to the entrance doors appeared in her view ahead, walking toward her. Montfort and his rescuer were there too. They blasted through the small group of men and women, causing cries of exclamation and anger.

"Stop them," Cariad shouted. "They're Natural Movement terrorists."

At her words, the engineers turned, but Montfort and the other man were already gone, racing down the final section of tunnel. As Cariad caught up to the group one of them said, "We have to stop them opening the doors."

A third impact above reverberated from above. Cariad's mind flew to Addleson and the rest of the crew of the *Mistral*, who had to be engaged in battle with the aliens. She continued running toward the entrance. A second later she reached it. The doors were wide open. The sky was no longer starry—it was lit with a red glow. She ran up the stairs, the engineers following her close behind. Where was Osias?

Blinding light flared. A hiss came from above and a split second later another impact struck. Debris showered down the stairs.

"Osias," Cariad yelled. Where was the man? And what had happened to Montfort and the other terrorist?

She reached the top of the stairs and gasped at the sight that greeted her. The settlement was on fire, flames and smoke reaching high into the night sky. Silhouetted against the backdrop were the figures of two men: Montfort and his Gen rescuer. They had their arms raised high as if in supplication to the attacking alien ship. They were shouting something but the roar of the flames drowned out their voices. They got down on their knees and bowed their heads to the ground before raising their arms again. Insanely, they were welcoming the aliens' attack.

Then Cariad saw Osias. He was off to one side, calling out to the men. He was beckoning them, seemingly trying to get them to come inside the shelter.

"Osias," Cariad yelled again, straining her voice in her effort to be heard. "Osias, leave them! You have to come in now. We have to close the doors."

A great rending sound rose above the noise of the fire. The side of a burning building was collapsing. Horror freezing her, Cariad saw Osias try to run out of the way, but he was too late. He disappeared under the remains of the wall.

"Come inside," shouted an engineer, grabbing Cariad's arm. He pulled her down the stairs.

There was another flash followed by a hiss and a boom. The world turned silent. Cariad could see the engineers shouting but she couldn't hear what they were saying. She was fighting to return to the top of the stairs, but they were forcing her down.

"Osias," she said, though her voice was dim and distant.

Someone was shaking his head at her. Above, the doors closed, shutting out the fiery sky.

CHAPTER THIRTY-NINE

Numb at the loss of Osias, Cariad sat in the comm room in the bunker watching the live feed from the battle raging overhead. The *Mistral* was engaged in a fire fight with the alien ship. She could see the intense activity on the bridge and also the incoming fire from space. The crescent of the aliens' ship was too distant to see on the visual but the *Mistral's* crew could clearly pinpoint it with their scanners.

Aubriot was leading the defense and seemed to have taken over from Addleson in that capacity. From what Cariad could tell, the pilot was doing his best to maneuver the ship to the most advantageous position to mitigate the aliens' attack on the settlement.

Cariad hated to think what the current bombardment would have been like without the *Mistral* to defend them. The bunker would probably be a hot, molten ruin if it weren't for the Guardians' ship. As it was, the situation was just about under control in the shelter, despite the devastating death of Osias. The colonists were staying calm and keeping the young children occupied to try to distract them from the regular reverberations of attacks that had avoided the *Mistral's* defense.

Cariad's comm chirped. It was Florian.

"How's everything going down there?" he asked.

"We lost Osias," Cariad replied.

"Oh, no!"

"And Bob Montfort ran outside with another man—I guess it was another Natural Movement follower—they must both be dead by now too."

"They ran outside?!"

"I think they wanted to welcome the aliens, or something like that. They were both behaving like maniacs. They seemed to be welcoming the aliens like they were avenging angels, turned up to punish us for building the colony. Osias was killed while he was trying to make them come inside."

"Shit," Florian said. "That's terrible."

"What's happening up there?" Cariad asked "Are you and Cassie okay?"

"We're fine. No attacks on the *Nova Fortuna* yet. It looks like the aliens are more interested in destroying the settlement."

"Well, they're certainly succeeding at that." A dull boom echoed and the floor shook. "I got a look at the damage when the bombardment started. I doubt there's going to be anything left of the place."

"All that work gone to waste," said Florian.

"It's okay. We can rebuild. There are still plenty of materials and equipment aboard the *Nova Fortuna*. We can improvise. What's most important is that we don't lose anyone else."

"Perhaps the *Mistral* can persuade the aliens to retreat, or blast them out of the sky."

"I hope so." Cariad didn't say any more, but she had a feeling that the battle was only a skirmish. The aliens had only sent one ship. If they really wanted to erase the human colonization they would definitely send more. "How are the gestation systems holding up?"

"The babies are all fine," Florian said, "so you don't need to worry on that account."

"That's good to hear."

Raised voices on the bridge of the *Mistral* distracted Cariad from her talk with Florian. The crew were cursing and yelling and Addleson was making fast adjustments to the ship's controls. It took Cariad a moment to figure out what was going on, but when she did her heart rose into her throat. "Florian, I think the alien ship's altered course. It's heading for the *Nova Fortuna*."

Florian's pleasant expression turned grim. "Okay, I have to go and get Cassie to a crash seat. Don't worry. We're ready."

"Please take care," said Cariad.

"You too." Florian closed the comm.

Cariad put her head in her hands. After Ethan's and Osias' deaths, she couldn't bear it if she lost her lovely techs too. Hardly daring to look, she lifted her eyes to stare at the battle unfolding on the screens in front of her.

On the external visual from the *Mistral*, the

Nova Fortuna came into view as Addleson brought his ship around. The massive colony ship looked tiny in the distance, suspended above Concordia's globe. Cariad imagined the empty corridors and silent rooms. The only living beings on the ship that had sustained thousands over the duration of its long voyage were Geisen in her pilot's cabin, Cassie and Florian monitoring the gestation systems, and the one hundred and twenty-three tiny babies in their sacs.

Why were the aliens targeting the colony? Why couldn't they leave them alone? They weren't doing any harm. Or were they? Cariad recalled the intelligent thread creatures in the lake—the fila as Kes had called them. Was this attack something to do with Concordia's sentient species? Had the fila contacted a distant arm of their kind and summoned them to drive the humans off the planet?

A bolt flashed across the screen coming from somewhere beyond the *Mistral*. It hit the *Nova Fortuna's* wheel and splashed fire that dissipated into space. It was impossible to tell what part of the ship had been hit.

Cariad comm'd Florian. When there was no reply she tried Cassie.

"Yes?"

"Are you okay?" Cariad asked. "Have you been hurt? I saw the ship take a hit."

"We felt it but we're okay. Florian's giving the systems a final check before he straps in."

Another bright orb lit Cariad's screen and smashed into the *Nova Fortuna*. This attack hit the spindle. Cariad sucked in a breath. The ship's engines were in the spindle.

"Cassie!"

"I'm here."

"If the situation gets too bad, leave the ship. Geisen can fly you out on one of the shuttles. There won't be anything you can do for the babies but you'll have a chance to save yourselves."

"Okay."

"Promise me."

"I promise."

A third bolt of light sailed past the *Mistral* in a flash. The ship tried to shoot it down but failed and it scored another hit on the colony ship's spindle. The effect of this impact on the *Nova Fortuna* was noticeable. The ship's attitude altered and Cariad thought she detected its spin slowing down. Losing artificial gravity wouldn't be a big problem for her techs or their charges, but the ship couldn't withstand this continued attack. What was happening on the *Mistral*? Why couldn't they defend the colony ship?

The *Nova Fortuna* was growing larger as the Guardians' ship drew closer to it. Was the *Mistral* trying to position itself between the colony ship and its attacker?

Cariad listened in on the talk on the bridge of the *Mistral*.

"We're in a bad position," Aubriot was saying. "Every time I try to deflect their fire I risk hitting our ship. The margins are too narrow."

"I'll alter our approach," Addleson replied. "Give you some leeway."

Another bolt hit the *Nova Fortuna*. This time the effect was unmistakable. The wheel was noticeably slowing.

Cariad comm'd Cassie, and then Florian, but there was no answer. She tested the line and found that it was dead. The attack on the ship had taken out the comm system.

"She's lost an engine," said someone on the *Mistral's* bridge.

Aubriot cursed. "We're doing this wrong. Turn the *Mistral* around. We're going after that ship."

More bolts were impacting the *Nova Fortuna*.

Someone exclaimed, "Another engine's gone."

Cariad hoped that Cassie, Florian, and Geisen were doing the sensible thing and abandoning the ship.

The view from the *Mistral's* perspective was changing. First the planet surface came into view and then open space. The crew seemed to have decided to abandon their defense of the settlement and the *Nova Fortuna* in favor of a direct assault on the attacking ship.

As the *Mistral* drew around, another view of the *Nova Fortuna* appeared in the edge of the screen. Had it altered position? Had it dropped a little lower toward the planet surface? With two of its engines down, the *Nova Fortuna* would lose velocity and would not stay in orbit. Concordia's gravity would drag it in.

If the *Nova Fortuna* fell to the planet surface it would be a disaster, and not only for whoever remained aboard the ship.

"What's happening?" said a voice at the door to the control room. Cherry stood there, leaning on the jamb. "Nothing's hit us for a while. Is the bombardment over?"

"I don't know exactly," Cariad replied. She explained what she'd seen. "I think the *Mistral* was deflecting the assault on the settlement, then it was trying to defend the *Nova Fortuna*, but now they're trying to take out the alien ship."

"So what's happened to the *Nova Fortuna*? Has it been destroyed?"

"No, but it's damaged. I'm not sure it can stay in orbit."

"Oh no." Cherry came into the control room, her animosity toward Cariad momentarily forgotten in her desire to understand what was happening. She sat down next to Cariad and watched the screens.

Far above, the *Mistral* was growing more distant from the *Nova Fortuna*, though the colony ship remained visible at the edge of one screen. Aubriot was letting go with all weapons forward, streaks of light streaming into the darkness of space. Still, the alien ship didn't show up on the visuals. It was like they were firing at an invisible, malevolent ghost.

Suddenly, the bridge of the *Mistral* erupted in whoops and cheers.

"Yes," Aubriot exclaimed. He leapt from his seat and collected high fives around the room. The *Mistral's* crew hugged and punched the air.

It seemed a safe time to contact Addleson. Unlike the rest of the crew on the bridge, he wasn't elated. He looked serious and sad, bent over his controls.

"What's happened?" Cariad asked.

"Bastards turned tail," Addleson replied. "They ran. I wish we could go after them and finish them off, but their ship's about ten times as fast as the

Mistral."

"Thank the stars," Cariad said. "Do you think they'll be back?"

"Probably not for a while. Aubriot got some good hits in. I think that's why they chickened out. They'll have to make repairs. Or maybe wait for the rest of the fleet."

Cariad clenched her jaw. "That's what I was thinking." Though the colonists seemed to have beaten off the aliens, she doubted that was the last they would see of them.

"Do you have comm with the *Nova Fortuna*?" Cariad asked.

"Nope," Addleson replied. "It's been dead for a while." Then he said, "Holy shit!"

"What?"

"She's dropping out of orbit!"

"I thought she might be," Cariad replied. "I was hoping I was wrong."

"No, unfortunately."

"Are your scanners picking up anything on a shuttle leaving?"

After a pause, Addleson replied. "No. Geisen should abandon ship soon though. A couple more people are still aboard too, right?"

"Yes. My techs."

"Don't worry. I'm sure she'll get them away. More importantly, what's going to happen when the ship hits?"

"I'm trying not to think about it," said Cariad. Billions of tons of starship impacting the surface of Concordia would be sure to wreak utter devastation.

"Better keep everyone down there in the shelter

for now," said Addleson.

"Yes. It isn't like there's anything left for us to return to anyway. Is your system giving an estimate of the time of the impact?"

Addleson checked. "The remaining engines are working to slow the fall. I guess that's Geisen's doing. Hopefully she'll put the ship on auto and evacuate soon. Uhhh... The ship's going to hit in about six hours."

"Where?"

"The ocean to the east of you," Addleson said.

Cherry asked, "That's better than it hitting land, isn't it?"

***

As each minute leading to the crash of the *Nova Fortuna* passed, more and more of the sheltering colonists were drawn to the control room. They crowded inside and leaned in at the door. The *Mistral* had its scanners and cameras trained on the colony ship, tracking its smooth descent.

No shuttle had launched. The generally accepted reason was that the alien attack must have damaged the shuttle bay. Whether that was true didn't really matter. There was clearly an insurmountable problem preventing Geisen, Florian, and Cassie from abandoning ship. The comm lines were dead, so no one would ever know.

Cariad was trying not to imagine her techs spending their final hours together, knowing their inevitable fate. She wished with all her heart she'd fought harder to persuade them to come down to the planet and shelter in the bunker with everyone else. Or that she'd convinced them to change places with her.

Kes had joined her in the room and had his arm around her shoulders.

On the visual from the Mistral, the sun was dancing at the edge of the horizon. Morning would be arriving at the settlement soon, and along with it would come the after-effects of the impact of the *Nova Fortuna*.

Addleson comm'd Cariad. When she answered he said, "I need to speak to you in private."

Cariad pushed out of the comm room, through the crowd of people staring, zombie-like, at the screens. When she told Addleson he could speak freely he said, "I asked the *Mistral's* computer to calculate the repercussion of the *Nova Fortuna's* impact. You need to get everyone out of the shelter immediately. Though the ship will hit hundreds of kilometers away, the tsunami will be so massive it's going to reach as far inland as where you are."

Cariad cursed. "But what can we do? We can't climb on roofs. The settlement's razed."

"I don't know. But if everyone stays there you'll all drown. You have to get them out and on to the highest ground you can. You only have a couple of hours at most."

"Okay." Cariad closed the comm. They had already lost everything above ground and they were about to lose everything aboard the *Nova Fortuna* too. Would the onslaughts against the colony never cease?

CHAPTER FORTY

"Out. Be careful. Out. Be careful." The voice had droned on for what seemed like hours. It was driving Ethan insane. Ganika was sitting hunched up, her hands over her ears, rocking. Her father was doing his best to comfort her, but the strain of hearing the constant repetitions of the voice was showing on his face.

At first, Ethan had entertained a wild hope that the threads were about to set them free. What else could they mean by *Out*? But no means of leaving the chamber had materialized and the word had turned into a cruel taunt. *Out* was the one thing they wanted more than anything yet they would never achieve it. What the threads meant by *Be careful*, Ethan had no idea. Imprisoned as they were, they had no option about being careful or careless.

The only upside to the previous few hours was

that the pain from Ethan's severed limb had lessened somewhat. Either that or he'd become more accustomed to it. Whatever the cause, he found he was now able to think straighter than he had when he'd first returned to consciousness in the cell.

Over the sound of the threads' endless message, he and Rudra had managed several conversations. Ethan had told Rudra more about his experiences outside the settlement and in the threads' chamber under the river, and Rudra had spoken about colony life up until the point that he and Ganika had been captured.

The latter wasn't particularly informative for Ethan. It turned out that Rudra and his daughter had been dragged into the lake not long after Ethan had left on his expedition. All he discovered was that Cherry had been conscientiously managing both his farm and her own, and that Cariad was spending time at the settlement conducting some sort of assessment on the progress of the colonization. That had struck Ethan as rather odd considering the amount of work she already had on her hands restocking the gene pool.

When he could block out the drone of *Out. Be Careful*, Ethan thought a lot about Cariad. It was both heartening and heart-breaking to know that she was so near at hand and yet utterly unreachable. She probably thought he was hundreds of kilometers away, cataloging Concordia's life forms and assessing their potential danger to the colony.

Maybe she was wondering when he would return. Eventually, she might begin to worry that he'd been gone so long. Finally, perhaps years in the future, she would give up hope and accept that he was dead. Only he might still be trapped in a chamber in a lake only kilometers away and she would never know.

"It has to stop some time," Rudra said hopefully, over the droning voice. "There's no point in them continuing to harass us with this sound."

Ethan replied, "I don't think we can begin to guess why the threads do something, or whether they have any point. They aren't from Earth. Who knows what they think?"

"Maybe. I just wish they were trying to speak to us."

"I thought I made some progress with communicating with them," said Ethan, "but after days of work we'd only managed to exchange a few words and even then I wasn't sure that Quinn understood me."

"Quinn?"

"That was what I called the creature that I was communicating with. Giving it a name made the process easier."

Rudra said, "I guess they've been trying something different with me and Ganika. I must have said those words thousands of times since we were captured. I've talked a lot about getting out and I'm always telling her to be careful. The threads must have built something that replicates human speech and now they're observing how we react."

"Yes," Ethan agreed. "I don't know what's the best response to it. Maybe the threads don't understand that we don't communicate by endlessly repeating the same words. From what I've seen of them, they're constantly in motion. Perhaps this sound we're hearing is the equivalent of their communication style, except in human speech."

"Whatever the hell it is, I wish it would stop," Rudra said.

And it did.

The silence pressed in on Ethan's ears as he and Rudra stared at each other in surprise. Before they could say anything, however, the floor jerked. Ethan placed his hands on it, expecting it to drop and water to flood the cell. But when the floor jerked again, it moved upward.

"Daddy?" Ganika clambered to her feet and threw her arms around her father's neck.

A grinding, groaning sound came from all around and the floor began to rise steadily. The walls diminished in height as they slipped below the rising surface. Ethan looked up at the glowing ceiling, which was drawing rapidly closer.

If the floor didn't stop rising, he, Rudra, and Ganika would be crushed against it.

"Daddy," Ganika repeated insistently, as if expecting her father to do something to make the scary sensation stop. But Rudra could only grip his daughter tightly, fear written all over his face.

What could be done? The rise of the floor was relentless.

Ethan stood up awkwardly, balancing on his intact leg, leaning against the wall. The ceiling was just above his head. He reached up and prepared to brace himself against it. Rudra saw what he was doing and followed suit. Perhaps, between both of them, they could halt the progress of the rising floor. Ganika grabbed her father's leg and wailed.

The floor pushed Ethan's head against the ceiling. His effort was having no effect. His head was forced down and his shoulder took its place. Rudra was grunting with effort as he too buckled under the pressure of the floor.

Ethan was forced to his knees. His stump complained loudly.

"Ethan," Rudra said, grimacing. "It's been good knowing you."

Before Ethan could reply, the floor stopped.

The two men and small girl were in a space only about a meter tall. The warm, glowing ceiling and smooth floor were the new boundaries of their world. Depriving them of space as well as everything else in their lives seemed a particularly cruel joke.

"Well," said Rudra, "at least we aren't dead."

A clunk sounded. Lines defining a square appeared in the ceiling. The square lifted up and away.

Daylight shone in.

Shock froze Ethan for a moment. Rudra was similarly affected. Ganika crawled toward the hole.

"Quick," Ethan exclaimed. "Get out. Get out. I think they're setting us free."

Rudra scooted over to the square space, grabbing Ganika under one arm along the way.

"Thank the stars," he shouted. "Sunlight! I can see sunlight." He stood up, lifting his daughter with him.

Ethan watched Rudra's legs as the man climbed out of the hole. As Ethan followed, he squinted hard against the brightness of the light, even though the sun was only just rising. The first thing he noticed was a fresh breeze, blowing the sweat from his body.

"Ethan," Rudra shouted. "This way." He was walking over the roof of the chamber, holding Ganika's hand. The chamber was close to the lake shore and soon the man and his daughter were splashing and scrambling through the waves.

Ethan's eyesight had been confined to small spaces for so long, it took him a moment to take in his surroundings. As he climbed out of the chamber he noticed an electric fence stood all around the shoreline. That hadn't been there before. A familiar farmhouse stood not far away. His own. Or it had been his. Perhaps someone else lived there now.

"Quickly," Rudra shouted. "Let's get out of here. Before they change their minds." He was over at the fence.

Ethan crawled over the roof of the chamber and into the shallow water that lay between it and the shore. He half-crawled, half hopped through the waves. When he reached the lake's edge, he turned back to look at the rectangular roof of the threads' prison, half expecting one or more of the creatures to rise from the lake. A wild joy took hold of him, almost a madness. He had a vision of Quinn's tentacle lifting out of the water and waving goodbye.

Finding himself unable to hop in sand, Ethan set off crawling to join Rudra and Ganika at the fence. Rudra was trying to lift the bottom of it to give Ganika space to crawl through but when he saw

Ethan's progress he abandoned his effort and ran back to him. He helped him rise to his feet and supported him as they returned to the wire boundary.

"Hey," Ethan shouted, his hands cupping his mouth. "Hey!" He thought his voice would be heard at his old farmhouse but after several more attempts to announce their presence, no one replied. Perhaps the house was empty after all.

Both men exerted their all their strength trying to lift the bottom of the fence, but it had been secured in place with heavy staples, driven deep into the ground.

"They must have done this to prevent other children from going under it like Ganika did," said Rudra.

They tried some more, but neither of the men could loosen the staples with their bare hands.

"It's no good," said Ethan. "We'll have to climb over."

"Can you manage?" Rudra asked.

"I'm going to have to. Can you carry Ganika?"

"She can hold on like a monkey, can't you?" Rudra asked his daughter.

"Yes, Daddy," Ganika exclaimed. She was still clutching Rooty to her chest.

Ethan wondered if she would keep the toy and if, in the years to come, she would remember her weeks of confinement.

They set about scaling the fence. It wasn't easy for Ethan to do with only one foot but his arms helped to compensate for his missing appendage. As he reached the top, he saw a wide view of the farming district. It struck him as odd that, among the fields and farmsteads dotted among them, no one was about. Though the hour was early, farmers usually began their working days soon after the sun rose.

Out, the threads had said. Their captives were now "out." But what had the creatures meant by, *Be careful*?

CHAPTER FORTY-ONE

Cariad was one of the last to leave the bunker. Cherry and other colonists had organized the evacuation of the shelter and were helping everyone find the highest ground available before the tsunami hit. Addleson had sent down both of the *Mistral's* shuttles to collect as many children, elders, and sick or injured as possible. Both shuttles had departed crammed, but there was no time for them to make a return trip. All the settlers who remained planetside would have to do the best they could to survive the tsunami when it arrived.

A view on a screen of the slowly falling *Nova Fortuna* occupied Cariad's attention. She couldn't stop wondering what was going through her techs' and Geisen's minds as they awaited their fate, trapped aboard the ship. She imagined they were probably together somewhere, comforting each other, trying to stay strong to the end.

She wished she had a final chance to say goodbye and tell them how much they meant to her. On the other hand, if the comm channel was open, seeing them and not being able to help them would be almost unbearable.

Addleson had told her the *Mistral's* computer calculated the tsunami would reach the settlement about forty minutes after the colony ship impacted the ocean. She knew she should leave and try to find somewhere out of the reach of the tsunami, but she couldn't seem to tear herself away from the screen.

The true size of the *Nova Fortuna* became more apparent as it neared the planet surface. In all the years that she'd worked on the colonization project on Earth, of all the possible scenarios for how the project might unfold, Cariad had never once imagined that the ship would meet its end by crashing into the destination planet. The ship's wheel had entirely ceased turning, but the *Nova Fortuna's* last three passengers would already be feeling the gravity of Concordia pulling them to its core.

The portion of the planet *Nova Fortuna* was passing over was in daylight, and the ship's battle scars were easy to see. Scorch marks were scored across large swathes of its skin and in places the metal was buckled and torn. It wasn't hard to imagine that the shuttle bay had sustained such heavy damage that evacuating in one of the vessels was impossible.

"Cariad! What are you doing still here?" Cherry was standing in the control room entrance as she had only hours before, though it felt like days ago to Cariad.

"I... " In truth, Cariad didn't know why she was still there.

Cherry didn't wait for an answer. "Come with me, quickly. Unless you want to drown? I've tried it and, believe me, it sucks." She walked into the room and took Cariad's hand. "Come on. I don't know what's gotten into you."

Cariad stood mechanically, feeling like a child. As Cherry led her from the room, she took a final look over her shoulder at the screen. The *Nova Fortuna* was dropping at speed toward the ocean. She hit. A massive wave arose. Then Cariad left and saw no more.

***

The churning, roiling tsunami approached, its surface thick with displaced vegetation. Sluglimpets could be seen in it too, upending or spinning in the current, their legs wriggling. The settlers stood on the roofs of the handful of settlement buildings that remained standing, or clung to the branches of tall tree-like vegetation. The electric fence had been turned off, and a few men and women had chosen it as the structure least likely to be knocked down by the wave. They perched precariously on top.

Cariad and Cherry were squeezed into a narrow space on the roof of the Leader's residence. Cariad had looked for Osias' body among the ruins as Cherry had guided her there, but she hadn't been able to see him. Most of the place had been burned to ash, so it wasn't surprising.

So many deaths. With the loss of the babies on the *Nova Fortuna* along with all the reproduction equipment, the colony's death warrant was already signed. It was only a matter of when its execution would take place. If they survived this moment and into the future, the end of the colony wouldn't happen in Cariad's lifetime, but at some point several or even many generations hence, a final few inbred humans would be the last gasp of humanity in the galaxy. The efforts of the thousands of *Nova Fortuna* Project participants and those of Steen, Mina, and the rest of the Guardians' creators would have been in vain. The flickering flame would finally go out.

Cries of fear and despair rose all around. The tsunami was nearly upon them. The terror of the colonists was almost palpable. Cariad was frozen, hardly able to watch what was about to happen yet also unable to tear her gaze away. Cherry's grip on her arm was hurting. She took the woman's hand and together they faced whatever fate awaited them.

The wave hit the settlement fence, sparking screams and shrieks. A man slipped, fell, and was immediately dragged under. The water rose higher, reaching the hanging legs of settlers as they clung on. It was sweeping through the wires, which wavered under its weight. But the fence was holding.

The wave advanced, picking up the burnt remains of the settlement buildings, until the water was no longer visible. Only a tide of black and gray debris moved closer, engulfing the ruins of houses. It was as if destruction had taken physical form and was bearing down on the settlers, preparing to devastate whatever lay in its path.

The wave hit what was left of the hospital. The part of the building's roof that remained intact was crowded with figures. Cariad clasped Cherry's hand tighter. Her heart was in her mouth. But as the wave passed around and through the hospital the structure stood firm.

The Leader's residence was next.

"We'll be okay," Cherry said. "We'll be okay."

"I hope so," Cariad replied.

"But just in case we aren't," Cherry went on, "I'm sorry for being a bitch."

Cariad turned to her, tears of terror and gratitude in her eyes. "No. I'm sorry. For everything."

The two women returned their gazes to their potential approaching deaths. The building shuddered beneath their feet as the debris piled against it, driven relentlessly on by the swirling water. Cariad gasped, remembering to breathe.

The wave pushed on, testing the strength of the only thing that stood between her and oblivion. The building was holding. The water was all around them now, and the Leader's residence hadn't collapsed. For the moment, they were safe.

CHAPTER FORTY-TWO

It took Ethan and Rudra all day to walk to the settlement. Ethan had fashioned a crutch from a broom Rudra found in what was left of one of the farmhouses. He could walk but only slowly. The pain from his wound hampered him and the crutch quickly began to hurt the underside of his arm. Rudra couldn't travel much faster anyway as he was forced to carry Ganika. Both men also faced the challenge of navigating the sediment from the tsunami.

The wave had obliterated the fields and the crops that had been growing in them. The road was also gone from sight, though Ethan guessed it probably still lay fairly intact somewhere underneath the mud. They had to guess the direction of the settlement but the layout of the farm buildings helped. Most of the structures had withstood the giant wave, as had the fence around the lake.

Ethan would never forget the sight of the wave approaching. First, he'd noticed the cloud of smoke rising into the sky from the spot where the settlement lay, then he'd heard Rudra gasp. Turning, Ethan had been greeted by the sight of something impossible. The ocean had risen up and traveled inland, an hour's flitter ride or farther.

He'd never heard of such a thing. But he'd barely had time to wonder what could possibly have caused the wave before he'd realized he and Rudra and Ganika stood a good chance of being swept away by it and drowned.

They had no time to run. The water was traveling too fast. And where would they run to? There was no high ground for miles around.

"Hold on," Rudra shouted. Like Ethan, he'd reached the top of the fence.

"I am," Ethan shouted back. Then the wave had hit. Ethan felt the force of the water in the trembling of the wires. For long seconds, His pulse surged in his ears as he waited for the fence to fall, carrying him into the murky, rushing water.

Then the crisis point seemed to pass, and Ethan and Rudra watched in horrified fascination as the wave pushed on, drowning the fields, turning the land into a shallow sea. Later, they'd waited hours for the water to subside, until clinging to the fence wires became painful and Ganika grew frantic with her requests to go down.

Ethan had little idea of what they might see when they reached the settlement, but even so he wasn't prepared for the bare, burnt out, muddy devastation that awaited him. He recalled the plume of smoke he'd seen that morning, which had been driven from his mind by subsequent events. The settlement had been burning, of course. But why? Had there been another Natural Movement attack? Had an arsonist set fire to the place?

The first people they saw were at the settlement's electric fence. The colonists were fixing it—a sensible precaution as night would arrive soon, bringing sluglimpets with it, though Ethan guessed their numbers would have been significantly reduced by the wave.

Both Ethan and Rudra were too tired to shout loudly for help. But as they hobbled closer, wading through mud, a young woman noticed them. "Hey," she called to a fellow worker and pointed at Ethan and his companions. The man saw them and climbed down from the fence. He walked over, looking at the two men curiously.

It wasn't until he was closer that he finally realized who they were. Giving a shout of surprise, he turned to the woman who had alerted him, and called, "It's Ethan! Ethan's back." He said to Rudra, "And who are you?"

"My daughter and I were dragged into the lake by the thread creatures."

"You don't say," exclaimed the man. "I heard about that. And you survived?"

"Well, here we are," Rudra replied, rather nonplussed.

Shouts and calls were rising up all through the settlement as the news was passed along.

"Here," said the man. "I'll carry your girl."

After some small protests, Ganika allowed herself to be passed into the stranger's arms.

The woman who had first seen Ethan and Rudra

had come over. "Lean on me," she said to Ethan. "You walked all the way from the lake? You must be exhausted."

Ethan gratefully put an arm over the woman's shoulders, easing the pressure of his arm on his makeshift crutch. He hobbled a few steps. A crowd was gathering at the fence. The gates were open, and settlers were passing through, staring at Ethan.

He wondered what they saw. He was crippled and disheveled to an extreme. Probably many of them would hardly recognize him as the man who had played a role in the Gen rebellion. He didn't really mind what they saw or what they thought, however. He was only profoundly glad to be free from captivity and back home.

Though another disaster had clearly befallen the colony, they would be able to rebuild it in time. As he understood, plenty of materials remained stored aboard the *Nova Fortuna*. And as soon as he had a chance to clean up, he would comm Cariad. She would probably come down to see him soon and he could tell her how he felt about her.

A figure burst through the crowd, then stopped dead. It was Cariad. What was she doing down from the ship? She was staring at him.

"Ethan," she gasped, "what happened to you?"

But before he could answer, she ran to him. She was in his arms, holding onto him like she was holding on to life itself. "I can't believe it. I thought you were dead."

Ethan's crutch dropped away. He was balancing on one leg, clinging to Cariad as she was clinging to him. "I thought so too, for a while. But I made it back."

"You did." Though it hardly seemed possible, Cariad gripped him closer. "You made it back."

Cariad & Ethan's story continues in...
THE SCYTHIAN CRISIS

SPACE COLONY ONE BOOK 3

Author's note

Welcome to the end of *The Fila Epiphany*. I hope you've enjoyed the ride so far. The *Nova Fortuna* colonists certainly have a lot of challenges ahead of them, haven't they?

The fila in the book are inspired by an order of marine animals called siphonophores. The Portuguese man o'war is the most well-known of these organisms, but there are many other weird and wonderful examples that you can waste considerable amounts of time watching on Youtube (believe me, I should know).

The tsunami that inundates the settlement is a megatsunami. Unlike tsunamis caused by tectonic activity, megatsunamis are the result of a large object or large amounts of material falling into an ocean or sea. In *The Fila Epiphany*, the object is the colony ship, but in Earth's history megatsunamis resulted from landslides and meteor impacts. One of the most famous impact craters is at Chicxulub, and the effect of the impact is thought to have resulted in a tsunami 100 meters high that spread into Florida and Texas. In the book, Geisen slows the fall of the ship, so the effects aren't quite so devastating.

Ethan's attempts to communicate with the fila are based on my many years of experience teaching English as a second language. I used to teach complete beginners without being able to speak my students' language. The kind of bootstrapping technique that Ethan figures out was often the only way of teaching in those circumstances, though I had an advantage over him in that my students used language and not another form of communication.

As the series progresses, we may see more of the fila, though I'm not promising anything. If we do, it might be wise to never expect to have a clear understanding of how they think. After